AMISH PEACE VALLEY 3-BOOK COLLECTION

PEACE VALLEY AMISH SERIES

BOOKS 1 – 3

RACHEL STOLTZFUS

Copyright © 2017 RACHEL STOLTZFUS

All rights reserved.

ISBN-13: 978-1545014561
ISBN-10: 1545014566

Download the Rachel Stoltzfus Starter Library for FREE.

Sign up to receive new release updates and discount books from Rachel Stoltzfus, and you'll get Rachel's 5-Book Starter library, including Book 1 of Amish Country Tours, and four more great Amish books.

Details can be found at the end of this book.

TABLE OF CONTENTS

ACKNOWLEDGMENTS I

AMISH TRUTH BE TOLD 1

CHAPTER ONE 3

CHAPTER TWO 19

CHAPTER THREE 31

CHAPTER FOUR 45

CHAPTER FIVE 57

CHAPTER SIX 65

CHAPTER SEVEN 83

CHAPTER EIGHT 97

CHAPTER NINE 111

AMISH HEART AND SOUL 125

CHAPTER ONE 127

CHAPTER TWO 141

CHAPTER THREE 151

CHAPTER FOUR 163

CHAPTER FIVE 169

CHAPTER SIX 191

CHAPTER SEVEN 205

CHAPTER EIGHT 221

EPILOGUE 245

AMISH LOVE SAVES ALL 247

CHAPTER ONE 249

CHAPTER TWO 261

CHAPTER THREE 277

CHAPTER FOUR 289

CHAPTER FIVE 299

CHAPTER SIX 309

CHAPTER SEVEN 321

CHAPTER EIGHT	333
CHAPTER NINE	347
CHAPTER TEN	357
A WORD FROM RACHEL	373
ENJOY THIS BOOK? YOU CAN MAKE A BIG DIFFERENCE	377
ALSO BY RACHEL STOLTZFUS	379
ABOUT THE AUTHOR	391

RACHEL STOLTZFUS

ACKNOWLEDGMENTS

I have to thank God first and foremost for the gift of my life and the life of my family. I also have to thank my family for putting up with my crazy hours and how stressed out I can get as I approach a deadline. In addition, I must thank the ladies at Global Grafx Press for working with me to help make my books the best they can be. And last, I thank you, for taking the time to read this book. God Bless!

AMISH TRUTH BE TOLD

Shame. Deception. Truth.

Inside the Amish community of Peace Valley lurks a shameful double standard. When two women, Lizzie Lapp and Annie Miller, are told by their husbands to abandon their dreams of work outside the home, will they have the strength to protect themselves and their families? Can the light of God's truth transform their community, and their husbands' hearts? Or are some secrets too painful to reveal?

CHAPTER ONE

Caleb Miller's neck veins bulged out as he yelled at his wife, Annie. "*Nee*, wife! You need to quit working at that shop! Sell it!" Completely in the grips of his frustration and anger, Caleb set his coffee mug down hard on the table's scarred wood surface. As the cup made impact with the hard wood, the force behind the slam caused the sturdy clayware to shatter.

As the cup broke into several pieces, the hot, black coffee within splashed over Caleb's hand, wrist and the table's clean surface. "Awww, look at what you made me do! Naomi, get the cloth and clean this up, right now!" Standing, Caleb raised his fist over his head as he glared at Annie.

Annie, seeing the large, raised fist, took a step back, then stopped. *Nee*. I can't show him fear. Standing her ground, she allowed her eyes to take in details of Caleb's appearance. His eyes were bulging, distorted by his anger. His shoulders pulled up toward his ears—he would soon be complaining of a sore neck.

"Caleb, please listen." In contrast to her husband's yelling, Annie's voice was quiet, although it held a quaver that betrayed strong emotion. "We planned to have a *gut* harvest of the wheat and corn, but *Gott* had other plans. He sent too much rain, then not enough. I won't go into our finances because you know them probably better than I do. What I want to point out is that, as your wife, I want to stand next to you, bringing in some money. I'm the shop owner, and I have two other workers. We get lots of business, which means my shop is popular. I cannot quit and close it. I'd put two other women out of work and, in this economic..."

Caleb growled, signaling his impatience with Annie's explanation. "Annie, you are my wife! Women should stay at home and raise the children... because *Gott* made them inferior. All you can do is take care of this house and keep watch over Naomi. I expect you to tell me when you have a plan for closing that blasted store! Daughter, are you finished cleaning that table? You are no better than your *mamm*."

Naomi, long used to her *daed*'s clueless insults, still felt this one to her core. Closing her eyes, she gripped the wet cloth and hurried back to the sink, rinsing it out. Clenching her full lips tightly together, she bit back words of anger. "*Mamm*, may I begin clearing up from supper? I need to finish my current quilting order because it's due to my customer in less than two weeks."

"*Ja*. We'll work together. Caleb, we'll speak about this later on." Annie refused to allow her husband to ride over her plans and dreams. She had worked hard to get her quilt shop started and nobody was going to take it away from her, unless it was *Gott*'s will. Waiting until Caleb had gone back to the barn to finish the last of his day's work, she made sure the door was closed before she began speaking quickly. "Naomi, we aren't closing the Quilt Place. Don't you worry about that. We've worked too hard to give up now."

"*Ja*, but *mamm*, why does he talk this way? He puts you and me down and it hurts!" Naomi swiped her soapy hand over her cheek, brushing hot tears away.

Annie was quiet for several seconds, thinking. "He grew up in a time when our *Ordnung* was much more conservative. It's what he's used to. His *daed* was even more strict, if you can imagine that."

"Did *grossdaudi* allow grandmother to work? Or was she restricted to taking care of the house and children because '*Gott* made her inferior?'" The tone of Naomi's voice was heavily sarcastic as she spoke. She glanced through the kitchen window, keeping an eye out for her *daed*.

"Naomi, please be careful. These are your grandparents we're talking about. . . though I agree with you about their beliefs. We are not inferior. We are just as able as any man is." Drawing in a deep, calming breath, Annie glanced quickly outside the window, then continued. "We are supposed to be valued in our homes, daughter. Your *daed*, his brothers and the rest of his family have taken the leadership role too seriously. If you look at other families here in Peace Valley, you'll notice that the husbands and wives are actual partners with each other. The wives have their own businesses, such as baking and selling their goodies at the market or quilting as you do. A few even work outside the. . . oh, he's coming in." As the back door opened, Annie shifted into another topic. ". . . So, because we will be hosting the Sunday service in two weeks, you, your sisters and I will need to begin cleaning the house top to bottom."

Naomi was so grateful that her *mamm* could shift topics so quickly. Drying the dishes and putting them away, she nodded. "*Ja*. Okay. When will we start?"

"Monday. *Ja*, Monday. That will give us time to get every room in the house and make it ready for services."

"It's time for devotionals." Caleb's low voice rumbled from the living room as he held up his worn Bible.

"We're coming, husband." Annie finished wiping surfaces down, then looked around. The kitchen gleamed. "Okay, let's go."

"I want to talk about Ephesians, Chapter five." Caleb began reading the familiar chapter. When he had finished, he looked closely at Annie, who was praying. "Wife, husbands are supposed to love their wives and wives are expected to be submissive to their husbands. Their *kinner* are expected to obey their parents and honor them."

"*Ja.* I understand. We are submissive to our husbands here. Our children obey us and do as we command them. If they sin, we punish them. Caleb, if you'll look at our children, you'll see that they have obeyed you and me. We have rarely had problems with them."

The devotional session ended when Naomi pointed out that she and Annie both held Caleb in high esteem. "*Daed*, I see you as being strong and wise. I see *mamm* as being a complement to you, helping you whether things are good or bad for us. And that makes me want to honor you. As I grew up, I saw my brothers and sisters all had the same opinion of you. We all wanted to grow up and follow your examples."

Caleb was grateful for the calm and, while he wanted to use the moment to press Annie again, something held him back. Smiling at Naomi, he pointed to her quilting room. "Go. That quilt won't sew itself."

Smiling, Naomi stood and, giving her parents quick kisses, she skipped to her quilting studio. As she hurried in, she released a quiet sigh of relief. Tonight's devotional could have gone completely off the rails. Closing her eyes, she thanked *Gott* that everyone had stayed calm as they discussed His Word.

As she worked, piecing quilt pieces together and sewing them with her sewing machine, she thought. *Helpmeet.* Partner. Loved by husbands as Christ loved His church. So, *mamm*, her friends and I can still work outside the home and still not violate *Gott*'s law or our *Ordnung*.

How do I learn more? Who do I talk to? Quickly cutting the sewing thread to release the row of quilt pieces from the machine, she vowed to think more about their situation. Because seeing *daed* raise his fist at *mamm* really didn't feel like love. Conscious of the sounds in the rest of the house, Naomi continued to work. Soon, the sounds of her parents quieted down. They had gone upstairs to bed. Yawning,

Naomi finished sewing the second row of quilt pieces together, then began to straighten out her studio, putting things where they belonged. Blowing out the lantern, she moved quietly through the rest of the house and made sure everything was securely locked up.

After brushing her teeth and showering, she combed out her long hair, still thinking.

Maybe I can talk to Bishop or to Deacon King. The deacon would be easier to approach and talk to. In her room, Naomi stood in front of her window, peering out at the dark, star-studded sky, praying about her family's situation. She knew she wanted to have the freedom to make the choices she would need to make with her future husband, rather than be constrained by what she believed was an outdated belief. Lying down, she thought of her boyfriend, Jethro Yoder. She had dated a couple of Amish boys before beginning to see Jethro. Thinking back, she remembered, even then, knowing she wanted a partner who would view and treat her as an equal in their marriage. Sitting back up, she leaned her back against her pillow. Her smooth forehead creased as she tried to remember the word that the English used in connection to not allowing women to be equals. Giving up, she opened her stand-up closet, where she had stored her old textbooks.

Looking for her notebook, she leafed back to one of the last assignments she had turned in. "*Ja*, here it is. Miss Mary had us work on an assignment about the differences between the Amish and the English." Opening the notebook, she began reading the essay. "Men and women, *ja*, here it is . . . Men and women are viewed as more equal in English communities, although women still lag . . . There it is! 'Sexism' is the word I want!" Dropping the notebook on her bed, Naomi grabbed her dictionary and looked up the definition for 'sexism.'

"The belief that one gender, almost always the male, is superior to the female, which enables him to dominate in almost every area of life. Sexist discrimination in the US in past years has kept many women from achieving the opportunities they want."

As she read quietly, her words slowed down. Sitting back on her bed with her dictionary in her hands, she thought. So it is in Amish life as well. Our men, *daeds* and husbands are acting on the assumption that they are superior to us. And that's why *daed* is acting as he is toward *mamm*. Because he believes she is inferior to him. Once we go to work tomorrow, I want to show this to *mamm*. She needs to know where *daed*'s beliefs come from. With that decision made, she slipped her dictionary and notebook into her carryall so she could show them to her *mamm* the next morning.

Yawning again, she slid under the covers, ready for sleep. Unfortunately, her sleep that night was troubled, punctuated by near-nightmares featuring her parents fighting, with her *daed* striking her *mamm*. After one particularly vivid dream, Naomi sat up, gasping wildly as she tried to come out of the nightmare. Looking around, she touched the cool wall of her bedroom, trying to orient herself back to reality. "It was a bad dream, that's all."

Hearing a sound from downstairs, she looked at her alarm. Seeing that it was almost time to get up, she fell back onto her pillow and groaned softly. "I need more sleep!" She sat up, feeling reluctant to leave her bed when she remembered her decision of the night before. Slipping out of bed, she made her bed and got dressed.

Combing her hair and arranging it in a braided bun, she settled her *kapp* on her head. In the kitchen, she set her carryall against the wall, out of the way of both of her parents. "*Gut* morning, *mamm*. How are you?"

"I'm *gut*, how are. . ." Annie paused, seeing the circles under Naomi's sleepy eyes. ""Ach, you didn't sleep well, did you?"

"*Nee*. Where is *daed*? In the barn?"

"*Ja*. What's wrong?"

While Annie's and Naomi's voices were quiet, they communicated the tension of the situation. "After I went to bed last night, I was thinking." Naomi's words were soft and rushed because she wanted to get them out as fast as possible. "I looked for one of my last essays. It was on sexism. We don't have time right now because *daed* will be back inside soon. But what he's doing is the exact definition of sex discrimination. I have the books in my carryall,* and I'll show you on the way to the store."

Annie was stunned. She realized the level of thought Naomi had put into their situation. "You really want to do something about this, *ja*?" As Naomi nodded, she went on, feeling the pressure of time. "Ours isn't the only family experiencing this. I'll tell you more on the way to the shop. Meanwhile, I see that *daed* is coming back. Get the bacon going, please."

She and Naomi were uncharacteristically quiet as they got

breakfast ready. Annie stirred the scrambled eggs and oatmeal as Annie worked on the bacon. Looking up, she smiled quietly at Caleb as he stomped his feet on the outside door mat.

After breakfast, Caleb complimented Annie and Naomi. "*Gut* breakfast. I will be back for supper. We'll be working at the Stoltzfus farm on their harvest, so I'll have dinner over there. It's the last harvest of the season, so we'll be done within a week or two." Giving Annie a rough caress on her arm, he left.

Annie shook her head. She loved the man, even though his beliefs seemed to be stuck back in the 50s. She laughed quietly as she thought, the 1850s.

"What's funny, *mamm*?" Naomi's dark eyes were large with curiosity.

"I love your *daed* with all my heart, daughter. But he has some real old-fashioned beliefs. I laughed because he is stuck in the 50s."

"The 1950s? But *mamm*, that's like, almost 60 years ago. Even then, *daeds* were more, uh, evolved?"

"Annie began laughing. "*Nee*, Naomi. The 1850s! It's funny in a sad way. I laugh because, if I didn't have that, I would be crying. And I am so amazed at your insight. You caught onto our situation so quickly last night, because you are living it. . . let's get the dishes done and kitchen cleaned up so we can go.

We'll talk on the way to the shop."

After Naomi and Annie cleaned the kitchen and packed their lunches, they left for the shop. While Annie guided the team of horses, Naomi read the definition she had found in her dictionary. Then, she explained how she had chosen her previous boyfriends and current one. "*Mamm*, I know that I don't want to go through what *daed* does to you. I love him, but *ja*, he is stuck back in a very old-fashioned way of thinking. My first boyfriend could have been *daed*'s son, for his way of thinking. That's why I only dated him for a few months. My second boyfriend. . . well, he talked *gut* about believing that women should be able to make decisions. But when it came down to talking about what his future wife would be 'allowed' to do, I found out that she wouldn't be able to do much more than bake or quilt and sell what she made. When we talked about it, I brought up your shop and he told me, 'I would make my future wife sell the shop or quit working outside the home. Once we get married, she gives up her rights to work away from home.' *Mamm*, that's the night that I broke up with him. When he brought me home, I told him I wouldn't be seeing him anymore. He tried to get into an argument with me. I jumped out of the buggy and ran, even though I twisted my ankle. He wasn't going to do anything to me!"

Annie was stunned. Naomi had never shared this with her. "Wha. . . Naomi! Why didn't you say anything?"

Naomi was silent. "I don't know. I was embarrassed and

ashamed."

"Daughter, please, don't ever be ashamed when someone does something to you! You are a strong young woman, just like your sisters. You did the right thing by running away from him. But please, if ever anyone does anything like that to you again, tell me!"

Naomi nodded, feeling shock. "*Mamm*, I just wasn't sure if you or *daed* would believe me. And, I thought that, by bringing up you and your shop, that I brought all of his words and actions on myself."

"*Nee*, Naomi! His beliefs. . . and his insecurities. . . made him act out against you. It wasn't your fault. It's too late for us to go to the elders now. Please promise me that, if Jethro acts like this, you'll tell your *daed* and me right away."

"*Ja*, I will. Jethro hasn't ever tried to get physical with me. I don't think he will, either, because, when we've talked, he has agreed with my position on how wives can be the equals of their husbands. *Mamm* . . . before Jethro and I started dating, I took the time to find out what he believed. I didn't bother with that with John. And I regret that. Well, I nearly regret it. I learned what I don't want in a relationship with my future husband."

"I shouldn't ask, but is there a possibility that you and Jethro might marry?"

Naomi blushed because parents normally wouldn't find out about their children's plans to marry until the couple got engaged. "We. . . we've talked about it, but we haven't really made a decision yet. Besides, we still need to get to know each other much better."

Annie was quiet for several minutes. Rousing, she realized they were almost at her shop. "We're almost at work. Thankfully, Leora won't be here for about half an hour. That should give us time to make sure we can talk about what you brought to work with you. Because I really want to know."

***

Inside the shop, after preparing the cash register and putting sales flyers on the counter, Annie and Naomi sat, discussing what Naomi had dug out of her closet. "*Mamm*, sexism is the belief that one gender, usually the men, think they are superior to us. This leads to sex discrimination. . ."

"What is sex discrimination?" Annie's brow crinkled in confusion.

"That's when people—usually men—stop women who are just as qualified as they are from sharing in the same opportunities. Like getting a job or even having the right to work at all."

Annie's first reaction was a widening of her eyes as she understood what Naomi was saying. Then, her being radiated sadness as her eyes dimmed. "You mean. . . like what your *daed* is trying to do to me."

RACHEL STOLTZFUS

CHAPTER TWO

Naomi's mouth filled with a sour taste as she nodded. "*Mamm*, I really hate seeing you like this. It's hard, I know. But we can keep on doing what we're doing. Remember, your store gives so much good to so many here! Leora works here. The women can sell their quilts on consignment, which helps them earn money for their families. And the English tourists love the quilts! *Ja*, you're unusual because you own your business. But other Amish women own their businesses, too."

Annie smiled, grateful for Naomi's sensitive words. Feeling her love for her daughter welling over, she gave her a rare hug. "*Ja*, that is true, isn't it? You know, before I opened my shop, I worked out of the house. As more and more women brought quilts for me to sell, Caleb got upset because they took up so much space. He told me, "Just find a building on the edge of town and rent that. Sell from there." Another memory bubbled up to the surface of Annie's mind. "Then, he said. . . he said, "I don't mind you doing this because it's women's work."

Naomi's eyebrows came together as she frowned. With great difficulty, she refrained from saying anything, knowing it would be disrespectful of her *daed*. "Am I right in remembering that, another time, he told you, "Your business has kept us from going under when things haven't gone well with the crops?"

"*Ja*! He did! More than once! Daughter, we'd better get ready for our work day. It will be busy because I have that promotion starting today. And look, there's Leora."

The bells on the front door tinkled as Leora came in. "*Gut* morning! It will be a warm day today. We should have lots of tourists coming in."

***

While Annie and Naomi were discussing Caleb's issues with Annie's shop, another Peace Valley family was having its difficulties. Lizzie Lapp had served as the manager of the Peace Valley Quilt Place until her husband, Wayne, had forced her to resign her position. This morning, Lizzie had suggested that she return to work on a part-time basis, so they could help their daughter and granddaughter with medical expenses. "Barbara's *boppli* has that asthma now, and the supplies are expensive. Her husband's income doesn't quite stretch to cover the nebulizer, which the baby needs so she can breathe better on bad days."

"They're borrowing one from the clinic, aren't they?" At Lizzie's nod, he shook his head. "*Nee*. You stay home. Period. This is where you belong, taking care of home, meals, Leora and our grandbabies."

"But. . ."

"No buts! You remember that last time we discussed this!" As he yelled, Wayne raised his fist in a threatening way.

Lizzie remembered only too well the beating she had gotten from Wayne. It had been the first time he'd ever hit her, although his temper and raised voice had long been an issue between the two of them. Backing up and moving into the spacious living room, she raised her hands in a defensive way, shaking her head. "*Nee*! Don't hit me, Wayne! I'll go to the elders if you do!"

Leora came into the kitchen at that point. Seeing her *daed*'s raised fist, she dropped her black cape. "*Daed*! *Nee*! Don't hit her!" She backed up and, standing next to Lizzie, she wrapped both arms around her mother's shoulders.

Wayne, seeing his wife and daughter standing huddled together, dropped his arm and his attitude. "Wife, you just remember that I make the decisions here! I've decided you're not working outside the house, no matter what! If you want to earn more money, give quilts to Annie for her to sell. Bake. But you're not working outside the home! And Leora, the day you marry, you're staying at home, in your husband's home. No need for you to work outside the home, either." He was about to raise the point that she could work from home, but seeing the defiant, angry look on Leora's face, he decided to wait. "Don't think that Annie Miller's going to have that shop for much longer. I've been talking with Caleb. He'll get her to close it. Leora, that means you'll have no choice but to work from home." Slamming his straw hat on his head, he gave a stern nod and left through the kitchen door, slamming it behind him.

"*Mamm*, did he hit you?" Leora allowed her eyes to roam over Lizzie's face and neck.

"*Nee*. You came in at the right time. I wish he didn't have this notion that women aren't supposed to work outside the home! Your sister needs that machine for baby Anna."

"He won't even let you work part-time?"

Lizzie shook her head. "Well, there's nothing for it but to finish that quilt and take it to Annie's store. Would you please let her know that I'll be donating quilts on consignment?"

"*Ja, mamm*, you know I will." Leora felt her head cover and hair, making sure they were smooth and straight on her head. "I'd better go now. I'll be home before supper. But tomorrow, Annie has an all-day sale, so I may not be home until shortly after you put supper on the table. I have to be at work by nine tomorrow morning."

"*Gut.* You go. Just remember, bring your pay home and I'll put it away for you. Let me know if you need anything from your pay so you can buy it."

"I will. Bye, *mamm.*" Leora waved as she left the house. On her walk to the store, she thought, wondering why some men were so stern about women working. I'll talk to Naomi on our breaks and see what she says. She knew she could never bring up the fact that her *daed* threatened physical violence against her *mamm*. To do so would bring shame on her family. Hurrying up the porch steps to the shop, she forced herself to smile and think of a happy topic.

Annie's words about the English tourists was prophetic. She, Naomi, Leora and their other two employees were kept busy, running from the back room to the cash register, ringing up sales and wrapping up quilts and smaller blankets.

"Naomi, you and Leora take the first break today. Rebecca and Miriam, you'll get the second break today." Annie rushed by, a quilt and blanket set in her arms ready to wrap and ring up.

"Let's go to the back. I brought some cookies and milk we can enjoy." Naomi grinned at her friend, feeling better about the day.

"Naomi, why do some of the men here don't like letting us women work outside the home? *Mamm* wants to come back to the shop, but *daed* won't let her. He says she can earn money from home if she wants to. Oh, she's going to send a quilt with me in a couple weeks."

Naomi finished chewing her cookie before answering. Wiping her mouth, she thought. "Well, *mamm* and I talked about sexism and sex discrimination. Remember that paper that Miss Mary had us write in our last year of school? Mine was about how women have to deal with sexism."

"*Ja*, now I remember! I think men and women are equal. We can do a good job earning money for our families."

"*Ja*, we can! *Daed* still wants *mamm* to close the store. She doesn't want to, because we employ you, Rebecca and Miriam. Women in Peace Valley can make quilts at home, then sell them here. So everyone wins."

"Well. . . everyone except for the men. They think." Leora's voice was droll as she threw that into the conversation.

Naomi, about to take a drink of milk, put her glass back on the table and began laughing hard. "*Ja*, that's for sure and for certain, isn't it? I don't want to disrespect *daed* or your *daed*. But. . ." Her voice dropped to a whisper. "It's so ridiculous. It's like they're afraid that we'll show them up or something."

Leora's grin faded. "Naomi, listen. *Daed* was saying that

he's been working with your *daed* to make your *mamm* close the store. Your *mamm* needs to know that."

Naomi's giggles stopped, just as if someone had shut off a spigot. "What?" Her eyes roamed around the small, neat and comfortable break room. In her mind, she pictured the bright, spacious display and sale area. This was her second home! She'd grown up spending her days with her *mamm*, beginning to work for her after she finished school at fourteen. Looking at the remaining cookies in the bag, she zipped the bag shut, no longer feeling hungry. Covering her travel mug, she stored the rest of her milk back in the small refrigerator. "Leora, are you sure? Did you misunderstand your *daed*?"

"*Nee*. He said so this morning, that he's been talking with your *daed*. He said that your *mamm* won't have the store for much longer. We need to let your *mamm* know!"

"Can you stay a little late tonight so you can talk to my *mamm*?"

Leora grimaced. "I wish I could! I promised *mamm* I'd be home in time to fix supper with her. *Daed*'s mood wasn't very good because I heard her ask him about coming back here part-time. She wants to help Barbara out with the *boppli*'s medical expenses. He said no, that she could bring quilts here to sell."

"We want her quilts. But does he realize what harm he'll do if he and my *daed* succeed in getting *mamm* to close her store? Okay. Denki. I'll tell *mamm* tonight so she's warned and can be ready."

After storing their snacks back in the refrigerator, both girls went back to the sales floor to relieve the two other employees. As they worked, straightening out displays and cleaning counters, they were both quiet.

Annie noticed the new moods Leora and Naomi appeared to be in. Pulling them in close to her during a small lull, she referred to their change. "I hope you'll be able to greet guests to the store and make them feel welcome. What happened while you were on break?"

Naomi looked at Leora, who shrugged. "*Mamm*, I see new customers walking up. I'll let you know tonight, okay?"

Annie had no choice but to accept that—several customers came into the shop, each veering to different areas of the store and asking several questions. The remainder of their day was busy with few lulls. At lunch time, Annie gratefully locked the front door and flipped the door sign to "closed."

Sitting in the back with her daughter and employees, she ate and rested her aching feet. Looking at Naomi and Leora, she was relieved to see they had regained their high spirits. All four girls talked and giggled as they ate, discussing the sing they would be attending on Sunday night.

"*Ja*, Vernon and I will be at the sing. Naomi, will you be there with Jethro?"

"*Ja*, of course! Rebecca, Miriam, what about you?" Naomi's cheeks were flushed as she asked the question.

Miriam nodded, blushing. "*Ja*. John asked me to go at the last sing and I told him I would."

Rebecca was the sole girl with no plans to attend with one of the boys in their community. "*Nee*. I broke up with Abe."

Naomi gasped. "Rebecca, why? You seemed to be getting along so well!"

Rebecca shook her head. "*Nee*." As she spoke, she absently rubbed her left forearm. "He. . . doesn't like that I work here. He'd rather that I earn money by working from home, like most of our mothers do. He brought it up the last time we got together. He came over to visit on Tuesday or Wednesday night. We got into an argument when I told him that my parents use some of my earnings to pay off the loan at the bank. That I'm happy to be able to help out. Well, he told me I could work from home and I told him I wouldn't earn as much as I do now. He grabbed my arm and tried to twist it and force me to agree to quit working here. . ."

Annie leaned forward and, holding Rebecca's hand, she gently raised the long sleeve of her dress. Seeing the livid, purple bruise on her employee's arm, she gasped. "Rebecca! Did you tell your parents about this?"

"*Ja*, after I broke up with Abe and told him never to come

back." She chuckled slightly, then her voice caught. "He wasn't. . . wasn't too happy when he left."

"Rebecca, does that hurt? Would you like some ice or something for it?" Naomi stood up. "We still have some time for lunch before we need to open back up."

"*Nee*, I'm fine. Denki. *Mamm* has been putting ice and a rub for sore muscles at night, then wrapping it. Today's the first day I've gone without the wrap."

"*Mamm*, I want to tell her about my own experience. Please?"

Annie nodded. "I think we can dispense with our usual custom of courting secrecy for this."

"Rebecca, I had two boyfriends before I began dating Jethro. My first boyfriend was just. . . well, outright firm that he didn't want his future wife working outside the home. We had only been dating for a couple months, so he wasn't too upset when I broke up with him. My second boyfriend talked a good game about supporting our right to help support our families. But, when we talked about marriage, he said he'd 'make' his future wife stop working outside the home. I told him we wouldn't be seeing each other anymore when he pulled into our yard. He tried to get into an argument with me and he tried to grab me. I just jumped out of his buggy and ran into the house. Now, before I begin dating anyone, I find out, for sure and for certain, what a young man believes about his girlfriend or wife working outside the home."

Leora leaned forward. "I do the same."

"Rebecca, Miriam, *mamm* and I talked about sex discrimination and sexism on our way here this morning."

Annie stood, needing to walk while Naomi and the girls talked. She kept her attention on their conversation, ready to jump in if needed. Looking outside the window of the back room, she saw Caleb and Wayne Lapp walking to their buggies. They were deep in conversation. For some reason, Annie didn't have a good feeling about what she was seeing—she remembered how hard Lizzie Lapp, her previous manager, had tried to continue working outside the home, until the day she had had to stay home, 'sick.' Annie had run into her at the next Sunday's church meeting. Lizzie had a large bruise on her cheek, which she had tried to cover with her black bonnet.

RACHEL STOLTZFUS

CHAPTER THREE

"Lizzie, what happened? Your cheek!" Naomi had been stunned.

Lizzie looked around and, not seeing Wayne, she gestured to the house. "Let's go inside." The meeting had been at the Lapp house that Sunday. "Annie, I am so sorry, but I'm going to have to resign as manager at the shop." Looking down, Lizzie had gulped, seeming to struggle with tears.

"Lizzie, what's wrong? This is about more than just resigning, isn't it?" Annie's intuition had begun to warn her about something bad.

"*Ja.* Close the door, please." After Annie had closed the bedroom door, she joined Lizzie on the side of the bed. "Annie, Wayne hasn't liked it that I work in your shop. He wouldn't like my working in anyone's business. That's. . . well, that's how this happened." With one hand, Lizzie had indicated the livid bruise on her face. "He. . . beat me and now, I have to quit." Turning her face to the side, Lizzie began to cry quietly.

Annie felt sick, knowing her intuition had told her right once again. "Lizzie, I'm so sorry! I hate having to accept your resignation, but we know the *Ordnung* says we're to obey our husbands. Much as I don't like that he used physical force to make you agree. I don't want you to put you in any danger of more beatings. I value your friendship too much." Annie sighed, not wanting to cry. "*Ja.* I accept your resignation. Reluctantly." She had hugged Lizzie, trying to give her what comfort she could. "The shop has been doing very well. I'll be giving you severance pay on top of your regular pay. And you know that, if Wayne felt differently, I would have you back right away."

Lizzie had tried to smile. Carefully wiping tears away, she nodded. "*Ja*, I know. Thank you!"

Looking back around at the girls, Annie slid away from the window. If she could see Caleb, he could see her. Sitting back at the table, she forced her attention to the girls' conversation. I need to tell Annie and Leora what I just saw. When we close tonight. "Girls, we need to finish here and get opened again. It's nearly one and we close at four." By the time the end of the day rolled around, Annie was grateful. Counting the day's receipts and preparing the bank deposit, she reminded the girls to be on time the next day, "It's Saturday tomorrow. That, along with our sale, means we'll be very busy. I will see you here bright and early! Oh, Leora, can you stay for just a minute?"

"I'm sorry, but I promised *mamm* I'd get home as soon as we closed. She and *daed* had a. . . discussion this morning and. . ."

"Okay. But please, listen. I was looking out the back window at lunch today." Annie's words rushed together in her hurry. "I saw Caleb and your *daed*, walking together and having a conversation. They seem to have been buying supplies. Or they met, just to talk."

Leora's eyes widened and her mouth opened as she gasped. "Oh, no! Annie, *daed* said he would be talking to your husband about how to make you close your shop! They must have been talking about that! I'd better go. I'm. . . I'm sorry. I wish I didn't have to tell you that." Turning, she rushed out of the shop and began jogging home.

Annie looked down and grimaced. "No doubt she's right. Naomi, let's go home. We'll get here early and straighten out the rest of the shop and get ready then. We don't need to anger your *daed* any more than he already is. We need to be ready for anything he says or does." Annie was so preoccupied with Leora's news that she nearly forgot to lock the shop.

"*Mamm*! You forgot to lock the door! Here, let me have the

key." Naomi made sure the door was secure. "Bank and deposit. If we hurry, we can be in the kitchen before *daed* comes inside."

"Let's go. And, denki." Annie smiled, feeling a little of the tension in her shoulders easing. After depositing the day's earnings, she headed the buggy for home.

***

"Ach, yes! It's only four-thirty! We can start supper—and thank *Gott* I cut the vegetables for the stew already. Come. . . you work on the biscuits and dessert while I cut up the meat and make the stew."

Thirty minutes later, the stew was bubbling and ready to be served. Naomi pulled the biscuits out of the oven just as Caleb came into the kitchen.

"This smells *gut*! Now, this is just what I like to see. My women, working hard at what they are best at. Taking care of the family." With a self-satisfied smile, he ran upstairs to change his shirt and wash his hands.

As he was upstairs, Annie and Naomi exchanged a long gaze that said everything they couldn't say out loud. Annie put her finger over her lips. "Shhh, we'll go outside for a walk after supper and cleaning up."

Naomi, not trusting her words, just nodded. Setting the

table, she tensed as she heard her *daed*'s familiar footfalls when he entered the kitchen.

"Stew! One of my favorites! What's for dessert?"

Annie spoke. "Apple pie with ice cream."

During dinner, Naomi didn't contribute much to the conversation. Instead, she simply ate her meal, waiting until she and her *mamm* could go walking.

"Naomi, why aren't you talking? You're normally not this quiet." Caleb took a huge bite of one of her biscuits.

"I'm just thinking about going to pick up quilts from some of the women next week. And about getting together with Leora and Vernon."

"Vernon? Vernon King? He seems to be a good boy. Although his parents seem to have some strange ideas."

"*Daed*? I'm going to start cutting the pie. Are you ready?" Naomi was aware she had brought up a potentially sensitive topic.

"*Ja*, I am. This is *gut*! Who made it?"

"Me." For the first time, Naomi smiled. "Denki." Her pie did taste good.

After cleaning the kitchen, Naomi and Annie went on their walk. Holding flashlights, they walked alongside the road, talking. "*Mamm*, how are you going to deal with *daed*, especially on weekends?" Naomi was seriously worried, especially after learning what she had heard that day.

"I already have tomorrow under control. We'll prepare the meat, fruits and vegetables for supper. Your sister is coming over so your *daed* can have a hot lunch after finishing his work. He's going over to the Hofstetter's to help them unload benches and tables for the Sunday service, so he's going to be out of the house most of the day. We'll get home again before five and put supper on the table. You are going to open the shop every day next week while I clean the house and do the laundry. In fact, I'm thinking. . . about keeping the shop, but stepping back from day-to-day operation. What would you think of stepping up to become the manager? You're single. You say Jethro is okay with you working outside the house? What would he say about this?"

Naomi was stunned. Looking at her *mamm*, she forgot to breathe for a few seconds. Inhaling audibly, she closed her mouth and blinked as she forced her mind to function. "Umm, oh! Wow! *Ja*, I would be happy to help as manager! But I would need to learn how to take care of all the paperwork. Hiring, pay, firing, all of that."

Annie giggled, feeling nervous. "And Jethro?"

"Jethro would be fine with it. But, just to be sure, I will talk to him the next time we're together. *Mamm*? Will you be in the shop at all or stay home full-time?"

"I would be in the shop at least two days a week, maybe four. I haven't decided whether that would be from noon to close or if I would spend a full day there or not. I'm just trying to make it to where your *daed* stops acting like this."

Something about her mother's last statement bothered Naomi. Looking at the ground, she focused on that as she watched the pool of light from her flashlight. "*Mamm*? I'm going to say something and please, don't get upset. Because I love you."

"I. . . okay. What is it?"

"Why are you trying to placate *daed*? He needs to stop. I'm sorry. I hope that's not disrespectful, but he has been disrespecting you with his threats. I like your idea, because you will get more time away from the shop to relax. But you shouldn't do this just to make him more comfortable."

Annie looked at Naomi and her mouth fell open. Ouch! Out of the mouths of . . . ow! "Well, I have also been thinking about going to talk to the bishop. Or one of the ministers. I want to find out exactly what the *Ordnung* says about our women working out of the home."

It was Naomi's turn to be surprised. Shaking her head, she peered closely at Annie. "About. . . "

"Surely, our district's *Ordnung* allows married women who are working to provide for their families to work, either in or out of the home. I want to find out if your *daed*'s thinking goes against the *Ordnung*. If he needs to adjust his thinking." Annie remembered what she had seen during lunch. "Oh! I forgot about this. During lunch, I was looking outside the window at the back of the store. I spotted your *daed* and Wayne Lapp walking down the street, just talking."

"Okay... Oh! He forced Lizzie to quit her job! *Mamm*, this could mean trouble. Do you think they were talking about how to make the shop close?"

Annie's heart squeezed painfully. "I hope not! That's why I want you to think about this manager's position. Don't make a decision right away. If your *daed* is up to something, I want to be ready with a plan. We'd better go back."

The two turned around. "*Mamm*, when do you need a decision?"

"As soon as you get an answer from *Gott* and Jethro. Seriously."

This brought home to Naomi the urgency of her mother's situation. "Okay. I'll be praying about it."

***

The next morning, Naomi worked, moving from counter to

stock room and back to the counter. As she did, she mulled over her mother's idea, wondering if she could really manage the shop.

Shortly after lunch, Lizzie Lapp came in, holding a heavy quilt. " Annie, I have several more in the back of my buggy, if I could get some help with them."

Annie sent Leora and Naomi out to help bring the remainder of the quilts in. As they placed them on the shop's counter, several English shoppers crowded around. "Ladies, I still need to price these and write up the description. You'll be able to look at them, possibly on Tuesday. Lizzie, do you want to fill out this consignment paperwork so I can start an account for you?"

Lizzie let out a soft sigh. "Denki! Yes, I will." Moving to the back of the shop, she filled out every page, knowing she had found a compromise that, hopefully, would make Wayne happy. Bringing the sheets of paper to Annie, she looked around while Annie created an account for her on the small computer allowed by the Amish. "Annie, if I can bring in a quilt a month, I would like to do so."

Annie's grin beamed absolute happiness. "*Ja*! Your work is so beautiful and I know it will sell fast. You know my consignment structure—60/40, with you getting the 40 percent. Because these are full-sized quilts, they will be priced at a minimum of $500."

Lizzie's eyes rounded. "You've raised your prices!" In her mind, she was figuring out her 40 percent split and thanking *Gott*. Now, she could give Barbara *gut* news about helping with the nebulizer and medications for her granddaughter.

"*Ja*. My rent has gone up, so I had to raise my quilt prices. If you bring in smaller quilts, such as for dolls or cribs, those are priced lower. Doll quilts are $25 and crib quilts are $125."

Lizzie put her hand over her mouth as tears threatened to overwhelm her.

Annie saw the powerful emotion coming over her old friend. "Come. Let's go to the back. I'll get you some water." Wrapping her arm around Lizzie's slender waist, she comforted her. Getting a bottle of cold water, she sat her friend down. "What is it?"

"Barbara's youngest has been diagnosed with asthma. The medications are so expensive. I tried to get Wayne to agree to allow me to come back, even part-time and he raised his fist to me. I'm making and selling quilts so I can help Barbara and her husband afford these medications and the nebulizer."

"Oh, my! Of course, I'll help in every way I can. I'm running a big promotion, so you brought your quilts in at just the right time—I'm running low of quilts made here. I'll position them front and center so customers see them. I know they're going to want to buy them!" As Annie chattered, she decided she was going to change the consignment split for

Lizzie, from 60/40 to 50/50. Her friendship with Lizzie warranted this, as did Lizzie's family situation. And Lizzie would be the only one who received this split.

As Leora worked outside, she overheard snatches of the conversation between her *mamm* and Annie. As she processed what Lizzie was saying, she solidified a decision in her mind—she was going to go to talk to Jethro and see if she could talk to his *mamm* and *daed*, because something told her that her own *daed*'s treatment of her *mamm* was wrong and against the Ordnung.

***

As Leora walked home, she tried to allow the beauty of the spring day to calm her down. Gazing around, she saw the young wheat and corn stalks swaying in the gentle breeze. The sky was endless, seeming to go up forever. And, as she walked, Leora heard and felt the crunch of the rocks under her shoes. Inside the house, she dropped her carryall in her room, washed her hands and ran back downstairs to help Lizzie with supper.

"There you are, daughter! I'm working on the meat, if you'll work on the vegetables and brown the potatoes. Once they are nearly done, add the sliced onions, pepper and salt. I'll let you know when to put the pie into the oven."

Agreeing, Leora worked alongside Lizzie. As they worked, they talked quietly, about their respective days.

"*Ja*, it was busy. You saw when you came in with the quilts. Oh, we've already had one sale! An English tourist bought the Hunter's Star quilt! Several were interested in the Miniature Hearts crib quilt you made, and they'll come back in on Tuesday with money! Annie wants to know how many you can make a month."

Lizzie closed her eyes, sending up a silent prayer of thanksgiving. "Maybe two a month, if I work every day. Oh, thank the Lord!"

After dinner was over, Leora left with Vernon, who had made plans with her to spend the evening together. Before they left, Wayne tried to give Leora a hard time. "Daughter, you're going to see each other tomorrow night at the sing! I want you back in early because we have services tomorrow."

"*Ja, daed*, I will be in early. I promise." Leora struggled to keep her frustration out of her voice. Once in the buggy, she sighed.

"That doesn't sound *gut*. What's wrong?"

"Let's wait until we're down the road a bit. *Ja*, this is serious and I'll be asking for your help."

"Oh. Would you like to go and get some milkshakes so we can talk?"

"*Ja*, denki! That would be wunderbaar!" Leora loved pineapple milkshakes—she imagined they tasted how Hawaii looked.

At the milkshake shop, they took their shakes to a table that was set off from the main grouping of tables. "So, what is it?"

Leora swallowed the sweet, icy taste and exhaled nervously. "Vernon, this has to stay strictly between you and me. Please!"

Vernon studied his petite girlfriend. Her green eyes were vivid. "Okay. I promise."

"*Denki*. Remember that my *mamm* used to manage Annie Miller's quilt shop?" At Vernon's nod, she continued. "*Daed* forced her to quit. He doesn't like his wife to be working outside the home, believes she should be content staying at home. Only. . . my older sister's youngest has been diagnosed with asthma and the medications are expensive. The nebulizer is also expensive. She took several of her quilts into the shop today and it looks like they are going to sell fast."

"Well, it looks like she's found a solution for that, right? What's going on?"

Vernon didn't know it, but he was about to get a life lesson from Leora.

Leora sent a look of disbelief toward Jethro. Turning around, she looked around the milkshake shop, taking in the other customers, the activity level and the scents of the different milkshakes being prepared. "Vernon . . . really?"

Scooting her chair closer to him, she leaned inward. "Come here." Her voice had dropped to a low whisper.

Vernon obeyed, scooting much closer. "What is it?"

"It's not just a matter of *daed* making *mamm* resign from her job at the quilt shop. He did more. He beat her, Vernon. He left her with bruises on her face. And, because she didn't want that treatment again, she gave in. She knows he's going to start working on me. But because our *Ordnung* says that, because I'm unmarried, I can work outside the home as long as my work doesn't violate any part of the *Ordnung*. Vernon, tell me if I'm wrong. Can *daed* force *mamm* to quit her work? Or did he violate the Ordung?"

Vernon's mouth slowly fell open as he fell back against his chair. He shook his head and exhaled with a loud whoosh. "Leora, I am so sorry! I know only what my *daed* has said. Our *Ordnung* doesn't say anything specific about married—or single—women working outside the home. I need to ask him about the written part that governs all our districts. But I've never heard tell of anything that said women can't work outside the home. He is definitely violating our *Ordnung* by assaulting your *mamm*."

CHAPTER FOUR

Leora's appetite for her frozen confection disappeared. "Mei *Gott!*" Remembering what Annie had said about seeing her *daed* with Annie's husband came back. "Oh, no. . . Vernon, I think my *daed* is giving Annie Miller's husband ideas about how to force Annie to close the Peace Valley Quilt Place. That might include beating her or even Naomi."

"You think so?"

"For sure and for certain, if he—Mr. Miller— is successful in forcing his wife to close the shop, it could put a lot of us out of business. Even my *mamm*. She is making quilts at home and taking them to the Quilt Place. See, the Quilt Place accepts quilts on consignment and sells them for those women who bring them in. Not having that as an option would hurt those women."

Vernon pressed the heels of his hands into his eyes in reaction. Looking up, he looked outside the large window of the shop, seeing people walking and driving by. "Leora, aren't you afraid of living under your *daed*'s roof?"

Leora thought for a few minutes. As she did, her attention was pulled away by a small English toddler who was determined to run off her energy in the shop. She smiled slightly at the little girl, who was wearing light-purple leggings, a fluffy white-and-purple top and sneakers with flashing red lights in the soles. Feeling Vernon's warm hand on her wrist, she came back to the present. "Oh, uh, *Nee*, not really. When I come into the kitchen or wherever they are and he's been. . . bullying her, he stops when he sees me. I tell him to stop and he does. Stop, that is. I think he's ashamed of what he does, even thought it got him what he wanted."

"Okay, so you're safe. . . for now. About finding out if what he does violates the *Ordnung*, I need to check with *daed*. Do you mind if I do?"

"*Nee*, go ahead."

"He may want to have the elders come and talk to your *daed* if he asks me how I know this."

Leora caught the warning right away. "That doesn't matter. He fears the elders. He is so worried about breaking the *Ordnung* that he orders us not to do anything that will reflect on him! If he knows that someone talked to one of the elders, he may stop."

Vernon ruffled his hair as he thought. Running his hand back and forth over the top of his head, he was in danger of creating a rat's nest until his hand stopped moving over his head. "*Ja*, it could make him stop. But I'm thinking my *daed* should not be one of those visiting him. Or he'll think you told one of us."

Leora shivered as she thought of the consequences. "Uh, *ja*. Good point! Denki for listening to me." Pulling the shake back toward her, she began to drink it down before it melted completely.

***

Over the next few days, Leora waited for word from Vernon. She also worried, wondering who would come to visit her *daed*. One morning, as she was on her way to the Quilt Place for work, she realized she was beginning to obsess over the question. Releasing a deep sigh, she sent up a quick prayer then forced herself to take in the beauty around her.

It was full summer and the morning was already warm. Smiling slightly at the caress of the breeze on her cheek, Leora felt herself beginning to relax. A small dimple in her right cheek peeked out as she smiled. Her wavy bangs responded to the slight breeze, moving around her forehead and, as the wind picked up momentarily, flying back over her head covering before setting on her forehead once again.

"Leora! Wait up!"

Leora turned, hearing the pounding of shoes on pavement. "Vernon! *Gut* morning!"

"*Gut*. . . morning! You walk fast, don't you? I've been calling your name for a minute."

"Oh! I'm sorry! I was trying not to be so obsessed about. . . well, you know. I was rejoicing over the wonders we have all around us."

By now, Vernon had caught his breath. "I just wanted to let you know. I told my *daed* what you told me. He agreed with me. The elders need to visit your *daed*. And that will happen this afternoon or this evening. The deacon and the other minister will visit him. They won't reveal that you're the one who spoke up."

Leora closed her eyes in relief. "I'll be home by then. Will they want to talk to him by himself?"

"*Ja*, I would imagine. They'll probably talk to your *mamm* as well."

Leora stopped. Her vivid green eyes opened wide in fear. "Oh, no! I didn't want her to be involved!"

"She is. She's a victim. When you think about it, you are, too. They have to talk to her and, depending on what she says, they may want to talk to you as well. Leora, don't worry so much! If he knows that he's in danger of being put in the *Meidung*, he may stop forcing his will on your *mamm* and you."

Leora nodded, her mind obviously elsewhere. "Should I say anything to Mrs. Miller?"

Vernon began to ruffle his hair once again, thinking. "You said he might be giving ideas or guidance to Mr. Miller, *ja*? I would tell her something, but in private."

Leora's bright smile made her look even prettier than she already did. "Denki! I will—I don't want to see the shop closed because... my *daed* and Mr. Miller aren't willing to come into the 21st century."

"Okay. I'll see you later this week?"

"*Ja*! I'll be there!" Leora kept walking to the shop while Jethro returned to the market, where he was buying replacement parts for one of the saws.

Leora was almost at the shop when she saw her *daed* driving his buggy in the opposite direction. Forcing herself to smile at him, she waved, trying to seem like a carefree young woman focused on her job.

Wayne saw Leora and, raising his hand from the reins, he waved back. Instead of smiling, he sent a scowl toward his daughter.

Leora, seeing the frown, stopped smiling. Opening the door quickly, she slipped in and tried to forget the image of her *daed*'s face. Seeing that she still had some time, and that the other workers were still not there, she gestured toward Naomi and Annie. "I have some news! Fast! Before the others get here."

In the back of the shop, Annie looked at Leora, wondering what had happened. "What is it?"

"I told Vernon what's been happening with my *daed* and with your husband, Annie. He spoke to his *daed*, who spoke to the bishop and the other elders. My *daed* has violated the *Ordnung* by beating my *mamm*. The deacon and the other minister are going to come to our house later today and talk to my *daed*. Annie, they are aware that my *daed* has been giving your husband suggestions to make you close the shop and stay at home."

Annie was stunned. Looking toward both rear and front doors, she licked her dry lips. "So, that means the elders may also stop in to speak with Caleb."

Leora shook her head, raising her hands. "*Nee*! I don't know! That depends on what they talk to my *daed* about. I'm just telling you so you know what has been happening. That, if the elders persuade my *daed* to stop beating and bullying *mamm*, he may actually back down. I don't know. All I know is that his behaviors and his attitudes have been. . . sexist. I mean, what would happen if he were to die some time? How would *mamm* support herself? He doesn't think about that."

Annie needed time to think. "Leora, let's go for a walk, you, Naomi and me, at lunch time. We'll tell Rebecca and Miriam that we're talking about. . . oh, about something else and we'll be back before it's time to re-open after lunch. I'm not mad at you. You just surprised me. *Gott* knows, I want this to stop. Wayne hasn't hit me, but he has raised his fist to me. . . meaning he felt the impulse."

Not wanting to rattle Annie again, Leora filed her thought in her mind so she could bring it up on their walk later. If Mr. Miller hears about the elders' visit to my *daed*, he may decide to back down. I wonder if there are any resources for us if we are hit by our husbands or boyfriends? "Okay, Annie. Denki. I just don't like how my *daed*, your husband. . . or any other men here sometimes treat their wives and daughters. It's wrong. We are just as capable as they are."

Annie stifled the impulse to sniffle and cry. Swallowing hard, she smiled, running her hand through the hair made visible by her head covering. "Denki. I am so grateful to *Gott* that you and Naomi are such good friends!" She turned her head as Naomi, Rebecca and Miriam came into the store, chattering all the while.

"Girls! I want to have a short meeting before we open up. Come!" Walking toward the back of the store, Annie arranged five chairs just behind the cashier's counter. "I want to see the front window, so we'll talk here. Now." Looking at her notes, Annie continued. "Our promotional sale went very well. Between last Tuesday and this Saturday, we sold progressively more and more quilts so that, by Saturday, we doubled our normal Saturday sales!"

She waited until the squeals and cries of "Wunderbaar!" died down. "This means that, if things continue in this way, I may be able to give each of you raises early next year. But I don't want to count the chickens before their eggs are laid. So, let's just plan on working as hard as we have been doing. Naomi and I will work on more promotion ideas and we will have additional sales between now and the end of this year. Ideas?"

Naomi looked around. She already had a few, but she wanted to give the other girls a chance to weigh in. She smiled as Miriam raised her hand.

"How about an end-of-school promotion? We could focus on the lightweight, summery quilts."

Annie jotted the idea down, nodding her head.

Leora tossed her idea in: "I'm thinking that, with Wedding Season at the end of the harvest, we can offer wedding quilts and quilts in general for people wanting to give them as gifts."

Annie liked that idea, putting a small star next to her

handwriting.

Rebecca was the last to weigh in. "I know we focus more on His birth at Christmas, but why not have a Christmas sale? I know my own *mamm* gets very busy in the months and weeks before Christmas and she doesn't always have time to work on finishing the quilts she wants to give to others."

Annie gazed into the far distance, thinking. "*Ja*, I like that. Because Wedding Season and Christmas—and Thanksgiving, for that matter—are so close together, it is difficult for us to spend much time in our quilting rooms. If we focus more on taking some of the stress off the mothers and wives and less on the 'sale' aspect, we should be okay. Although I do want to speak to Deacon Hannes and get his input first. Okay, I see people starting to wait outside. It's about that time, so let's open up. Remember, customer service with a smile! Oh, Leora and Naomi, let's go for a short walk during lunch. I want to refine some of these ideas a little. Rebecca, Miriam, would you please stay here and keep an eye on the shop while we're gone?" Standing, she hurried to the door and unlocked it.

"*Ja*, we'll be happy to," Miriam said as she smiled.

The morning was busy for the quilt shop. While it wasn't as busy as it had been the previous Saturday, everyone still moved quickly from customer to customer, explaining various quilting designs, then ringing up sales.

***

Caleb waited impatiently at the side of the store, looking for Wayne Lapp. The other man had asked for the meeting so he could offer suggestions for getting Annie to close her blamed quilt shop. "Well, there you are! I'm a busy man and my crops won't wait."

"C'mon, I'm sorry. I had to shake Lizzie off my trail because she knew I didn't have plans to come into town. Sometimes, it was easier when she was working. But it violated the natural, God-given order of things. That's why I ordered her to quit her job at your wife's shop. And that's what I want to discuss with you now. What I did to get Lizzie to quit. You have time for some coffee?"

Caleb gazed at the sun's position. If he didn't linger too long, he should be okay, he thought. "*Ja*, sure. Long as it doesn't take too long. Let's go to that English diner on the edge of Peace Valley."

"*Ja*, I know the one. I've stopped patronizing the little restaurant here. It's run by Mrs. Zook, Miriam's *mamm*. Her husband should talk to her and make her close it. He's a farmer. He makes enough to support all of them."

Caleb nodded, though something about Wayne's last statement rankled him. "'Woman-owned.' Two of the most unnatural words in the English vocabulary. If her husband owned it, that would be correct."

Wayne grinned at his friend. "True. But Tim Zook is one of them new-thinking men, believing that it's just peachy for his wife to own her own business. I know it's not in the *Ordnung*, but it should be—that only the husbands should own and work the businesses here in Peace Valley." By now, they had gotten to the diner. Escorted to a booth by a male server, they ordered coffee and slices of pie. "Now, this is what I did. . ." Looking around, he verified that nobody would overhear what he was telling Caleb. "My wife was real resistant to quitting her job as the assistant manager. So, I. . . convinced her. With a beating."

RACHEL STOLTZFUS

CHAPTER FIVE

Caleb had just taken a sip of hot coffee. Inhaling at his shock, he choked painfully as the brew burned. Coughing and spewing coffee over the table, he shook his head. "Warn a man, wouldn't you?"

Coughing a few more times, Caleb swiped at his streaming eyes with the back of his weathered hand. He repeated Wayne's furtive gesture, looking around. "You mean you raised your hands against your own wife? You do know that violates the *Ordnung*, no?"

Wayne flushed with irritation. Sitting back, he pondered leaving, then he decided he needed the support more. He chose to glare at Caleb instead. "Hey, you want help or to see your wife continuing to work?"

Caleb's mouth opened and closed twice as he decided he wanted the help. "The help. But go easy on your wife! Remember, they do still have roles in our community. Doesn't

Lizzie still make quilts at home, then sell them?"

"*Ja*, but that's from home. That don't violate the *Ordnung*. *Ja*, the money comes in real handy, but I don't want her working outside our home! She saw the wisdom of my decision real quick. That's what I'm suggesting to you. *Ja*, your wife owns her business, but it's diminishing you and your role in your family. It's also diminishing your role in Peace Valley. She could own her own home-based business and she should be just happy with that. Lizzie's perfectly happy making quilts at home, even though she cries and moans about wanting to help Barbara, her husband and newest baby."

"What's happening with them? I knew they had a new little one. She sick or what?"

"*Ja*. The English doctor diagnosed her with asthma and loaded her *mamm* up with medicines and some machine called a 'nebulizer.' Because the baby's so young, she doesn't know how to breathe in the medicine from an inhaler, so Barbara has to pour liquid medicine into a little cup and attach that to the nebulizer. It works by making the medicine into a mist. The baby wears a small, I don't know, mask over her mouth and nose so the medicine gets into her lungs."

Caleb scratched his cheek. "Ain't all that stuff expensive? Barbara doesn't work, right? So they rely on her husband's income? How are they affording all that?"

Here, Wayne shifted, feeling vaguely uncomfortable. "*Ja*. It is. And Lizzie was whining about needing to go back to work at the shop so she could help them with the baby's medicines. I stopped all that real fast."

Despite his misgivings, Caleb was curious. "How?"

Caleb glanced around again. He was grateful that he'd chosen a table closer to the kitchen. "Just before she finally saw the light and quit her job, I administered a 'reminder' to her. I knocked her around a little. That week, she took a resignation letter in to Annie and now, she's staying at home. When Barbara came to us about the medicine and Lizzie started making noise about wanting to go back to work, I just stood over her. . . you know how little she is. . . and I just raised one fist at her. She knew what I meant and she backed down." Remembering that morning and the night he'd beat Lizzie, Wayne's grin became predatory and somehow, frightening.

Caleb, seeing this, leaned back. He regretting eating his pie so quickly—now, his stomach was squirming just as though he had eaten a passel of snakes. Smothering a groan, he looked again at Wayne. "Okay. Suppose I did what you suggest. What's to say that Annie. . . or even Naomi, won't go to the elders with that?"

"That's when you let them know that what happens behind the front door of your house stays right there. You worried about the money?"

Caleb raised one shoulder in a slight shrug. Any more

movement, and he was afraid he'd toss his pie all over the table. "*Mebbe*. Farming's not a sure science. The weather gets strange and there go the crops for a full season."

Wayne grunted in sympathy. "*Ja*, I know. I get an unreliable or dishonest customer and I can kiss a good sum of money goodbye. That's why I decided to. . . 'allow' Lizzie to make quilts from home and take them to your wife's shop. She gets a portion of the sale from each quilt. And *ja*, she is able to help with the baby's medicines."

Swallowing a little more of his coffee, Caleb shifted in his seat. "So. . . raise my hands against my wife. That'll work? What about if I just do what you did last time? Stand over her and raise my fists as though I'm going to hit her?"

"Caleb, you have to be ready to take every step possible! That's the only way. . . shhh." Taking a gulp of his coffee, Wayne shifted to a different topic. "So, the customer told me I had done a bad job with the headboard and dresser. He threatened not to pay me. It took me and my shop foreman to remind him that we had made everything exactly to his specifications." Glancing around with his eyes, Wayne assured himself that the server was now gone.

"If you're going to be successful in forcing Annie to sell the shop and stay at home, you have to hit her. Try not to bruise her too much, although that's not always possible. After the beating is over, apologize and just tell her that it's the stress that made you do that. Remind her how much you love her. . . then have the idea of, if she wants to work, she can work from home. And only from home. If she needs any reminders, just stand over her. She's tall, I know, but she's slender, ain't?"

Caleb nodded. "*Ja*. She is. I'm stronger than she is. It might work." Grimacing, he sighed, forcing back sudden nausea. "Okay. Next time it comes up, she gets a beating." Looking outside, Caleb saw that the shadows had shifted. "And now, I really got to get home." Pulling a few bills out of his wallet, he tossed them on the table. "Denki and I'll be seeing you."

Forcing himself to stand straight, Caleb strode outside and made a beeline for his buggy. The entire time he walked, his mind kept playing with him. And his stomach kept getting more and more messed up. His fists connecting with his wife's lovely face. The bruises and cuts on her face and body. Annie, crying and moaning.

By the time he got back to his buggy, the images had nauseated him completely. He had climbed to the seat and was ready to signal his horses to head back home, but his stomach had had enough. Leaning over the side, he lost his snack. The discussion with Wayne was so upsetting that he was sick two more times before finally pulling into the barn at home. I need medicine. Walking into the house, he looked around. Empty. As always.

In the bathroom, he swallowed medication intended to calm

his stomach. Downstairs, he sat on the dark-blue sofa and leaned his head back on the sofa's back, willing his stomach to behave. A few minutes later, groaning, he ran into the downstairs bathroom and vomited again. *Nee*, no way can I eat lunch. But maybe I can turn this into a situation that works for me. I'll just rest for a while, then go to the barn. Caleb worked through his idea slowly, mindful of his tender stomach. When they come home tonight and see that I'm sick, I can say that the leftovers went bad. And I can start using that as a reason for her to sell the shop. Caleb gave a slight grin, then closed his eyes. I'll just rest for a few minutes, allow the medicine to do its work.

***

While Caleb was suffering the aftereffects of his meeting with Wayne, Annie, Naomi and Leora were walking slowly down the street, discussing what Annie and Leora had talked about earlier.

". . . And Leora told me that what her *daed* and your *daed* are doing is sexist. I was thinking, while we were between customers, that our community's *Ordnung* does allow us to work outside the home. We're not as conservative as the Old Order Amish, right? So your *daed* and your *daed* are behind the times. It's going to take us some time to convince them of that. Naomi, try to think of ways to remind your *daed* that my business has helped our family to keep our heads above water when crops have not grown as they should have, or when they have failed outright. I want you and Leora to study this sexism thing more closely so we can develop more defenses against what the men try to tell us. Me? I will go and talk to Lovina King, Hannes' wife. We are friends and I am thinking that I could get some valuable information about violations of our *Ordnung*. It may be that what your *daed* did violated the *Ordnung*. . ."

RACHEL STOLTZFUS

CHAPTER SIX

Here, Leora jumped in. "Annie, it is! Vernon told me that. That's why the elders are going to talk to my *daed* today. His *daed* won't be one of them, because Vernon talked to him. Once the elders talk to him, they'll have a better idea of whether he's going to comply with the *Ordnung* or whether they have to promise the *Meidung* to him. I'll try to get information from Vernon and let you know what happens. Do you want me to talk to him about what your husband is doing?"

Annie shook her head. "*Nee*. Not yet. I'm praying that Wayne will tell Caleb what happened and that will make them stop their behaviors. If need be, I can talk to Lovina and ask her to tell Hannes what is happening. It's time to get back to the shop. Remember, learn as much as you can about sexism so we can develop a plan."

***

Arriving home that night, Annie was surprised when she opened the refrigerator and saw that Caleb hadn't eaten any of the dinner she'd made for him.

"*Mamm*! Bring the cleaners with you, please! *Daed* was sick earlier and he didn't clean it up. Ewww." Naomi gulped back her own nausea and backed out of the first-floor bathroom.

Grabbing the needed cleaners, plus a pair of cleaning gloves, Annie hurried to the bathroom. "Oh, my! No wonder he didn't eat this afternoon. Go. Outside and get fresh air so you don't get sick."

Naomi obeyed instantly, running to the back door, where she inhaled deep breaths of fresh air. Sighing, she closed her eyes in relief—the nausea was subsiding.

Annie quickly cleaned up the bathroom, erasing all signs of Caleb's illness. After putting the cleaners, gloves and soiled cloths away, she hurried to the barn. "Do you feel better, Naomi?"

"Much. Denki. I'll stay out here for a little while more."

"*Gut*. I'm going to the barn to see if I find your *daed* and see what's wrong with him." Hurrying, Annie nearly ran to the barn. "Caleb? There you are! What happened to you? You were sick—I just cleaned it up."

"Up or downstairs?" By now, Caleb had built up a head of steam, justifying what he was about to do. His nausea had long since departed.

"Upstairs, too? I'll clean that up right away. Did you pick up a bug?" Annie was concerned. Money was already tight and they didn't need for Caleb to be laid up until he got well.

"Wife, I got sick from the food you stored in the refrigerator for me! While you should be at home, you're in that infernal store of yours, chatting and gossiping with the other wives and your. . . workers instead of being at home, cleaning and making our meals fresh! I felt this sickness building last night with stomach cramps. Even though I took antacids, it kept growing inside my stomach, until this morning, when I got horribly sick. *Nee*, I didn't eat what you left. I couldn't! And now that I have finally gotten all that poison out of my system, I am fairly starving! I want you to close that store, sell it, whatever you need to do. Soon!"

By now, Caleb was physically looming over Annie, who had backed up against the wide counter inside the barn. He raised one arm, hand fisted, implying that, if she didn't agree, he would strike her.

Annie, seeing Caleb's raised fist, gasped with fear. Seeing a slight opening between his body and the counter, she edged out as fast as she could, then, without giving him an answer, she ran out of the barn and back toward the house.

Naomi heard her *daed* yelling at her *mamm*. Running toward the barn, she ran headlong into her *mamm*, who was white-faced and fighting tears. "*Mamm*! What happened?"

Annie didn't speak. Instead, she gripped Naomi's arm, pulling her toward the kitchen. In the house, she caught her breath and wiped away tears. "Your *daed* threatened me. Said that the food I put away for him went bad and made him sick. We'll make supper, then you will go to oh, either Leora's or the King's house. Let them know what just happened."

"*Mamm*, I'd better go to talk to Deacon King. If I go to Leora's, her *daed* will know what is up. And that we were the ones who alerted the deacon through Vernon."

Annie, her thoughts still scattered, nodded, realizing Naomi was right. "Okay. Just be back before bedtime. That's all I ask. I need to clean the upstairs bathroom. *Daed* was sick up there as well."

Gathering the cleaning items once more, Annie went upstairs. Holding her breath against the foul stench, she cleaned, still feeling shaky. Once the bathroom was cleaned, she threw the soiled cloths into the wash room and washed her hands before starting supper.

Caleb came silently into the kitchen, feeling somewhat ashamed of his outburst in the barn. Not liking the feeling, he scowled. "Well? Did you give thought to my ultimatum?"

Annie drew in a shaky breath. Not wanting to show fear, she stood tall and straight. "*Ja*. I did. It's not going to be easy to sell the shop in this economic downturn. Naomi, please stay. You need to know what goes into the thinking and planning." Feeling her thoughts coalescing around a theme, Annie felt more calm. "Caleb. I'm not buying medication or medical equipment for a seriously ill child. But I am employing five other young women here, one of them your daughter. To sell the shop, I would have to spend valuable funds on advertising. Hire an English attorney to draw up paperwork and pay more money to him. Find a buyer and pay even more money to run a credit check on them. Your crops are doing well—this year, thank *Gott*. But, what happens if a drought develops next year? Eventually, Naomi will get married and we need to save money for that. We're still paying off the loan to the bank for the equipment you had to replace. We also pay your employees. I'm not going to say no about selling, but I am telling you we have to think very carefully about how I would do this."

Caleb's scowl slowly lessened. "So, you aren't saying no? Just that we need to take some time?"

Annie's heart squeezed as she nodded. She didn't like to tell lies. "If you feel better, supper is ready."

"*Ja*. I do. Denki."

Supper was a quiet, strained meal that night. The usual talk and laughter that accompanied their meals was absent.

"*Mamm*? *Daed*? Do you mind if I go to visit with Leora?

She asked me to stop by after cleaning up from supper. She wants to talk to me about one of our friends and some troubles she having." Twisting her fingers painfully, Naomi sent up a silent apology for her own lies.

Annie pretended to be upset. "Tonight? Why didn't you talk on our lunch break?"

"*Mamm*, it's because the other girls were there. We couldn't exactly talk about our friend in front of them, could we?"

Sighing, Annie relented. "Okay, *ja*. As long as you are back before it gets full dark. It's summer, but I don't want you out after dark. Do you understand?"

"*Ja*, denki!"

"Daughter, I'm happy to see you trying to help your friends, but I do agree with your *mamm*. I don't like you traipsing all over the place, so be back before the moon comes up."

"Denki, *daed*. I will." Grabbing the cloth, Naomi cleaned the kitchen as Annie washed dishes, then she helped her *mamm* dry and put them away.

***

Riding to Vernon's house, Naomi breathed deeply, willing her heart rate to fall back to normal. On the way, she sent a fervent prayer to *Gott*, asking him to open her *daed*'s heart to the reality that her *mamm* needed to work. When she arrived at

Vernon's, she gulped back a sob. Knocking on the door, she waited, nerves causing her to wring her hands.

"Naomi! Come in! This is a wunderbaar. . . Naomi? What's wrong?" Vernon was very familiar with her expressions and he knew she was frightened right now.

Naomi dragged in a large breath, willing herself to stay calm. "Vernon, is your *daed* here? And your *mamm*?"

"*Ja*, they are. Come into the kitchen." Vernon curled his hand around Naomi's upper arm, trying to give her comfort. "*Daed, mamm*? Naomi's here. I think. . . something happened at her house. She asked to speak with you. Naomi do you want me to stay or leave?"

"Oh, please stay! I need you to know this as well." Naomi grabbed Vernon's hand in both of her own as she begged for his presence.

"Come, Naomi. Sit. Would you like some water or lemonade? It appears you don't need coffee right now." Deacon Hannes King's kind brown eyes took in Naomi's upset. He was sure he knew what it was about, but knew that Naomi needed to say what happened.

"Lemonade, please. Denki, Mrs. King." She took a gulp of the tart beverage before sinking into a chair. Closing her eyes, she saw the frightening scene outside the barn, which caused her to shudder. "Deacon, thank you for seeing me so unexpectedly. My *mamm* knows I'm here, but my *daed* thinks I'm at my friend's house. I know the other elders are meeting with Mr. Lapp this evening. *Mamm* said she saw *daed* walking down the street with Mr. Lapp a few days ago. We're concerned that Mr. Lapp is giving *daed* ideas and suggestions about how to make *mamm* quit her quilt store.

"Well, this afternoon, we got home at our usual time so we could make supper. Only *daed* had been sick, so *mamm* cleaned that up, then she went to the barn when she couldn't find him in the house. He got so mad at her, deacon!" Naomi sniffled, trying to hold tears back. Wiping her cheeks, she continued. "He blamed her for his sickness today, saying that the food she had prepared for his dinner earlier in the week was bad. He accused her of giving him food poisoning. I heard him yelling at her and ran to the barn. Deacon, I saw. . . I saw. . ."

Here, Naomi had to stop. Her sobs were too strong. Lovina and Hannes King took her hands, helping her to calm down. Naomi finally calmed down enough to continue. "I'm sorry. I saw. . . my *daed* trapping *mamm* between his body and the work shelf in the barn. He had one arm raised like this. . ." Here, Naomi imitated a man about to strike someone else. "His hand was in a fist."

Lovina looked at Hannes, silently communicating to him.

Hannes caught the message and nodded. "Naomi, you were brave to come here and tell us what you saw today. *Ja*, the elders are talking to Mr. Lapp at this moment, offering him help and reminding him that, if he continues to threaten his wife—or his daughter—in this way, he faces the *Meidung*. I am thinking we need to go and visit with your *daed* to give him the same message. "

Lovina began speaking when her husband finished. "Naomi, I don't know if you're aware of this, but we do have some families here who are willing to help families struggling with domestic violence. The English communities frown on this kind of treatment of men's wives. I'm also aware that some English wives actually physically abuse their husbands. We don't want or need any of that kind of treatment here, so Vernon's *daed* and I have been working with some of the volunteer couples. I would like to introduce you and your *mamm* to one of them. They have agreed to work with families in need of attention, prayer and. . . well, if you want to call it that, 'retraining' in handling disagreements in a loving, safe way. I want you to tell your *mamm* all of this because she and your *daed* would have to agree to this work. If Hannes, along with other elders, visit with your *daed* and let him know they are aware of what happened today, they will remind him of what he is risking if he refuses."

Naomi listened closely. "*Ja*. I can talk to her while we're on the way to the shop tomorrow. Mrs. King, do you and your husband know what 'sexism' is?" Naomi had recovered her usual calm and presence of mind so that she was not afraid of bringing up this topic.

Lovina nodded. "I do. Hannes and I have no doubt that what is happening between your *mamm* and *daed*, as well as the Lapps, is because of sexism, when one gender believes it is superior to the other gender. Now, do you mind telling me something?"

Naomi nodded. "Okay. What?"

"Well, tell me two things, please. First, what is Mr. Lapp trying to get your *daed* to do? And second, why did your *daed* threaten your *mamm* today?"

Naomi sighed. "We think Mr. Lapp is explaining to *daed* how he forced his wife to quit her job at the quilt shop. I mean, it's not like the two of them have been the best of friends before. I've seen them together at least twice and *mamm* saw them this week."

Vernon was angry that anyone could think he was superior to anyone of the other gender. Needing to walk off some of his anger, he gestured to Naomi and his parents that he would be back in a few minutes. "I'm just so upset at all of this. I need to walk it off."

"That's fine. Just don't be too long." Hannes sent a stern look to his youngest son.

"I won't. Naomi, I promise, I'll be back in soon." Vernon tried to smile.

Naomi nodded. Seeing the effects of her story on him worried her. "Vernon, I'm okay. I just hope we can get help for the Lapps, my *daed* and my *mamm*. After Vernon had walked out the back door, Naomi continued. "We believe that Mr. Lapp is trying to get my *daed* to attack my *mamm* physically. *Mamm* remembers that, shortly before she quit, Mrs. Lapp came into work with a huge bruise on her face. She tried to explain it away, but my *mamm* wasn't fooled. Mrs. Lapp finally admitted that her husband beat her up. Leora remembers the beating as well. And, this is what *mamm* and I have been talking about so much. *Daed* is trying to force *mamm* to give up and sell her quilting shop. But *mamm* doesn't want to. Her shop employs four of us. Five if she's able to find an assistant manager. He tells her that women belong at home, cleaning, cooking and taking care of the children.

"Tonight, *mamm* reminded him that her store allows women who make their quilts at home to sell them through the store and earn some money. I. . . I hope I'm not betraying any confidences here, but Mrs. Lapp has begun to take her quilts into the shop. Because her newest grandchild has been diagnosed with asthma. And her medicines and that special machine are so expensive. So, that's what Mrs. Lapp is doing with the money she earns from selling her quilts at our store."

Hannes had heard enough. Getting up, he began to stride around the kitchen. "*Nee*, Naomi, don't worry. I'm feeling the same as Vernon—frustrated, angry." After a few minutes, he calmed down and Vernon came in at the same time. "Naomi, I got so frustrated because both your *daed* and Mr. Lapp are missing the importance of their wives' work outside the home. Our *Ordnung* has been modified, allowing married women to hold outside jobs. I don't know if you remember this, but didn't one of your *daed*'s crops almost fail a year or two ago, when we had that long drought?"

Naomi's mouth dropped open. She knew where the deacon was going with this! "*Ja*! It did and it was only *maam's* ownership of the shop that allowed us to keep going, get food on the table and keep paying the note at the bank for *daed*'s new equipment! *Mamm* and I talked about that because she wants me to be as aware of finances as possible."

"Wise woman." Lovina smiled. "Naomi, I think my husband wants the elders to use this reminder to show your *daed* that your *mamm* and her shop are valuable and precious to your family."

"My wife knows me well, Naomi." Hannes gave a small smile. That's exactly what I want to do. I will go see the other ministers and the bishop tomorrow and we will stop in to visit with your *daed* and *mamm* later this week."

Naomi experienced competing feelings. First, she felt absolute relief, then fear of what her *daed* would do or say.

Vernon watched as Naomi's face changed. "Naomi, don't worry. He won't do anything to you or your *mamm*. The elders will make it clear to him that, by threatening physical violence against your *mamm*, he violated our *Ordnung*. And that he is risking the ban."

Closing her eyes, Naomi forced herself to calm down. "Okay. I know that he doesn't want to go under the *Meidung*. Mrs. King, who are these families that are helping you?"

"I'm sure you're very familiar with one of them, as our son is dating Leora. You're also familiar with them. Eli and Lizzie Yoder."

Naomi smiled, her first genuine smile since coming into the house. "They are perfect! I like how they treat each other and their children. And they treat other families with kindness and respect."

"That doesn't mean they'll allow abusers to get away with their bad behaviors." Hannes raised one finger as a reminder. "If they hear or witness anything, they will report it to the elders, and they will require couples to commit to treating each other with respect."

Naomi felt more comfortable with the idea by the minute. Closing her eyes and sending up a brief prayer, she nodded. Opening her eyes, she spoke. "*Ja*. If this helps my parents to stop fighting about the shop and it keeps *daed* from harming *mamm*, then let's do it. Also, if *daed* would just open his blamed eyes and see that the shop has kept his farm from failing in rough years so he stops bothering *mamm* about closing or selling the shop."

Hannes smiled at Naomi as he realized she was very intelligent. "Those are excellent goals and definitely reachable. Don't tell your *mamm* this until tomorrow. I would like to stop at your house tomorrow, at the earliest, but that depends on the other elders' schedules."

"I need to get home. I promised both *mamm* and *daed* I'd be home by the time it got dark and it's close to that now. Denki!" Standing, she got ready to leave the house.

"Let me follow you, please. Just to the end of your lane so I know you got home safely." Vernon didn't like the idea of her driving late at night.

"*Ja*, that's fine." Naomi walked out with Vernon and waited as he checked to make sure the horses were properly hitched to the buggy. Settling on the seat, she waited as he led his own team out of the barn.

"You go ahead and I'll follow." Vernon waited for Naomi to signal her horses to move.

On her way home, Naomi thought about everything she had discussed with the Kings. Knowing that another Amish couple could help her parents correct their relationship's course was a huge relief to her. Feeling better and better by the minute, she gave Vernon a genuine smile as she turned onto her lane.

"I'll see you on Friday!" Vernon said, just loud enough for her to hear.

"That sounds *gut*! See you then!" Hurrying the rest of the way, Naomi was relieved that the sun hadn't yet fully set. Pulling into the barn, she was surprised to see her *daed* working at his worktable. "Hi, *daed*! Are you feeling okay?"

"*Ja*, daughter. I'm better, denki. How was your visit with Leora?"

"*Gut*. We talked about quilt patterns we want to try, as well as our plans for the weekend." Naomi had already come up with things she and Leora had already talked about so she wouldn't really be lying.

"Plans for the weekend? You mean with Vernon and Jethro? Hmmm, as long as your work here is done. And, if you insist on working at the shop, that's not going to give you much time. Weeding? Cleaning the house?"

Naomi knew what her *daed* was doing. "*Daed, mamm* and I got the cleaning done earlier this week, when the shop was closed. And I got the weeding done in the morning, before it got too hot."

Caleb knew he'd been outsmarted by his own daughter. This didn't improve his mood. His voice settling into a low growl, he pointed at her. "Daughter, you'd better make very sure that all of your work here has been done. I am still your *daed* and I still have authority over you."

Naomi's mouth dropped open. "*Ja, daed*, I know. I was just letting you know that I got all of my chores done already. I also checked the garden again and ensured that there are no weeds there."

Annie came into the barn as Naomi finished speaking to her *daed*. "Caleb? What's wrong?" She sent a frown to Naomi, along with a silent message in her eyes.

"She was sassing me and I was reminding her that I still hold authority over her. She told me that she, Leora and their boyfriends have already made plans for this weekend. And I reminded her that she needs to finish her work here first."

"Naomi, you know our rules here at home. Work first, pleasure last. If your work is truly done, then yes, you can spend time with your friends. But if it isn't, you'll need to make adjustments and let them know. Do you understand?"

"*Ja, mamm*. I'm sorry, *daed*. I didn't intend to come across like I was sassing you. *Mamm*, my work is done. I'll. . . I'll get supper started."

"*Nee*, daughter. I have that underway. I need your help with the biscuits and dessert, and, when you're done with that, look through our work calendar for this month to make sure we have everything ready for tomorrow and next week."

"*Ja, mamm.*" Naomi made her voice meek and quiet. Lowering her head, she tried to give the impression that she was disappointed with herself as she went to the house. Pulling the ingredients out for the apple crisp, she thought about what her *mamm* may have been trying to tell her. She overheard her *daed* talking to her *mamm*.

"Annie, I still have a few things left to do. The new boy is still slow at his work, so it's up to me to get it done."

"Ach! How long has he worked for you?" Annie was sympathetic.

"Only for a few weeks. I'm giving him another three, maybe four weeks before I decide whether he stays or goes. I'll be in by the time you put supper on the stove."

"Okay." Annie hurried back to the house. Inside, she checked Naomi's progress on the apple crisp and biscuits. "Naomi, you handled that well. Have you decided whether you're comfortable moving into the manager's position?"

"*Ja*, I think I can handle it. When are you going to make the announcement?" Annie finished peeling the apples and began mixing the crisp as she watched the outdoors, looking for her *daed*.

"I'll bring it up tomorrow afternoon, after we get home. What I want to do is spend mornings only at the shop."

CHAPTER SEVEN

Naomi's hands stilled in their work. "You mean I would be responsible for everything in the afternoons? Including counting out the day's sales and making the deposit?"

"Exactly. But I want to bring this up with you as though we had never discussed it, understand?"

Naomi understood perfectly. "I like your ideas. Discussing them in front of *daed* will take some of the pressure off of you."

"That's my hope and prayer, daughter. I hope he will see that I am serious about making a good home for him and you while keeping ownership of the store."

Naomi gave a quick look out the window. "*Mamm*, I think he wants you home full time, with no shop at all."

"*Ja*, that's what he says. Deep down though, he knows that my little shop has saved our family and farm when conditions have made it impossible for him to have a good harvest. I hope that, when you go out with your friends tomorrow after I break my news and inform you that you're the new manager, that he will want to talk with me."

"*Mamm*, but I think it's safer to have that discussion while I'm around! What if he gets mad at you and. . ."

"There's a repeat of what you saw in the barn?" Annie continued stirring the vegetables as she considered Naomi's point. "Good point. Then you verify your plans for tomorrow with the others and let me know while we're on the way to the shop."

Naomi sighed. "*Ja*, that's better." Putting the biscuits into the hot oven, she indicated the back yard. "*Daed*'s coming in."

Annie nodded. Moving to the salad, she broke up a head of lettuce and began cutting up a tomato. "Naomi, is the crisp almost ready?"

"*Ja*, I'm about to put it in with the biscuits." Naomi's head swiveled around as she heard Caleb scraping dirt from his shoes. "Hi, *daed*! Supper will be ready in a little while!"

"*Gut*. I am powerful hungry, daughter. What did you and your *mamm* make tonight?"

Annie answered. "Fried chicken, baked potatoes with the fixings, salad and mixed vegetables. Naomi made the biscuits and some apple crisp."

Caleb closed his eyes in anticipation. "You two made my favorite meal! Denki!"

Annie and Naomi smiled at each other. As they did so, Naomi wondered if her *mamm* had planned this particular meal on purpose.

After dinner was over and Caleb was nursing a fresh cup of coffee, Naomi rose from the table. "*Mamm*, I'll clean the kitchen and do the dishes."

"And I'll dry. Thank you." By the time Caleb had finished his last cup of coffee, leaving the kitchen, Annie was ready to clean the table.

"I'm going to get ready now. Jethro should be here before long and I want to comb my hair and put on a fresh head covering."

"Okay. Just do not be too late. Understand?" Annie motioned toward the living room with her eyes.

"Okay. I'll let Jethro know I need to be home early." In her room, Naomi considered everything her *mamm* was doing. Fried chicken and telling me to be in early. She's trying to soften *daed* up! Given how he's been treating her, I think she's right to do so. If we can get him to stay in a happier mood, he might eventually give in about her store.

Finishing her hair and setting a fresh head covering on her

head, she hurried downstairs. A few seconds later, Jethro knocked at the back door. "*Daed, mamm*, I'll be back early. I promise!" Naomi hurried out before her *daed* could say anything. "Jethro, I need to be back in earlier than usual. We're trying not to upset *daed*."

"Why would he be upset about us going out?" Jethro's forehead crinkled in confusion.

"He's been trying to make the point that, if I'm not at home, I can't get my chores done. I have some news for you when we meet up with Leora and Vernon. Where are we going, by the way?"

"We thought we would take you two over to the new coffee shop, enjoy some coffee and sweets."

"I hope I can make room! *Mamm* made fried chicken tonight!"

"Mmm, one of my favorites!"

Naomi giggled. "I'll make sure to get the recipe from *mamm*."

***

In the coffee shop, Naomi and Jethro sat down with Leora and Vernon. "I want to try one of these new coffees," said Leora.

"Me, too! Which one?"

"Let's look at the menu to see which would be best." Leora's eyes twinkled as she read through the small menu.

After both couples had placed their orders, they waited and talked. "Leora, *mamm* has news for me. She's going to break it to me in front of *daed* tomorrow after work."

Leora's eyes widened. "I think I know! But tell us!"

Naomi waited for a split second before she spoke. "She asked me to think about moving up to the manager's position. There's a couple reasons for this. I'm happy and I'm saying yes. *Mamm* and I are hoping and praying that, by my becoming manager, she'll be able to spend more time at home, where *daed* wants her. That, by spending more time at home, he'll stop with his demands that she sell the shop and stop working outside our home."

Leora became serious. "I pray that will be so. *Daed* is still very firm that *mamm* has to stay at home. He's only okay with her selling quilts on consignment because of my niece's health problems and the costs of her medications."

"Leora, has he stopped. . . physically threatening your *mamm*?" Naomi was tense, feeling her entire body beginning to tighten up.

"*Ja*, especially after the elders came by the other night."

Jethro leaned in toward Leora. "Can you tell us what happened? Or is that confidential?"

"Only because we know what's been. . ." Leora gasped as several coffee mugs went crashing to the ground. Along with her gasp, the others jumped as well. ". . . Going on. The bishop and two ministers came to the house and took *daed* outside. I tried to stick as close to the kitchen door as I could without being caught. They told him that they had been informed that he had attacked *mamm* a few months ago, leaving bruises on her face. He couldn't deny it, but he did try to defend himself with the *Ordnung* of all things."

Vernon let out a bark of laughter. "How? Physically assaulting someone else is a violation, period!"

"He tried to say that *mamm* was violating the *Ordnung* by working outside the house at all. He tried to say that, if she hadn't begun working at the quilt shop, he wouldn't have been forced to exert his husbandly right to discipline her. The elders were having none of that. They reminded him that our *Ordnung*, in its current form, does allow married and unmarried women to work outside the home so they can provide for the economic needs of their families. So, Naomi, if your own *daed* tries to say that your *mamm* is violating the *Ordnung*, she can tell him that he's wrong."

Vernon cleared his throat. "Speaking of which, Naomi. The elders are going to go and see your *daed* tomorrow after breakfast. I hope you and your *mamm* will either be away from home or working on chores."

Naomi felt chilled at the thought that her own *daed* would soon be confronted by the elders. Shivering, she picked up her cup of coffee and took a large gulp. "We'll be going to work. Saturday's a short day and *mamm* wants to make the announcement of my promotion to the others. Will the elders be speaking to my *mamm* as well?"

"I would think so. They spoke to Mrs. Lapp and she confirmed what happened and why it happened."

Naomi was troubled. "On one hand, I'm glad they'll be speaking to her, because she can tell them that she'll only be working at the shop half-time. On the other hand, she'll be at work and they won't be able to get her side of this mess."

"Ach, good point, Naomi. When I get home later on, I will let my *daed* know that so he can call the ministers and deacon. What time do you and your *mamm* usually leave for work?"

About eight-fifteen, more or less. That gives us time to make sure the store is presentable and put the till in the cash register. Also, it gives us a few minutes for a meeting so we all know what's happening."

"Okay." Vernon turned to a passing barista. "Excuse me, but do you have the time?"

"Sure!" He looked at his watch. "It's about nine-forty-five. We're closing in forty-five minutes."

"Denki." Looking at the others, Vernon pointed toward the door. "We should get home. Naomi can't be getting into trouble. And I'm sure Leora feels the same way."

The two couples left, climbing into the courting buggies and headed back to Peace Valley. Naomi was quiet, thinking of the coming meeting.

"You okay?" Jethro gave Naomi a worried look.

"*Ja.* I'm just thinking about the meeting tomorrow. If *mamm* hasn't gone to bed yet, I'll let her know that we should find a way of leaving a little later than usual. But if she's in bed. . ."

"Just wait until you're making breakfast?"

"*Ja.* While *daed* is feeding the livestock. I'm sure we can create a reason to leave a little bit later. Vernon said he would be telling his *daed* that they need to get here before we leave. . ."

"Vernon's smart. He'll work things out and tell his *daed* what time you leave, so that they are there well before your usual departure time."

Naomi relaxed a little at that. "*Ja,* that is true. Leora picked a good man, and so did I."

"Thank you! I need to ask you this before we get to your parent's house. What do you think of my *mamm* and *daed* helping your *daed* with his anger at your *mamm* working outside the house?"

"I like your parents. A lot. I like how they think. . . *ja*, I think it would be *gut* for them to work with my *daed* and *mamm*. She needs to know how to make him stop before he gets all riled."

"That is true. Okay, I'll tell them when I get home." After bringing Naomi to the front gate of the house, he leaned over and gave her a soft kiss, then drove the team into the yard, where he escorted Naomi to the front door. "I'll see you tomorrow evening?"

"*Ja.* You will. Good night!" Naomi smiled and waved at Jethro before walking into the house. Turning toward the kitchen, she prayed that her *mamm* was still up. In the kitchen, she sighed with relief. "*Mamm*, you're still up! Is everything okay?"

"*Ja*, just thinking of tomorrow."

"Me, too. Is *daed* already asleep?"

"Mmm-hmm. Long since. Why?"

"*Mamm*, Jethro, Leora and Vernon and I were talking about our family's situations." Here, she lowered her voice slightly. "The elders visited Mr. and Mrs. Lapp the other evening and got confirmation that Mr. Lapp assaulted Mrs. Lapp. And

Vernon told me that the elders are going to be here tomorrow. They are going to want to talk to *daed* and you. Is there any way we can leave a little later than normal?"

"Did you tell them what time we leave?"

"Yes, I did. Jethro's sure that Vernon is telling his *daed* what time we leave so they can be here well before we have to go."

Annie exhaled a deep sigh and dropped her chin toward her chest. "Daughter, I am just so grateful to *Gott* right now! He is working all things for *gut* here. Your *daed* is going to find out that threatening me and trying to force me to sell the store violates the *Ordnung* and he is also going to find out that I am making you manager so I can spend more time here. Thank you, Lord!"

Both women paused at a creak in the hallway. Annie looked toward the stairs. In a normal tone of voice, she offered water to Naomi.

"*Ja*, just water. We had coffee drinks and snacks and I don't want to get too full to sleep comfortably."

Waiting a few seconds more, they assured themselves that the house was just settling. Caleb was still asleep.

"So, I will pray that they get here much closer to seven than eight-fifteen. I'll be making eggs, home-fried potatoes and sausage tomorrow morning. You make biscuits. As far as your *daed* knows, we won't know anything of the visit from the elders. We'll be getting ready to leave for work, period."

"Okay. I'd better get to bed. Morning is going to come. . ."

"Awfully quickly. Denki, daughter, for telling me about this." Annie hugged her daughter.

∗∗∗

The next morning, the ministers gathered at the King home, which was closest to the Miller's home. "We need to get there *gut* and early. Mrs. Miller and her daughter usually leave home by eight-fifteen." The bishop looked at his ministers and the deacon. "I don't want this kind of thing threatening our families, so I want to make it very clear to Caleb that he has to stop threatening his wife and daughter. Are we ready?"

Climbing into the bishop's buggy, they set out for the Miller home. Pulling into the front yard and under a large, spreading tree, the elders jumped out of the buggy and walked up to the house. Knocking on the door, they waited.

Caleb answered the door. Seeing the four elders, his face paled and his eyes grew wide. "Bishop! I. . . hope nothing bad has happened."

"Caleb, I believe you know just why we are here. Come outside. We want to talk to you."

Caleb moved on legs that had lost all feeling. Collapsing

onto the porch swing, he waited, knowing what was coming.

The bishop took the lead. "Caleb, we have had some sad and disturbing news. That you have been trying to force your wife to give up her ownership of Peace Valley Quilt Place so you can make her stay at home. Further, we got word that you have been meeting with Wayne Lapp to get additional ideas on how you can prevail upon Annie to make her quit and sell her store. Is this true?"

Caleb nodded with reluctance. "The *Ordnung*. . ."

"Says nothing about wives and older daughters about being required to stay at home. You are aware, aren't you, that, after the Great Recession of 2008, we changed our rules so that our wives and daughters could work outside the home? We view them as full partners in our marital relationships and in our homes. By trying to force Annie to sell her shop, you are violating the *Ordnung*."

Hannes King spoke up. "Further, we have been told that, just a few days ago, after meeting with Wayne Lapp, you raised your fist to your wife in the midst of an argument. Is this true?" As Hannes asked the question, his face and eyes communicated real sadness and disappointment.

It was these emotions, more than anything, that got to Caleb. Setting his mug down between his feet, he wrung his big, weathered hands together. "*Ja*. It is. I have always held the belief that the women are supposed to stay at home. Partners or not, they can contribute from the home." He refused to bend.

"If that is what they wish and what they are able to contribute, *ja*, this is true." One of the ministers sat forward, gazing into Caleb's face. "But, if the wife or daughters have a skill or specialized knowledge, they are encouraged—not 'allowed,' Caleb—encouraged to use those skills toward providing support for their families. As I understand it, your wife was able to attend vocational training, where she took business classes. My own wife contributes quilts to her shop and the money she gets paid has helped our household out when my crops haven't done well. Now, would you rather rely on your pride and have your family suffering after a crop failure? Or would you rather elevate Annie to a position next to you, where she can make a full contribution from her skills, interests and knowledge?"

The bishop leaned forward once again. "Caleb, you know full well why we are here. You have a decision to make. Repent and continue within our community. Or refuse to repent and face the ban. We are going to go in and speak with your wife now. If you would come in. . ."

CHAPTER EIGHT

Standing and grabbing his mug of now-cold coffee, Caleb let the elders into the house. "Annie! The elders want to talk to you. I'll be in the barn, working." Filling his mug with the last of the coffee, he walked out through the kitchen.

Annie and Naomi looked at each other, their eyes wide. "*Mamm*, you go talk to the ministers. I'll finish in here before we leave."

Sitting at the kitchen table with the four ministers, Annie verified everything. "*Ja*, he has been trying to force me to sell my shop so I can stay at home every day. I've been doing everything I can to make sure that everything here is done—providing meals for his dinner, cleaning the house on Mondays, when the store is closed. My daughter has consented to becoming the store manager, which will enable to me to work half-time so I can give Caleb a part of his wish."

"*Gut!* You have been trying to work with your husband on this issue. You are aware that the *Ordnung*, as it is currently written, does allow you to work?" The bishop's gaze met Annie's face.

"*Ja*, bishop. I am. I want to work with Caleb on this. I don't want him getting angry at me and threatening to hit me. That's why I came up with the idea of promoting Naomi."

"*Gut*. He is thinking and praying over his options. He knows what they are. Before we go, I am going to go to the barn and let him know that you have been trying to work with him on keeping your store and giving him some of what he's been seeking. Does he know that Naomi is becoming manager?"

"*Nee*. She only made her decision yesterday and we haven't had the time to break the news to him."

"Then I will bring him back in here, unless you need to leave for the shop now?"

Annie checked the wall clock. "We still have some time before we have to go."

"I'll let myself out the back." The bishop hurried, knowing that time was vital. In the barn, he saw Caleb leaning over the work bench, his head lowered. "Caleb? Are you okay?"

"As okay as I'll ever be, *ja*. What is it?"

"I have a development that you may like, if you'll come

back to the house." The bishop smiled with encouragement.

Caleb grabbed his coffee mug and swallowed the last of his coffee. "What is it?"

"*Nee*, you need to hear this from Annie and Naomi. Come!"

Caleb swung the back door open and, after the bishop entered, left it open so a cool breeze could enter. "Annie, what is it?"

"Husband, would you please sit? I have news that I hope you might like." After Caleb took his usual seat at the head of the table, Annie took in a huge breath. Looking into her husband's deep, normally kind, brown eyes. "Husband, I asked Naomi to become the manager of the shop. She agreed to do so last night, but we didn't get the chance to tell you this then. She's going to work all day long at the store while I work half-days. I'll go in just after lunch and close with her. That way, I'll be here at home more as you wish me to be. But that also means that I will be able to continue contributing to our family's financial well-being."

Caleb nodded. This was, indeed a surprise! One he could be happy with. Knowing he couldn't push for more, he decided to accept the inevitable. But. . . "What about Naomi? What will happen if she and Jethro decide to get married after they are baptized?"

Naomi had been quiet the entire time, just watching and

listening. "*Daed*, Jethro and I have talked about this already. We haven't yet made a firm decision on getting married because we are still too young. At least I am. But, he has told me that, if I still want to work at the shop or anywhere else within Peace Valley, he is fine with that. He knows that I can make some valuable contributions to our family, if we get married." Knowing her *daed*'s temper, Naomi forced herself to keep looking at his face. Her voice became more steady the longer she spoke.

"Before we leave." The bishop raised his hand. "I want to bring up one more thought and offer, then we need to let Annie and Naomi get to the shop. Caleb, Annie, what would you think about sitting down for some informal chats with Eli and Lizzie Yoder? While Lizzie has chosen to work from her home, she and Eli fully support the rights of women to work outside the home. They aren't going to look down at you for our having come to speak with you. They just want to see you grow from this situation and become a stronger couple and family."

Caleb had taken in a lot that morning and he still needed to get into the barn. Dropping his face into one hand, he sighed. "Bishop, I am going to back off on Annie and Naomi working in her shop. I repent of everything I did to her and Naomi. I. . . Annie, Naomi, I ask for your forgiveness. I apologize and I won't try to make you sell the shop. Naomi, congratulations. I know you have a *gut*, loving heart and you will do a wunderbaar job as manager. And, thank you for agreeing so that your *mamm* can spend more time here at home. Bishop, can Annie and I discuss the offer to work with the Yoders? I will have Naomi get a message to you through Jethro."

"That works out very well. I am happy to see that you repented, because we just want to see you, Annie and Naomi living in loving, supportive relationships. And now, I believe your wife and daughter should be getting to the store. Annie, my wife has a quilt just about ready for consignment. She will take it in to you next week sometime."

"*Gut*! I look forward to it. Caleb, we will be home by mid-afternoon. If you want, there are fried chicken, a baked potato and some vegetables for you."

"Denki, wife. I will heat them up and enjoy them."

***

At the shop, Annie and Naomi had a short meeting with Rebecca, Miriam and Leora. Before the meeting ended, Annie broke the news that Naomi was stepping up to the manager's position. After the flurry of congratulations and squeals had ended. Annie clapped her hands. "We need to open up! I already see tourists waiting! Let's make it a good, productive day!"

"*Ja*, this is the Giant Dahlia quilt, made by one of our best Peace Valley quilters. It would make a wonderful anniversary gift! If you are ready to buy now, I'm happy to wrap it up for you. Or, do you need more time. . ."

"Actually, the price is well within my budget. I'll take it now, thank you!" The English woman smiled with excitement as she imagined her daughter and son-in-law seeing the gift for the first time. Pulling out her credit card she handed it to Annie, who quickly rang up the sale.

"Rebecca, Miriam, would you please box up the Giant Dahlia for Mrs. Thompson?

"*Ja*, I am so excited this one sold! Mrs. King will be so happy." Miriam glowed as she spoke.

After closing the shop for lunch, Annie, Naomi and her employees discussed the day's events.

"Girls, I have decided to tell you what happened today. You are aware that I have been struggling with my husband's demands that I close the shop. Well, with Naomi's promotion, that is no longer a possibility. He has promised he isn't going to try to make me sell the shop. Rebecca, I have been thinking and praying about what happened to you. Naomi and Leora actually told me that they purposely chose the young men they are seeing. Have you gotten to that point yet?"

Rebecca nodded as she swallowed her lunch. "*Ja*. I decided to take some time from dating. I want to be comfortable with who I am and with what I have to offer to a future husband and to Peace Valley."

"*Gut.*" This was Leora. "Take all the time you need. There are plenty of wunderbaar young men out there and someone is just waiting to be ready to meet and love you. Before you get into a dating relationship, try to find out how he feels, in the future, about his wife working outside the home. Contributing to the family's income."

Naomi jumped in. "We have a lot to offer to the young men we date. Jethro knows this. If we decide to marry, he knows that I will be a full partner with him, standing next to him, not behind him. He works as a farrier, so he has plenty of work. But if he ever goes through a period where the work just isn't coming to him, he knows that my work here will help keep us from sinking under the bills. If we get married!" Naomi sent an impish look to her *mamm*.

On the way home after locking up the shop and making the bank deposit, Naomi and Annie talked. "*Mamm*, would you have any problem with my talking to Jethro's parents? I know *daed* is still trying to make up his mind, but I would like to find out, ahead of time, what the Yoders would say to him and you."

Annie considered. "*Nee*, I have no problem with that. Tomorrow's meeting Sunday, so why don't you see if you can speak to Mrs. Yoder at lunch?"

"I will, *mamm*, thanks."

At home, Caleb sat down with Annie and talked about the morning's visit. "Annie, I am truly sorry about my actions toward you. It will never happen again. I was thinking about the Yoder's offer and I am willing to sit down with them when they can come here. Or if they want us to go over to their house."

Annie, overwhelmed, put her hands over her mouth. "Caleb, denki. Naomi actually offered to speak to Mrs. Yoder after meeting tomorrow and find out what they would like to speak with you about."

Instead of getting mad, Caleb understood now that his wife and daughter were doing everything they could to make life easier for him. "Well. . . hmmm. *Ja*. Okay. That's fine. Aren't they the parents of the boy she's dating?"

Annie grimaced slightly, knowing that Caleb might be uncomfortable with that. "Well, *ja*. They are. Is that a problem?"

Caleb sighed. "Will they tell their son what we talk about?"

"Oh, Caleb, *Nee*! They will keep our meetings between the four of us. All I know is that Mrs. King knew that they could talk to us and keep everything within our district." She held her breath, knowing what her unspoken words said.

"Within our district. Meaning that, if I hadn't met with the elders and I had continued to try and make you give up the store, you may have called the police?"

"If it came to that. Or if I hadn't been able to, someone else would have."

Caleb's breath whooshed out in a long sigh. "I guess I should view their visit this morning as a blessing, then."

Annie refused to back down. "It would seem so, *ja*. Oh, Naomi will begin her first day as manager on Tuesday. I will begin training her on what she hasn't yet learned how to do. And I will be home a little bit after dinner time, Tuesday through Friday."

Caleb looked into Annie's eyes. "So, that means that Saturday will be the only full day you'll work?"

"*Ja*. I get home shortly after dinner and work on things here. Housework, cleaning, shopping, whatever needs doing."

"Annie, if I hadn't been such a stubborn old man and had just given you the room you needed, would you have come to this decision?"

"Probably. I'll be honest, Caleb. I love working at my shop. It has been a dream of mine since I was a teen. That's why I took the vocational classes, so I could learn what I needed to do to open and operate the store. Let me ask you a question. At any time during our marriage, when the weather or the market have worked against your plans for your crops, has the money my store allowed me to earn been a consideration for you?"

Caleb paused here. He knew he was entering an area full of painful stickers. "*Ja*. I was always aware of it. Grateful that you had worked hard to earn that money. But I wanted to be the one who earned the money that fed and housed our family. Annie, while I am and have always been grateful for your contributions to our household, there has also been. . . resentment, because I didn't want to have to turn to using your money."

"Caleb! We are in a partnership! What's yours is mine and what's mine is yours. You see other families where the women work, either in the home or out."

Caleb raised one hand. "Wife, I have already consented to this. I'm not going to be able to step over an entire ocean in one giant leap. This is going to take time for me to get used to. Please, don't push me any further."

Annie saw the warning in her husband's eyes. "Okay. We'll wait. But please, take the time to see how it goes with the changes before you make any more decisions. Because we women are able to contribute much to our families and households. I will adjust to coming home in the middle of the day. . . and I suspect I will come to be grateful for that time. As my partner and husband, Caleb, I am asking you to look at your beliefs. Because they are what fueled your attitudes and actions toward Naomi, me and the rest of our daughters. Look at what our married daughters are contributing to their households. Because they are smart, strong women and they are contributing quite a lot."

Caleb nodded. Standing he agreed. "*Ja*. I will think about it. I may never come fully over to your way of thinking, but. . . maybe, in due time, I will be able to accept and understand it."

Sitting back, Annie thought. Then, she nodded slowly. "Okay. I can live with this for now. But. . . what is that English expression? About moving goalposts? Whatever. They will move from time to time. What do you think about meeting with the Yoders?"

Caleb sighed. "Do you want water?" At Annie's nod, he poured both of them glasses of water. Setting hers down in front of Annie, he sat once again. "I guess. I have heard Lizzie Yoder described as some kind of 'fresh breath of air.' And she does look happy much of the time. Jethro seems to treat Naomi well. What will we talk about?"

"Just learning how to see each other as equals and how this affects all areas of our marriage. That's all."

"I guess I can live with that." Sighing, he changed the subject. "So, I guess Naomi is going out again tonight? What ever happened to my little girl that she has become so busy socially?"

"She's friendly and confident. She attracts girls and boys to her. Her relationship with Jethro appears to be much healthier than the others she had before."

"Oh, no, wife. What happened?" Caleb knew he was about

to get an earful.

"Her first two boyfriends believed much as you do. One tried to grab her after she broke up with him and jumped out of his buggy. Her first boyfriend didn't try to manhandle her, but he told her that, if they got married, he would make sure she stayed at home. She wouldn't be allowed to work outside the home. That's when she began learning more about what the boys here think about girls, women and how they contribute to their families before she agreed to date Jethro."

"He tried to manhandle her? Who was it?"

"*Nee, Nee*! He and his family moved away. They live in a settlement in Colorado now." Annie chuckled. "I have to wonder how he and his *daed* feel about that, because from what I hear, that settlement is a little less conservative than what we have here."

"Wife, why didn't she tell me anything?"

"How did you just react?"

Caleb gasped as he understood what Annie was asking. Standing, he looked out the back door, seeing the patterns the bright gold of the sunlight made on the lawn, fence, porch and back swing. He closed his eyes, allowing that image to sink into his soul, calming him down. "Okay, *ja*. I came across as some kind of man who tries to own his wife and daughters."

Annie inclined her head. "I won't disagree. You're already

beginning to learn. Naomi learned from her mistakes. She has a good head on her shoulders."

CHAPTER NINE

"Okay. I see exactly what you're saying. So, when we meet with his *mamm* and *daed*, we're just going to discuss, what? More equality?"

Annie nodded quietly, knowing they were entering dangerous ground. "And that's all. They aren't going to try and give us any kind of counseling, because they aren't qualified. I suspect that they are going to simply use their own experiences and what they learned as examples. That's all."

Caleb shrugged. "Let them come by, then. If Jethro and Naomi decide to marry, it seems they're going become a part of our family, anyway. We may as well get to know them."

Annie smiled, feeling deep relief. "*Ja*. Would you like some fruit before supper?"

"That would be *gut*. I am feeling a little like my sugar is low, anyway. If I eat, I may be able to see all these changes in a more positive light." He accepted a pear and an apple from Annie. "*Denki*. I'll be out in the barn." He snagged a napkin on his way out the back door.

Annie sat and thought about what had just transpired. Shaking her head, she knew she was going to have to pull her husband, kicking and screaming all the way, across that path of change.

"*Mamm*, why are you shaking your head? Is everything okay?"

"*Ja*. It is, for now. *Daed* is willing to work with the Yoders. He recognizes the contributions my income has made to the family. He admitted that he resented having to accept my income because he feels that his income should be perfectly sufficient, even in bad farming conditions."

"Well, that's progress of a sort, isn't it? And he admits that he feels kind of. . . *ja*, resentful. What did he say about my new position and your coming home in the middle of the day?"

"He's happy. I suppose I'll get used to it in time. For sure and for certain, I will have more time to get housework done."

"*Mamm*, he needs to know that you've both given something up in gaining what you wanted. You gave up full-time management of the shop. He gave up his dream of making you stay at home full-time. He gets a wife who will be a little more relaxed now. And you get. . . elbow room to keep the store. If he can see that, then you are partway to full agreement with each other."

Annie thought, then slowly nodded. "That's true, isn't it? I'll talk to him about it from that perspective. Maybe the Yoders can start to come and visit before he begins to slip backward again."

Naomi shivered. "I'll talk to them tomorrow, then."

***

The next day's meeting was held at the Yoder's home. After the long service ended, Naomi paired herself with Lizzie Yoder. "Mrs. Yoder, have the elders spoken to you already?"

"*Ja*, indeed they have, my girl! We are going to begin meeting with your parents, right?"

"*Ja*, if you could start sooner rather than later, I would be so grateful. *Daed* got a wake-up call from the elders last week and I don't want him forgetting that."

Lizzie's smile was friendly and open. "No worries, Naomi. I'll speak to Eli this evening. Before Jethro takes you home, we will give you a note with the days or evenings that work best for Eli so your *daed* and *mamm* can decide what night they want to start working with us."

Naomi felt the accumulated tensions of the past several weeks sliding out of her. Her answering smile was shaky.

"Denki." After talking with Lizzie Yoder, Naomi sat with Leora and her other friends. Feeling better, she ate the rest of her lunch. Looking around at the summer day, she gave thanks to God for His love and generosity in giving to them.

"Naomi, look. Over there!" Leora had positioned her fork so that it pointed subtly toward Naomi's parents and the Yoders, who had joined the Millers. "It looks like they're going to set up a time to visit your *mamm* and *daed*."

Looking around, Naomi was aware she didn't want others learning of the turmoil that had taken place in her home. She whispered. "*Ja*, I asked them to meet with *mamm* and *daed* earlier rather than later. Let's keep it between us, please."

"I wonder if they would consent to working with my *mamm* and *daed*. *Daed* is behaving for now, but I just know he'll conveniently forget and start raging on *mamm* and me again."

"After they have agreed on a time with *mamm* and *daed*, why don't you go and ask them for help? Or do you think the elders need to get involved?"

"*Nee*. They're already involved. I think I'll just ask them to start working with them." Leora's eyes moved around, looking for her *daed*. As she observed him, she sighed.

"What's wrong?" Naomi put her fork down.

"Nothing. He actually looks more happy—happier than I

have seen him look in a long time! He's visiting with some of the other men, but I don't know what they are talking about. I'll be right back." Leora slid off the bench and hurried toward the house. Coming out, she carried pitchers of water and lemonade. Pouring either beverage into near-empty glasses, she slowly approached her *daed*. "*Daed*, would you like something to drink?"

"*Ja*, daughter! Denki! Lemonade, please."

Leora refilled several other glasses, then returned the pitchers to the house. Returning to her bench, she sat down next to Naomi. "I overheard him talking to one of the other men. They were discussing carpentry stuff. So, as far as I know, he's complying with the elders."

Naomi closed her eyes and whooshed out a deep sigh of relief. "That's *gut*. It sounds like you're keeping a close eye on him."

"*Ja*, I am. *Mamm* can't really, because he'd get too suspicious. But for some strange reason, I can." Leora lapsed into silence as she looked around the crowded benches, seeing what was going on. Families were eating and visiting with one another; children, finished eating, were playing, racing around, throwing a baseball and playing tag. "I'm going to go and talk to Mrs. Yoder. She just went into the kitchen. Right back!" Trotting into the kitchen behind Lizzie Yoder, she ramped up her courage. "Mrs. Yoder?"

"Yes, Leora, how are you?"

"I'm fine, thanks. I was just wondering, would you have time in your schedule to begin meeting with my parents? They are having similar. . . issues... to what the Millers are experiencing."

"*Ja*, the elders spoke to me and I spoke with your *mamm* and *daed*. We will be going to your house after lunch and cleaning up. I am happy to say, your *daed* was agreeable to working with us."

Leora was so relieved that she felt dizzy for a few seconds. Gripping the sturdy kitchen table, she steadied herself. "Oh, thank you! Really, I mean this from the bottom of my heart!"

Lizzie's smile was friendly and understanding. "Let's go into the pantry for a few minutes. I have something to explain to you."

Leora followed Lizzie into the large pantry. "What is it?"

"I have come by my knowledge the hard way. My *daed* used to beat my *mamm* because she wanted to work outside the home to help with the money. He used to tell her that taking care of the house and a large family should have been enough. But she trained us well, so we could help her finish all the work that a large family and home present. And *daed* couldn't always predict when a planting season would go bad. One year. . . well, there were constant rain and windstorms.

One day, we had a horrific tornado and it just ripped through the crops. *Daed* lost almost all of his crops and we were facing financial ruin. He realized that we had no choice but for *mamm* to go to work. She was able to find a job working in a shop like Mrs. Miller's quilt shop. If it hadn't been for her, we would have lost everything."

"Did your *daed* finally stop abusing your *mamm*?"

"*Ja*. He had no choice. The elders visited him and made it very clear that, if he didn't stop hitting her, he would be banned. One of the elders' wives came to our house and she worked with us like I am going to work with your parents and with the Millers."

"Did her work help your parents?" Leora held her breath, waiting for the answer.

"*Ja*. That, in combination with the threat of *Meidung*, forced my *daed* to understand that he could not stand in my mother's way. I realized something long ago, Leora. While we have our ways of doing things here and we stay separate from outsiders, we will struggle with sexism, just like the English do. Do you know what sexism is?"

Leora was stunned. Taking a big gasp, she responded. "*Ja*, I do. Naomi, my friend, her *mamm*, my *mamm* and the other shop employees have been talking about it. We would all agree with you. Our men just don't want to understand that we can be just as successful in providing for our families. We need to be able to bring this topic up in a way that won't violate the *Ordnung*, or we are going to be very busy for a long time."

Lizzie became sober. "I think you are right. Your parents and the Millers are just the tip of the iceberg. And that is what I want to tell the elders—that we need to be on the lookout for other families struggling with this issue and domestic violence."

Leora had heard the term before. "Mrs. Yoder? Is what my *daed* did 'domestic violence?'"

"Leora, call me Lizzie. We are going to be in your home a lot! Yes, he committed a wrongful act of domestic violence against your *mamm*. I know that this is still happening. So, expect to see the elders visiting many more families."

"Lizzie. It isn't just the fathers hitting their wives. I know of at least one instance where some of the teen boys here have either threatened, grabbed or hit their girlfriends. So, they seem to be. . ."

"Picking up on the attitudes of their *daeds*, right?"

"Yes. One of my coworkers is dealing with that now."

"Ach. Is her boyfriend baptized yet?"

"*Nee*. What would the elders do in that situation?"

Lizzie considered. "Well, if they are informed of the violation committed by this boy, they would go and talk to his parents. They might could be able to pick up on whether the boy's *daed* is the root of the problem. If so, we—or another more-enlightened couple—could probably work with them and the boy. What is his name?"

Leora considered the consequences of giving the boy's name out. "I need to talk to my coworker first and let her know. I think she broke up with him, but I'm not sure."

"*Ja*, please do. If she says yes, then the elders can see what is going on within his family. They might not be able to do very much, since he isn't baptized. But we could begin working with him. Of course, if the elders find that the boy's parents are struggling with domestic violence and an agreement on their roles here, the *daed* could possibly face the ban as well."

"Denki, Lizzie. I will talk to my friend later in the week and I will let you know what she says."

***

On Tuesday, Leora managed to get some private time with Rebecca at the quilt shop. "Rebecca, do you know who the Yoders are?"

"*Ja*. They're Jethro's parents, right? Why?"

"Please keep this between you, me and Naomi. They are working with both of our parents. I hope you won't get mad. But I told Lizzie Yoder what happened to you with your boyfriend."

"I broke up with him. I'm taking your advice and getting to know the boys who are interested in me before I decide to date them or not. It's fine with me if they work with Aaron and his parents. Maybe the next girl he dates won't be subjected to the same treatment I experienced."

"Lizzie told me one thing that really stuck in my head. We still have some time before we have to go back to work, so I have the time to tell you this: She knows what sexism is. And she told me that, when families are struggling with the roles of husbands and wives, sometimes, the husbands try to keep their wives 'in line' by beating them up. It could be that Aaron learned to treat you poorly from his own *daed*."

Rebecca sighed. Though it was long healed, she began to rub her forearm as though it still hurt. "You know, that night that he grabbed me really scared me. That's what convinced me that I had to break up with Aaron. The few times I was around his *mamm* and *daed*, I did pick up on his *daed* wanting to control what his *mamm* did and what she said. It was very uncomfortable. I asked Aaron to take me home as soon as it was polite enough to do so."

"Do you mind if I take this to Lizzie?"

"Go ahead! I won't be dating Aaron again. And he knows that. I think I disappointed him anyway, because I wouldn't give in and do what he said. He will be single for a long time until he learns that we women have rights, too."

"We need to get back, but I want to talk more with you about this. Okay?"

"*Ja*, that's fine."

Back in the front, the girls returned to work with Naomi in the leadership role. When the store closed at four, Leora and Naomi met up with Vernon, who escorted them to the bank to make the day's deposit.

"I need to get to the market. *Daed* needs some new blades for his saws and I told him I would get them. I'll see you later in the week?"

Leora smiled. "*Ja*, that sounds *gut*! We'll get home okay." After Vernon left them to go to the market, she and Naomi drove to their own homes. "Naomi, I had an idea after talking with Rebecca. She gave me permission to tell you this. Her ex-boyfriend's parents are also dealing with domestic violence because his *daed* won't allow his *mamm* to work outside the home."

Naomi shook her head. "You know, I'm not surprised. I saw Aaron with Rebecca and always thought he was trying to control her. What's your idea?" Naomi already had a suspicion that Leora's idea would be the same as hers.

"We older teen girls need to start communicating to

everyone—the boys we're seeing as well as the other boys in Peace Valley—that we are individuals, we are strong and we count. As it is, Lizzie Yoder and her husband already have two couples to work with. At this rate, they'll never stop working with anyone!"

"And if we can start educating the boys and girls our age that violence is wrong, that it violates the *Ordnung* no matter what the intent is, and that we can contribute to our society."

"*Ja*! Exactly! We need to talk to the elders about this. Then to the Yoders, because I want to get started just as soon as possible." Leora finished Naomi's thought.

Both girls were excited, not realizing the resistance they would face.

"Leora, please ask Vernon if we can meet with his *daed* and the other ministers."

***

Later in the week, both girls sat, feeling crestfallen. The bishop had just explained that, while their idea was wunderbaar, several of the families in Peace Valley would not want to change their ways. "Allow us to begin discussing the message that domestic violence is against the *Ordnung*. We will do so over the next few months. Once families realize this, we may get reports of other families like Aaron's. What you two need to do is get like-minded young women and stress the idea that you won't accept being made less than what you are. If you plan to work, either inside or outside the home, hang onto those plans. Get the vocational training you need. And start talking with younger girls, those who are not yet courting or in rumspringa. Because this will not happen overnight."

THE END.

AMISH HEART AND SOUL

Denial. Struggle. Redemption.

Though Caleb Miller and Wayne Lapp have been warned to follow the Ordnung and respect their wives, both struggle to stop their abusive behavior. A lifetime of habit is hard to break, and for one, denying the truth will put not only his marriage, but his life, at risk. What is the price of redemption? Can there truly be peace in Peace Valley?

CHAPTER ONE

In his barn, Caleb Miller strode back and forth as he struggled with his almost overwhelming anger. When traitorous thoughts of hitting Annie intruded, he squeezed his eyes shut and forced them out of his head. "*Nee*, Caleb. To do so would violate the *Ordnung* and you would get the *Meidung*." After repeating this to himself several times, Caleb pulled in a deep breath and let it out several times. Looking down at his chest, he saw his shirt front moving rapidly up and down in time with his furious heartbeat.

Realizing his techniques weren't working, he reminded himself that the earnings from the Peace Valley Quilt Place were almost the only thing standing between his family and financial failure should a crop fail. Finally, he felt his thundering heartbeat beginning to slow down. Easing his head back, he let out a few more breaths and unclenched his hands.

He hadn't realized that they were so tightly closed, let alone that he had clenched them in his frustration. Shaking the cramps out, he talked quietly to himself. "Go back into the house. She and Naomi are making supper. She's been home since dinnertime and *ja*, the house is clean. Go." Finally, Caleb was able to exit the barn, feeling relatively calm. Walking into the house, he felt guilt twisting his gut as he saw Annie's tentative glance at him.

"Don't worry, wife. I am fine. I just needed some time in the barn to calm down. I know you are right. I just have a hard time accepting that things, even here in Peace Valley, are changing."

Naomi spoke up. "*Daed? Mamm* did make me the store manager so she could spend more time at home. It's working. She likes the work I'm doing and I am getting comfortable as manager."

"And you are making sure the shop is profitable?" Caleb mentally shook his head. That his own daughter should be managing a store at her age stunned him!

Naomi's smile was impish and sparkling. "*Ja*, it is. *Mamm* has been looking at the receipts and accounts. It helps that we know our customers and the women who make the quilts we sell."

"Okay, *gutt*. Now, I am hungry after spending all day long

in the fields. I will be upstairs for a few minutes."

"Caleb, supper will be ready directly." Annie's voice was calm as she removed the biscuits from the oven. "Naomi, that was a good idea. Reminding your *daed* that the shop is making a profit helps him to accept the facts."

"*Ja*. Linda Yoder reminded me to use that fact every so often. I know he worries about the crops failing and that doesn't help his state of mind. But *mamm*, he needs to accept that you aren't going to sell the store eventually!"

Annie made a shushing motion with one finger over her rounded lips. "Enough time for that in the morning, girl. Put the vegetables and potatoes on the table. When is the next meeting?"

Naomi knew what Annie meant. "Our peer counseling group meets this Wednesday after supper."

"*Denki*. Okay. I'll make something quick that your *daed* loves that night."

"And I'll make that peach cobbler he loves so much."

Annie had enough time to smile at Naomi, then the recognizable sounds of Caleb coming downstairs grew louder. "Husband, supper is ready!"

While they ate, Caleb questioned Naomi on what her work involved. "So, you get to supervise three other employees? Do they take your direction well?"

"*Ja*, they do. If they don't, they know *mamm* will discipline them or fire them. But not without a discussion first."

After the kitchen was cleaned and dishes dried, Caleb invited Annie to go for a walk outside. "It's been a while since we've been able to connect with each other, because we've been so busy."

Annie was tired and wanted nothing more than to relax and read. But, knowing that their together times were rare, she smiled at him. Rubbing lotion into her hands, she made sure her prayer cap was straight on her head. "Naomi, we will be back before long. Stay at home!"

"*Ja, mamm*. Jethro is working late, anyway. He has a late appointment with a customer who just got back into Peace Valley after visiting family in Colorado."

***

On their walk, Annie and Caleb discussed his attempts to get comfortable with her ownership of the quilt store. "Caleb, I know you have been struggling to accept my store. Does it help you, knowing that, if something goes wrong in our family, that the store will help us out financially?"

"It does, *ja*. Not only if one of my crops fails, but if something happens to one of us, it will be there. What is this notion that Naomi has been taking about? Sexism. It almost sounds like something forbidden by the *Ordnung*."

Annie responded slowly and carefully. "*Nee*. Sexism is just an attitude that many people have toward others. Mainly from men to women. It forces women to deny themselves opportunities they should feel free to take. Like my store. At first, you didn't seem to have a problem with it. Why, I don't know. But quilting and merchandising are things I've been interested in since I was a teen. And, when I found out that the retail space was available, I took my savings and rented it. This was, oh, about two years before we got married."

Caleb remembered all of this. He nodded. "I don't know why it began to bother me. I suppose it always did, in the back of my mind. If I'm honest, I have to say that it bugs me that I am not your only support. That you have another source of support out there."

Annie sighed. This was what she had been praying for. "Caleb. I won't go into the worries about failing crops. We've talked that one to death. But what would I do if you were taken away from me? I pray every day that won't happen, but what would I do to support myself and Naomi? I don't want to have to accept charity, especially since I have knowledge and the ability to support us. Do you understand?"

Caleb stopped in the road. This was something he had never thought about. He looked at Annie. Really looked at her, seeing her gentle, hazel eyes. He saw the intelligence that sparked within her being. *Denki, Gott,* for bringing this woman to me! "Oh. When you put it that way, I admit I never thought about it. I mean, I hope *Gott* won't take me for a long time. You are right." Reaching out, he snagged her hand, holding it within his own. Looking at Annie's face, he saw her blonde hair, pulled into a strict bun at the back of her head. He smiled. "You are right. I am going to need some time to come to grips with the reality. I am doing my best, and I confess, I will have failures."

Annie nodded. Just as Caleb was regarding her, she really looked at him. Gazing into his gentle brown eyes, she sighed. "I know. I am going to say one thing. I have noticed that, when you spend time with one certain person in Peace Valley, you seem to be a little more. . . riled." Annie gripped Caleb's fingers more tightly. She knew she was running a risk here. Seeing an apprehensive look in his eyes, she licked her lips.

"Who? Who are you talking about?"

"Wayne Lapp. We all know the history he has. He has threatened force and actually hit Lizzie as he made her do what he wanted. I've seen the bruises on her face."

Caleb's face twisted. As Annie brought up the beatings and bruises, he felt the knowledge twist in his gut. He knew she was right. But. . . "Well, how did she come to you for a job?"

Now, Annie's brow creased in confusion. "What? What do you mean?"

"Did she go to you before she discussed her desire for a job with him?"

Now Annie understood. "*Nee*! She told me she had discussed it with him and he told her that, while he didn't like it, they needed the money at that time. He had been stiffed by an English customer who didn't pay him for the furniture he made. And it was a considerable sum. They had taken out a loan for his carpentry tools and saws. He also needed a new gas generator to power the saws. And the payments were due and, without that payment. . ."

"Okay. So, he knew before that she was going to get a job with you."

"*Ja*. It was only after he hit her that she quit working for me. And she hasn't been back since, except to make the quilts and sell them on consignment."

"So, what about Wayne is bothering you?"

"You come back all tense and snappy after spending time with him. It happens every time."

"Every time? Even after I've shared a table at lunch after services?"

Annie nodded. "Even then. It's like. . . I don't know. Like

he has a special talent for projecting his feelings onto you and maybe others around him. And

. . ." Annie hesitated.

"What? You might as well say it because now I am wondering."

"Just don't get mad at me. This is only what I am picking up." Annie let out a quick breath through pursed lips. Looking into the far distance, she worked her courage up. "I get the feeling that he has given you the idea to try and get physical with me." She sidestepped, wanting to be out of his way if he reacted.

Silence. Caleb stopped walking again. His mouth opened and closed several times as he tried to make his brain work again. "He. . . he believes that women belong at home. *Ja*, he has gotten physical with Lizzie. And. . .*ja*, he did suggest that I try the same with you. And then the elders intervened."

Annie had been praying that she wouldn't hear this. Taking in a long breath, she stopped walking and put her hands over her face. Shaking her head, she tried to make herself accept that fact. "Caleb! And you tried to hit me with Naomi in the house?"

Caleb was ashamed. Any anger he felt was directed at himself. "*Ja*. It was stupid. I know that now. It took the elders reminding me of everything I could lose. I am having a hard time with this, but I am really trying. I can tell you this. Right now, for today, I have made my peace with your store. I... it feels like a rival to me. And I have to start over at the beginning every day, making my peace with your store."

Annie listened to Caleb. He was telling the truth. She nodded. "Thank you for being truthful and honest. *Ja*, accepting my store is a daily thing, just like working at forgiveness."

"Will you forgive me?"

"Caleb, you know I will. But I want you to promise me one thing. You can't always avoid Wayne Lapp. But please, do not seek him out. If he invites you to their house, please come up with a reason you can't go. I get a real bad feeling from him. Like something is wrong with him. His anger at Lizzie is sometimes all out of proportion to her old job at my store."

Caleb sighed. "*Ja*. But if I run into him, I will talk with him."

"Caleb, have you ever gotten the feeling that, maybe something is wrong with him?"

"You mean, in his head? *Nee*, not particularly. Let's walk some more before it gets too dark." As Annie drew abreast of Caleb, he began walking again. He purposely looked at the beauty around him. The trees were becoming black outlines as the sun slowly sunk in the sky. The sky began to turn pink and purple. He stopped, taking in the view.

Annie slowed down next to Caleb. She regarded the sunset and view around them. As she did, she felt her spirit calming. "Let's go home, husband. I have some lemonade and shoofly pie in the refrigerator." As they walked home, Annie felt a little more relief. They walked home in silence.

As he walked alongside Annie, Caleb felt a little lighter. Truth was, he had been getting some strange, worrisome feelings from Wayne. "You know, when you say Wayne's anger is out of proportion to Lizzie's job, it almost feels like he is reacting to something that happened long ago."

"You mean, in his childhood?" Annie was confused.

"*Ja*. As if he is remembering something from when he was a boy."

This worried Annie. "Caleb, when you said earlier that you never got the feeling something's wrong with Wayne, did you not connect it to what you now feel he may be reacting to? From his childhood?"

Caleb took several seconds to respond. "Annie, I want to be honest. But I like Wayne. After he and his family moved here, we became friends as children and have been so since then."

"*Ja*, I remember. You were teens. But. . ."

"But, until you put your question as you just did, I never

made the connection in my mind. When I met Wayne's *daed*, I sensed the relationship was strained. He tried to stay away from home as much as he could, staying at our house for meals as often as he could. But I never cottoned onto anything his *daed* might be doing to him. That's the only thing I can think it could have been. That his *daed* was disciplining him too much."

"Caleb, we don't know very much about him. About his childhood. His *mamm*—she didn't live with them by that time, did she?"

"*Nee*, she didn't. I understand from Wayne that she left when he was, maybe, nine, ten years old."

"Caleb. Mr. Lapp died several years ago, right?'" At Caleb's nod, Annie continued. "So, we don't know what led to Mrs. Lapp leaving. It could. . ."

"Annie, the only thing I ever heard from Wayne about his *mamm* was that she took off in the middle of the night. He blamed her. . ."

"For leaving all of the *kinder* behind?"

"Let me finish, wife. *Ja*, that, but also for being the kind of woman she was."

"Ahhh! How frustrating!" By now, Caleb and Annie were back in their yard. Annie stalked toward the back of the house, not going inside. She didn't want Naomi to hear this just yet. "Maybe she was that kind of a woman. But you've heard him say the same about Lizzie, Caleb! When he is ranting about her working at my shop, he is accusing her of making plans to leave him and this community. *Nee*, husband, please let me finish. I think he is expressing his fear that Lizzie is going to do to him what his *mamm* did to his *daed* and him." Annie walked restlessly around the backyard. She really needed to walk off her head of steam! "What I am wondering is, whether Mr. Lapp abused Mrs. Lapp before she finally got scared or fed up and left. Maybe she intended to come back for the children. Or maybe. . ."

"Maybe. . . what?"

"She couldn't. For whatever reason. And that is why Wayne stayed with his *daed*, feeling abandoned."

Caleb lapsed into silence, thinking. Well, on the face of it, that could be. It does fit. But until one of us can sit down with Wayne and get him to open up. . . . Wayne raised one finger. "*Ja*. I think what you say is reasonable. But until he is willing to speak about that time in his life, we can't speculate. Nor can we gossip."

"Caleb! You know I wouldn't do that! *Nee*. I want to think about this for a while longer. But I do think we need to share our thoughts with the bishop and the Yoders. On the promise that they will keep it strictly between the five of us. He does deserve that. I have seen him trying to work on his anger and how he tries to control Lizzie."

Caleb's mind fixated on one word. "Five? Five people? Annie, you know how quickly that will become fifteen, then twenty-five?"

"Not if we tell them in strict confidence, with nobody else nearby. The elders have to keep confidences. So do the peer counselors. We can let them know that these are only private thoughts we have had because we haven't been able to talk to Wayne. And that it is up to Wayne to confirm or deny."

Caleb nodded. "*Ja*, that is true. If we talk to them with nobody else around. . . . and that includes Naomi, Leora, Jethro and Vernon! Who else is in this group?"

Annie named the peer group members, ticking them off on her fingers.

"Huh. Okay. Well, don't say anything to anyone until I have had time to think about it. You do realize we are going to have to find a way of talking to Wayne and trying to get him to agree to speak about his childhood."

"*Ja*, I know. And I think the ministers should guide us on that."

"That I agree with you on! We'd better get inside. It's nearly bedtime and I'm sure Naomi is wondering where we are."

Inside, Naomi was washing her glass and plate. "There you are! I heard you talking in the backyard."

"Daughter, did you hear what we were talking about?" Caleb was worried.

"*Nee*, I just heard your voices when you got back from your walk. I was upstairs and decided to have my serving of dessert with some iced tea. Would you like some tea?"

"What, you mean I can't have a serving of your mom's delicious pie?" Caleb's smile was teasing.

Naomi, happy the mood was so relaxed, giggled. "*Ja*, you can! You work it off in the fields every day!" She cut a large slice of shoofly pie for him, then poured glasses of tea for all three of them.

***

Several warm summer days slowly passed by, with Naomi becoming more comfortable in her managerial role at the quilt shop. Caleb mulled his discussion with Annie over in his mind. He wondered when it would be a good time for a talk with Wayne.

CHAPTER TWO

In the Lapp household, Lizzie and Leora hurried to put the finishing touches on supper. After removing the biscuits from the oven, Leora set the table and poured the iced tea as Lizzie took the Swiss steak, vegetables and mashed potatoes from the stove and set them all on the table. Lizzie looked at Leora and gave her a silent message and they heard the sound of Wayne's footsteps on the back porch. Don't say anything about the shop. Keep all our talk about home topics. Leora nodded quietly

"Well, supper's finally on the table. It's about time!"

Lizzie resisted the urge to look at the wall clock. She knew supper was on the table before five p.m. They had gotten home from errands not an hour and a half before and started on supper and cleaning just as soon as they walked in. "*Ja*, Wayne, it is on the table. One of your favorites."

"*Denki*. It smells *gutt*." After offering a silent prayer, Wayne dug into a large cut of Swiss steak. On his plate, he piled a large serving of mixed vegetables, mashed potatoes and gravy. After eating two large servings, he leaned back in his chair, sighed and drank his tea down in three gargantuan gulps.

Lizzie, eating her own supper, remembered Wayne from their courtship. He had been quiet and intense, but so much more open back then. While he had always been wary of allowing her to work outside the home, he hadn't been so dogmatic about it. She jumped as she heard Wayne's voice.

"Lizzie! Where are you? In that shop?"

"*Nee*, I was remembering our courtship, actually."

Lizzie's response threw Wayne. He hadn't expected that. "Oh? What do you remember?"

". . . "How much fun we had, how much we laughed. How I came to love you."

Wayne was surprised. "Oh! Well. . . I remember the same things. You were so shy, I was never sure I'd get two words out of you. I had to work for a giggle."

Lizzie blushed, looking down. "My brothers had already grown up and gotten married by the time I came along, so I was only used to having my sisters in the house."

"*Ja*, I remember. I also remember that, when I came to pick you up on Easter Sunday, your brothers were there. . . and they made it very clear that I would not hurt you. If I had. . ."

"I remember. Would you like some peach cobbler with ice cream?"

"Well, you went all out! *Ja*, I would." After receiving his plate of dessert, Wayne thanked Lizzie. "To what do I owe this *wunderbaar* supper?"

"I remember you said the other day you had a hankering for Swiss steak, the fixings and for peach cobbler. I put it on the menu for today."

"Well, *denki*." Wayne had enjoyed every bite of supper, but now he began to wonder just why Lizzie had chosen these items for their supper. *Maybe she's trying to fool me before she leaves. I can't let her go back to work anywhere. Ja*, she makes quilts and sells them to the store. . . *maybe she should stop that as well. My income is more than sufficient.* He promised that, after supper and devotions, he would discuss this with her. Indeed, after Leora went out with Vernon, Wayne tracked Lizzie down, finding her in her quilting room. "Wife, do you have just a few minutes?"

Lizzie sighed quietly. She was under a tight deadline for this quilt. Her customer wanted it before the weekend. "*Ja*, what is it, Wayne?"

"I've been thinking. My income as a carpenter is going up

quarter by quarter. I'm getting many orders. More than I did even a year ago. I think we can plan easily for you to stay at home. Who knows? Eventually, you may be able to stop sewing quilts for the English and for Annie's. . . shop." Wayne had to make himself say that word.

Lizzie looked closely at Wayne. He didn't appear to be angry. His shoulders were relaxed and she didn't see his eyes glowering out at her from beneath his bushy brows. "Well, we can talk. But what happens if you have some kind of accident? Carpentry can be dangerous and, if you cut yourself, you could be out of work for some time. If that happens—and I pray sincerely that it won't—we will need what I can earn."

"Lizzie, I am careful not to be hurt. My income is more than sufficient for our needs. Our bills are paid and we have nearly paid off the loan for my carpentry equipment. You will be staying home. Keep quilting from home, but at some point, I will require you to stop selling your quilts." So he wouldn't hear her objections, Wayne left before she could frame an argument.

Lizzie sat in front of her quilt, mouth open. She was stunned. A part of her was genuinely puzzled as well. She saw fear in her husband's eyes while he was delivering his ultimatum. Fear? Why would that be? Setting her scissors down, she began to walk around her quilting room, thinking. Then she remembered what he said about his *mamm* leaving when he was a child. My *Gott*! He is afraid of me leaving, but why? Well, I just need to let him know that I will never leave him. And that I work because I enjoy contributing to our family. With that decision made, Lizzie went in search of Wayne. She found him relaxing on the back porch swing, drinking a glass of iced tea. "Husband, I am really confused. You want me to promise that I won't ever work in Annie's quilt shop again and you even want me to stop selling my quilts in the future." She sat next to him on the swing, something she would soon regret. "When you were telling me this, I saw a certain expression on your face and I remembered your *mamm*. That she left when you were just a boy. Wayne, I love you and I would never leave you! All I am doing by selling my quilts is helping to build our. . ."

"WIFE! You heard me and my decisions are final! Now, I am being generous by saying you can continue to make quilts here at home and sell them through the shop. I can just change my mind and say you won't sell any of your quilts anymore, beginning today. Would you like that?" Hmmm?"

"*Nee*! I am working on a quilt for a customer and she wants it before this weekend. She's already paid her deposit and will pay the balance when I deliver the quilt to. . ."

"Then you need to remember that I am the head of this household. Don't question me! You will not go back to work at Annie's store. Count yourself fortunate that am not making you stop that quilt for your customer tonight! I am upset. I'll be in the shop, calming down." Wayne stalked off, hurrying to his carpentry shop.

Lizzie ran upstairs, feeling afraid of Wayne and his temper. Before she did so, she said one word: "Ban, Wayne." Slamming the kitchen door, she ran upstairs.

***

In his shop, Wayne stalked around, trying to get control of his temper. Finally, feeling his heartbeat slowing down, he turned to the decorative edging he was working on for an English customer of his own. Unfortunately, he was still angry enough that he wasn't paying attention to safety precautions— or the narrowing distance between his arm, hand and the router saw. Guiding the length of lumber through the saw, he felt the saw's edge biting into the skin, muscles, ligaments, tendons and bones of his right hand and forearm. Letting out a blood-curdling howl, he closed his eyes against the overwhelming, searing pain. Hissing his breath in and out from between his clenched teeth, he reached over to the side of the router and switched the router into reverse. This had the effect of pushing his bloody, mangled hand and arm backward. As soon as it was free, he shut the router off with his trembling left hand.

Looking at the torn-up skin, muscle and bone, Wayne swayed, feeling sick. Dark spots danced and shivered in front of his half-closed eyes. Grabbing a shop cloth, he tried to wrap it around his arm to stanch the flow of blood. Stumbling out of the shop, he shambled to the house, calling Lizzie's name. Once he was on the porch, he fell into the kitchen. "Lizzie! Lizzie, help me! I'm hurt!"

Upstairs, Lizzie heard Wayne's frightened voice. But she wasn't sure he was telling the truth and she was afraid of getting hurt if he was trying to fool her. A few minutes later, she went slowly downstairs, looking for Wayne in the living room, hallway and kitchen. "Wayne? Where are you?" Her steps were slow and reluctant.

"Here! In the kitchen. . ." Wayne's voice wavered and sounded close to tears. By now, he was slumped on the floor, against the back door. He held his left hand around his right hand and arm, which were both soaked in blood.

Lizzie gasped. Rushing to Wayne's side, she grabbed several clean dish towels, which she wrapped around his arm, heedless of the pain it might cause him. "Husband! What happened? Wait. Tell me on the way to the hospital. I have to go to the phone house and call a driver. I'll be right back." Racing outside, she hurried to the phone tree two houses away. She called a driver she had hired before. "Kevin, I hope you have the time to help us! My husband just hurt himself in his carpentry shop. . . *ja*, this is Lizzie Lapp. You know where we live. Can you take us to the emergency room?"

"Yes! I'll be there in just about ten minutes. Stop his bleeding! Go!"

"*Ja, denki!*" Dropping the phone back into its cradle, Lizzie ran back into the house, pulling her skirt close to her knees. Back in the house, she saw that Wayne was more pale than he had been a few minutes ago. His eyes were half-closed and he was slow to respond to her questions. She grabbed his arm and applied pressure, ignoring Wayne's weak growls of pain. The time seemed to walk by at the speed of a giant tortoise. Finally, hearing the beep of a car horn, she wrapped one arm around Wayne's back and urged him up. "Hold your arm so I can lock the door and get you down the porch stairs." She needed her driver to help get Wayne down the steps and into his car.

"Lock your house and come back. He really needs help." Kevin extended the seat belt, latching it on Wayne's other side, securing him to the seat. "Sit in the back with your husband." He hurried to town and the community hospital, driving just over the posted speed limits. At the hospital, he parked and helped Lizzie get him into the emergency room. "I'll wait here for when you are ready to go home. Mrs. Lapp, I'm a retired EMT. He's going to be in the hospital for a while. With that blood loss, he probably has some torn tendons and ligaments."

Kevin was right. After taking several X-rays and ultrasounds, the emergency room doctor decided that Wayne needed to be admitted for surgery to repair his arm. "Mrs. Lapp, what was he doing? It looks like he ran his arm through a saw!"

"That's just what he did. He wanted to get some more work

done for a customer, so after supper, he went back into his shop. I don't know exactly how he did it. . . can I see him?"

CHAPTER THREE

"He's passed out from the blood loss and pain. Besides, we need to get him into surgery right away. I do want to say that you prevented the possibility of infection. You acted quickly by wrapping his arm up. I suggest you go home and rest tonight. He's going to be in surgery for a few hours and it's already late." The doctor looked out the entrance. He was right—full dark had fallen and the parking lot lights had recently come on. "You can come back tomorrow morning and talk to his surgeon or me. Just leave his doctor's contact information with the triage desk and we will take care of updating them on what happened tonight."

Lizzie sighed. She was worn out. Hearing the doctor's competence coming through in his words, she was able to relax. "Okay. Thank you, yes. I will come back tomorrow. Will you be on duty tomorrow morning?"

"No, but ask at the front desk for your husband's room. The

nurses on that floor will get his doctor so they can bring you up to date on his condition." The doctor placed his hand on Lizzie's shoulder. "Go home now. Do you have a ride?"

"*Ja*, that gentleman with the gray cap right there."

"Ah, Kevin! Thank you for helping!" The doctor, with a broad smile on his face, strode over to the waiting Kevin, shaking his hand with energy.

"You're welcome, doc! I'm going to get Mrs. Lapp home. If she has any children still at home, they're probably wondering what's going on."

"Oh! Leora! *Ja*, I need to get home! *Denki*!" Lizzie hurried out with Kevin. She gave him a twenty-dollar bill when he pulled up in front of her house. "*Nee*, Kevin. Please, take this. You came out on a summer evening, when you could have been relaxing with your family. And you saved my husband."

Reluctantly, Kevin accepted the money. "Let me know if you need any more rides to the hospital."

"I will. *Denki*." She hurried back into her house, calling for Leora. No answer. "So she's still out with Vernon, thank *Gott*." She hurried to clean up the blood, as tired as she was. Wringing the cloth out in the sink and rinsing it, she heard Leora's key in the front door. "Leora!"

"*Ja, mamm*? What happened? What's that blood there?"

"Mrs. Lapp? What happened?" Vernon had come in with Leora.

"Leora, your *daed* had a carpentry accident." She explained Wayne's accident to Leora and Vernon.

"I'll go straighten out and clean the shop then lock it. "Vernon had an armful of old towels with him as he hurried out the back door. In the carpentry shop, he found large blotches of drying blood. Wetting the towels, he hurried to clean the floor, benches and machinery so they wouldn't stain. Looking around, he saw a length of lumber, lying askew on a router. "*Ach*, so this is where his accident happened." Vernon carefully removed the lumber from the router and closely inspected it. Seeing large splatters of blood on the wood, he tried to clean it, but quickly realized the blood had ruined it. "*Nee*. This wood is no *gutt* anymore. It has to be cut up or thrown away. I will put it over here and Mr. Lapp can make that decision when he is able." Looking around the shop one last time, he ascertained that everything else was in order. He locked the door, ensuring it was secure from the outside. "Mrs. Lapp, all is done in the shop. I cleaned the blood up and swept up leftover sawdust and put that in the barrel outside. Where do you store your dirty laundry?" He went into the laundry room and spread the still-wet cloths into a tub of hot water.

"*Denki*, Vernon, let me put bleach in there so the blood will be washed away."

"Mrs. Lapp, how bad is your husband's injury?"

"Bad. He ripped and tore the muscles and ligaments. His hand, wrist and arm are broken, so he will be out of work for some time. He will be in the hospital for several days."

"Not to mention, physical therapy."

Lizzie nodded, feeling somewhat calmer. "*Ja*. Would you like some tea? I made snickerdoodles yesterday. Have some."

"*Denki*." Vernon took a large bite of the delectable cookie. After swallowing, he spoke his thoughts. "*Daed* and I can go visit him while he's in the hospital to find out what orders he is working on. We'll find out what he has coming up as well. If his injuries are really as bad as all that, he will need us to help him meet his orders so he doesn't lose customers."

Lizzie's heart slowed down some, hearing Vernon. "*Ja*, he will. *Denki*, Vernon."

Leora had been thinking. "*Mamm*, do you think you'll have to go back to the shop to earn money?"

Lizzie sighed. She hadn't wanted to think about this, knowing how Wayne felt about her even working from home. "*Ja*, I will. It's almost for sure and for certain that I'll have to do so, so we don't fall behind on our bills. Taking quilts and selling on consignment won't be enough, even though Annie is giving me such a *wunderbaar* consignment percentage. Your *daed* won't like it. . ."

Vernon looked at Leora and shook his head. "Mrs. Lapp, if he doesn't want to lose what he has, he will have to agree to your working in the shop. I will let *daed* know about that so that, when your husband is alert, *daed* can remind him that he is not to try to force you to stay at home."

Lizzie's shaking was back. She knew that it would get bad with Wayne, his beliefs and his temper. Nodding, she swallowed hard several times, trying to keep the tears from bursting forth. Beginning to pace through the kitchen, she felt better. "*Denki*, Vernon. I am very tired, Leora. I'm going to go to bed. Would you and Vernon lock the house up when he goes home?"

"*Ja*, we will, *mamm*. Go to bed and pray." Leora gave Lizzie a strong hug, trying to communicate all her support and love to her *mamm*.

Upstairs, Lizzie undressed and slipped quickly into her lightweight, long nightgown. Taking her hair out of its braided bun, she ran her brush through the long tresses. Before she went to bed, she hurried into the bathroom and brushed her teeth, forcing her sobs back the whole time. Practically running back into her room, she closed the door and blew out the lantern. Falling face-first onto her bed, she buried her face deep into her pillow. She didn't want Leora to her crying. The hot scalding tears and throat-ripping sobs were quick to come. Her pillow was quickly drenched. Then, Lizzie heard a soft, quiet voice.

"*Gott* has everything under control. It is going just as He wants it to go."

Lizzie sat up, muting her sobs and wiping her face dry with her sheet. Rising from the bed, she walked to the opened window, praying with everything she had. "*Gott*, we need your help. Wayne needs your help. He was badly hurt and won't be able to work for quite a while. You know this means I have to go back to the shop to earn what we need to keep our household functioning. Please give Wayne the insight and good sense to stay away from me as I work to keep our family above water. And please, *Gott*, don't let him hit me!" Lizzie's tears began to fall down her cheeks again as she thinks of what Wayne could do to her and Leora.

***

In town, Wayne remained in the hospital, recovering from his accident and the subsequent surgeries he needed. In his accident, he had sliced deep into his hand and forearm, ripping and tearing several tendons, arteries, ligaments and muscles. First, the doctors wanted to forestall the possibility of infection, then operate on his hand and arm to repair the damage he had done with the router.

Wayne had several hours every day on his hands. Not

believing in television, he never turned the TV set on in his hospital room. Instead, he sat, thought, read his Bible and prayed. Knowing just how close he came to losing his lower arm, he realized just how instrumental Lizzie was in helping him to save it. He was grateful for her quick actions that night. It was this knowledge that helped him to stay calm when she came to him in the hospital and told him that, out of financial necessity, she had accepted an offer of employment from Annie Miller. "*Ja*, that's fine. Hannes and Vernon can only work for so long on my orders. I don't know if customers will continue to place orders while I am unable to work."

"Wayne, if they do, I will take the messages and speak to Deacon King. Maybe we can arrange something so you don't lose customers. . . and orders."

That thought curdled in Wayne's gut. He hated to accept charity, even from one of their own. I have no choice. The alternative is. . . disaster. If we are going to keep what we have, I have to accept their help. Releasing a long, gusty sigh, Wayne nodded twice. "*Ja*. Talk to him, please. If they can help me keep my customers and fill my current orders, plus any that may be coming in, that would be. . . so helpful."

At the end of her visit, Lizzie squeezed Wayne's good hand. She was hopeful. He hadn't lost his temper when she told him that she was going back to work.

In his hospital room, Wayne lay back in his bed, just

thinking. While he had been discussing his situation with Lizzie, he was uncomfortably aware of his own shameful role in his accident. *Ach*, that was my own fault, nobody else's. I went into my shop angry. Very angry, as it turns out. I should have been nowhere near my saws that night. Looking at his heavily casted arm, Wayne sighed. He knew just how close he had come to completely losing his arm at the elbow—too close. Getting out of bed, he slowly slipped his feet into slippers and, pulling slowly on the IV tubing, he stood at the window, just remembering back to that night. Remembering his anger at Lizzie as she told him she couldn't stop working on the quilting order she had, Wayne looked down, feeling very small. How do I continue to maintain this attitude about her working? I have no choice for now, and that's why I was able to accept her news. But what will happen when I am discharged? Wayne distantly heard the hated sound of his *daed*'s own voice as he yelled at his long-absent *mamm*. Squeezing his eyes shut, he shook his head, trying to force the voices and memories out of his mind. *Nee*, Wayne. She isn't going to leave you. She came to you tonight and told you that she had taken a job just to keep us afloat.

The next night, when Lizzie came into his hospital room, Wayne told her what he had been thinking the night before. "Wife, I am so ashamed of my actions that night. Our argument—*nee*, I didn't hit you, but I was overwhelmed with my anger. I did something stupid by trying to trim that lumber while I was still so distracted by my emotions. I wasn't watching what I was doing. And now. . ."

Lizzie was silent. With her right hand, she began rapidly squeezing her forefinger and releasing it—a habit she had picked up as a child. Her silence continued. Finally, she spoke. "Husband, please know that I love you deeply. We began as friends, then our relationship grew deeper, with *Gott*'s help. We have been struggling with this issue for a long, long time. Years. I don't know how I can help you understand that I am your helpmate. We are to stand beside each other, helping each other and providing support and love to each other. If that means that *Gott* wants me to stand beside you, offering help by working in the shop, then I will carry out His will. And I hope that, one day soon, you will understand that doing so is only to help our family. Not me."

Wayne felt more tuned into Lizzie than he had for several years. He kept his eyes focused on her expressive face, watching her eyes as he took in her words. As she spoke, he felt the truth of what she said sinking into him. Closing his eyes, he allowed her voice and message to move into his heart. Sighing deeply, he nodded, taking her hand with his own good one. He squeezed it, then as was his habit when he was thinking, he ran his hand down the length of his beard. "*Ja*. I hear you. I truly do, wife. I need to think about what you have said before the nurses come in to torture me."

Wayne's heartfelt tears caused Lizzie to begin crying.

Wiping tears from her cheeks, giggled just as she used to when she and Wayne had courted. "'Torture?' They are cleaning your wounds!"

"*Ja*, but it hurts! And I am starting therapy in two weeks."

Lizzie nodded. "Okay. I will leave now. Please, think about what I just said. I want to be your helpmate, husband. Nothing more. And nothing less. I have a good heart and I have a skill I can use to help our family."

Realizing the truth of Lizzie's words, Wayne ended. "I will pray for strength to accept the changes. And the torture." Wayne's eyes twinkled as he delivered the last.

Lizzie laughed outright. "Oh, husband! Leaning down, she kissed him, thanking *Gott* for the return of his sneaky sense of humor.

After Lizzie left to meet her driver and go back home, Wayne closed his eyes for a few minutes before the nurse came in to clean his wounds. *Gott*, Lizzie spoke the truth. After talking to the doctor and my physical therapist, it will take months before I can take on all of my regular carpentry work. We can't go for that long with no income. *Ja*, the other carpenters in Peace Valley are helping me with my current orders. But I will need to bring in more work so we can keep paying our bills, even though we do have money set aside.

And *ja*, Lizzie and Leora are going to have to work. *Gott*, I don't know why I get so angry at the thought of Lizzie working outside the home. I got warned months ago that, if I went after her again, I would lose the community after being banned. *Gott*, please help me with that! Because I don't know what else to do. Once he finishes his prayer, Wayne got up and moved over to his hospital room window, looking out at the activity outdoors. As he saw people entering and leaving the hospital, he became aware of a small, quiet voice.

"Wayne, you know good and well what is happening. You don't need to admit it. You want control over your wife. Lizzie. You don't want her to have any independence because you fear she'll do something bad with it. She was telling the truth. She only wants to help your family by working at the quilt shop. You need to step back and let her help you out, as you are letting the community help you. Or you will lose everything and everyone you held dear."

Standing at the window, Wayne allowed his forehead to rest against the cool pane. *Gott* has spoken strongly and lovingly to him and he knows that He is right. He vows, with *Gott*'s help, to work with Lizzie as partners in life.

CHAPTER FOUR

A few months later, Wayne is still undergoing physical therapy several times a week as he struggles to regain full use of his hand and arm. He has been able to stick to his vow to step back as Lizzie works at the shop. But it hasn't been easy for him—he has had several struggles to accept her words at face value.

Every so often, Wayne got flashbacks and memories of his *mamm*, who had worked as a baker in their Old Order Amish community before leaving his *daed*. The day she left was etched as clear as crystal in his memory. He had been no more than twelve years old. Running into the house from school, he stopped cold. The kitchen was dark, the stove cold. Spinning around, he ran around all the rooms upstairs and downstairs, looking for her. "*Mamm? Mamm? Mamm!* Where are you?" It was only when he ran to the barn to ask his *daed* where *mamm* was that he found out. "Wayne, your *mamm* cleaned out our bank account and left. She is gone. And she is not coming back!" Wayne remembered that his *daed*'s voice had been sharp with anger and even some fear. He had backed up from his *daed*, fearful of his anger—even at that young age, he had witnessed heart-searing scenes that no child should ever have to experience. His *daed*, smacking his *mamm* on the face. Pushing her against the kitchen sink and cabinets, yelling in her face. Seeing his *mamm*, tears shiny on her face as she sported yet another black eye or split lip.

Wayne also remembered the times he and his siblings cowered upstairs in their rooms after bedtime, trying not to listen to their *daed*'s shouts at their *mamm*. Hearing her scream, beg and cry out as her husband hit and pushed her. All of this had damaging effects on Wayne and all of his siblings. All of his sisters had married abusive men who refused to allow them to have any say in whether they worked outside the home or not. Wayne saw them come to family gatherings, huge with pregnancy, sporting mysterious injuries that they tried to pass off as accidents or clumsiness.

Coming back to the present day, Wayne drew in a shaky breath and opened his eyes. *Gott*, please help me to stop abusing her! For now, he was sincere in his desire to become a better, more loving husband.

Even though Wayne bore a dim knowledge that what his *daed* had done to his *mamm* was abuse, he was unable to explicitly admit it to himself. All the years that he continued to live under his *daed*'s roof, he silently accepted his *daed*'s condemnation of his *mamm*, nodding when his *daed* denounced her as a bad woman. Wayne and his siblings had never heard from or seen her again. They didn't know if she was still alive, where she was if she still lived or what she was doing.

Most mornings or afternoons, seeing Lizzie and Leora leaving for The Quilt Place, Wayne was grateful for the added money their work brought into their home. If he heard old, fear-inducing voices, he did all he could to shake them out of his mind, staying as focused as he could on the benefits of Lizzie's and Leora's employment. *Nee*! Get behind me, Satan! They are only doing good for our family. Our bills are paid. We have managed to pay off the bank note for my newest carpentry equipment. On these days, Wayne would take out the savings account book and remind himself that almost everything Lizzie and Leora earned was going into their accounts. Leora was managing to save a tidy sum for herself as well. Looking at the growing numbers helped Wayne to reorient himself in reality.

On his way home from one of his three-times-weekly physical therapy sessions, sitting in the hired driver's car, Wayne grimaced at the pain he felt from the session just past.

"So, how's your arm? Are you doing your exercises every day?"

"*Ja*, Kevin, I am. But it hurts!"

"Yeah, I understand. I wrenched my back a few years before I retired. My doc ordered physical therapy for me and it was mandatory for me before I was allowed to report back as a paramedic. I had to keep in mind that, as long as I did my exercises exactly as my therapist showed me, that pain was good. I was strengthening my muscles. What kinds of exercises do you have?"

"Strengthening and stretching. I have to squeeze a little tennis ball. Using my hand and arm. . . Kevin, that hurts!"

"I get you there. Yeah, I sure do. But just let your therapist know if any pain doesn't feel right. Do you use heat or ice after your sessions? Take anything for it?"

"*Ja*, for the heat and ice. I'm allowed to take ibuprofen or acetaminophen, but that's all. My doctor only wanted me to take the real powerful painkillers for two or three weeks."

"Those are pretty strong and you can get in trouble with those. Just keep doing what you're doing. I can see that you're getting more movement back in your arm and hand."

"*Denki*. I will. Here's what I owe you for today. Will you be able to pick me up on Friday?"

"Unfortunately, no. I told my buddy about you. His name's Andy. He drives a Ford F-150, dark blue. He'll pick you up at eight-thirty on Friday and bring you home. But I'll be back as usual on Monday."

"Ah, okay. *Denki*! I will look for him then." Getting out of the car, Wayne shut the door and went into his house, unaware that on Friday, his whole outlook would change.

CHAPTER FIVE

Driving their buggy home from the quilt shop, Lizzie and Leora chatted about their day of work. "How did you stay so patient with that tourist, Leora? I was biting my tongue, trying so hard not to scream at her!" Leora chuckled ruefully. "*Mamm*, it was hard! I was this close. . ." Leora demonstrated, with her finger and thumb nearly touching. ". . . to snapping at her."

"Well, Annie was, too. By the time you wrapped that woman's quilt up, she wanted to throw her out of the store. I was watching as I straightened all the inventory she was messing up. Ohh! I have to wonder just what her house looks like!"

Leora's clear, high laugh rang out. "Oh, *mamm*! Just the mental image! I was never more grateful to see someone leave than I was to see her backside walking out the front door."

Lizzie nudged Leora. "Shhh! I think that's her over there! Quick. Don't look at her. I don't want her recognizing us." Lizzie demonstrated by looking straight ahead at the road ahead of them.

Leora followed along. And, as they drew abreast of the nosy Englisher, she hid a grimace as the tourist did recognize them. "Ohhhh. . . "

"Hey! Excuse me! Yoo-hoo! Ladies!"

"Go faster! We need to get your *daed*'s supper on the table!"

Leora slapped the reins on the horses' backs. "Go! Now!"

The horses responded by springing into a fast trot. Several hundred yards down the street, Leora swung the buggy right and disappeared down that road. "*Mamm*, look to see if she's behind us, please. *Daed* wouldn't like it if a tourist followed us home."

Lizzie's eyes rounded and she looked behind them. "Ohhh! No, I don't believe it! She's following us! Oh, heavens, take a detour!"

Leora swung down a narrow dirt road then, immediately after, took a left down a third road, hurrying the team along. The horses were nearly in a gallop as they hurried toward the main road. "Whoa, slow down!" She directed them to turn right, back on the main road as they entered the final part of their journey home. "Did we lose her?"

"I don't know. . . I hope so. Just hurry. The sooner we're home, the better." Lizzie kept craning her neck back as she looked for the nosy tourist. "I don't see her, but let's hurry the horses into the barn." Both she and Leora unhitched the horses, fed and brushed them and closed the barn door. As they hurried into the back yard, Lizzie clamped her hand on Leora's arm. "Hurry! I see a car coming up the road!" Both women broke into a full-out run, trying not to be seen. Inside the house, she spoke quietly to Leora. "If she knocks, we'll try to ignore her. But if she becomes too insistent. . ."

"Ooooh, I can't believe the nerve of her. Coming to someone's house. Just because she wants to learn what she has no business. . ." Leora's mouth clamped shut as someone knocked on the door.

Both women backed up so they wouldn't be visible from the entryway into the living room. "Let's just quietly get things ready for supper. Maybe she'll go away. . . oh, no, she's not!" Lizzie's ears had caught the sound of the woman trying to see if their door was locked. "That's it. You stay here. When I open the front door, you make noise with the pots and pans." Stalking to the door, she swung it open. "Yes?"

"Oh, hi! I just had a few questions about your life. . ."

"Why? Are you writing a book?"

The tourist paused, taken aback for a few seconds. Then, she laughed. "Oh. . . no! I'm just curious, that's all!"

"Well, curiosity about the Amish is one thing. Snooping into our private lives and knocking on our front door is quite another. My daughter and I are getting ready to start supper. Now, if you don't mind. . ." Lizzie started to shut the door, thankful that the screen was locked.

"But wait! Don't your kind welcome our questions? I mean, it's good for you and all. Good for you as a tourist kind of thing, right?"

Wayne came into the kitchen, where Leora was loudly putting pans down and stirring as she started the evening meal. "Daughter, what is going on?"

"We had a tourist in the store and she was just so. . . snoopy! Now, she's at the front door, quizzing poor *mamm*."

Wayne's eyes widened. He didn't like this. He hadn't bargained for that when he had agreed that Lizzie needed to go back to work. Stalking into the living room, he joined Lizzie at the front door. "Lizzie, what is going on?"

"Husband, she won't leave us alone. Annie had to make her leave the quilt store after she made her purchase. She spotted Leora and I as we were on our ride home. She followed us!"

Wayne kept a strong grip on his feelings. Turning to the Englisher, he looked at her with no smile on his face. "What do you want?"

"I. . . uhh, I just want to know more about your lifestyle, that's all! Where I live we have no Amish living nearby. . ." The woman drew in more breath to speak, but Wayne beat her to the punch.

"Well, we live separately from Englishers like you for a reason. We want to keep our path to *Gott* as clear as possible. So we avoid temptations and technology that are common in your world. My wife and daughter didn't appreciate having you follow them home. So now, I am telling you to leave. Go back to your motel or wherever you are staying and do not come back here again!" Restraining his voice and temper with difficulty, Wayne swung the door shut with his injured arm. He winced only a little as he felt a twinge run up his arm as he used it in a way he hadn't been able to do in months.

"Well. . . but, I just. . . I'm just cur--" The rest of the woman's response was cut off by the shutting of the door. She knocked frantically, trying to get Wayne to open the door once more.

"Ignore her. I'm going outside and I am going to escort her to her car. If I see anyone else who can help me, I will get their help." Wayne hurried through the back door and to the front. "Ma'am! I was serious when I told you to leave! We aren't a curiosity or tourist attraction for you to gawk and point at. We are humans, trying to live the lives that *Gott* has ordained for us. Now, I will walk you over to your car. . ."

By now, the nosy woman had had enough. Glaring at him through lashes thick with black mascara, she snorted. "Never mind! You are rude! All I wanted was to learn more about you, your kind and your lifestyle. But forget about it! You can bet that, when I get home, I am going to put the word out to anyone who's thinking of coming here. This place isn't worth the money we paid to travel to this god-forsaken place."

"Wayne? Wayne! What is going on?"

Wayne looked up, never more grateful to see his neighbor than at that moment. "Deacon King! *Ja*, please. This woman followed Lizzie and Leora home from the quilt store. She knocked on our door and she wants to learn about our lifestyle, so she says. I told her why we don't mingle with the English. I shut the door and she knocked again, so I came outside through the back and offered to escort her to her car."

"Who are you?" This rude question came from the tourist. "My name is Sophie. And yes, he is rude. I am going to get online and tell all my friends about this."

"Madam, I am Deacon King. I would say that I'm pleased to make your acquaintance, but I don't want to lie. When Mr. Lapp here told you that you needed to leave, he did so for a very good reason. Several, in fact. You came to his and his family's house uninvited. You asked intrusive questions. And now, you refuse to leave."

"'Deacon?' Does that mean you're. . . a preacher? Or a priest? Or what?"

"Ma'am, are you a reporter or something?" The deacon had caught on to the woman's pushiness.

"No, just curious. So?"

"I'm just a man like anyone else here. *Gott* has lifted me and four other men to be the elders of our community. And now, may I escort you to your vehicle? Let's go, now. Mr. Lapp would like to break bread with his family and enjoy a quiet summer evening." The deacon pointed the way to the woman's red sedan, which sat, driver's side door open, in front of the Lapp home.

"Before I leave, I just want you to know that this man, his wife and daughter are rude. And yes, I am going to post a blog entry, talking about my disappointment in today's excursion and my experiences."

The two men looked at each other in confusion. The deacon mouthed, "What is a 'blog?'" to Wayne. Finally, he assisted the woman to get into her car and he quickly shut the door. "Have a safe trip!" Returning to Wayne's side, he spoke. "'Blog?' That sounds like something that doesn't taste very good."

"Maybe one of our teens knows what that is. Thank you for your help. . . *ja*, she is leaving." Wayne huffed out a huge sigh of relief. "Iced tea?"

"*Nee, denki*. I just wanted to find out how things are going with you now that you are in therapy and able to do some light carpentry work."

"*Gutt, denki*! I am actually beginning to earn again. While I can't operate my saws yet or lift heavy pieces of lumber, I am getting back to what I was doing when I got hurt."

"And, how is it going with Lizzie? About her working?" The deacon's look was sharp and searching.

Seeing this, Wayne knew he needed to be up-front. "It hasn't been easy, but when Lizzie told me that she wants only to be my partner and helpmate, it helped me to understand that, if I didn't want us to lose everything, I needed to change my thinking."

"Wayne, what makes it hard?"

Here, Wayne really had to fight to be honest. "My. . . my memories. From when I was a child in my *daed*'s house."

"Mmm-hmm." Hannes King's expression encouraged Wayne to speak on.

"I remember, as though it were yesterday, the day my *mamm* left. My *daed* was hard. . . on her. And us. My sisters, brothers and me. When she left, he turned his physical punishments on all of us. But particularly on my sisters."

"Wayne, I believe I've met a few of them. Are you saying he abused them?"

"Abuse..." Wayne struggled to stay in the present. "Uh, *ja*. And they met and married men just like our *daed*. Their husbands don't let them work outside the home. They can't even bake and sell their goods at market. They can't quilt and sell to customers."

"Mmmm, hmmm. I won't go into what their lives are like. Except to ask you a few questions. When you see them, do they appear to be happy?"

Wayne thought. "... I can't say they do. They put on a happy face. They say that their family lives are going well. But I have spotted black eyes. Bruises on cheeks. And I know that their finances are very tight because they have only their husbands' incomes to live on."

"And the *kinder*?"

Here, Wayne shook his head. He couldn't believe he had been like his nieces and nephews when he was a child. "They are so quiet. Like fearful little mice."

"*Ja, ja*. And are you determined that you are not going to be like your *daed* or your brothers-in-law?"

"*Ja*, deacon. I am, but it isn't easy."

"Will you consent to joining our peer group? Talking to some of the men and women about what they have learned about equal partnership?"

Wayne thought about it. While he didn't want to share his innermost feelings and thoughts with others yet, he no longer felt that the group was out to intrude in the private lives of others. "I'm. . . not yet ready to do so. Lizzie and Leora. . . I know they are involved and I know it helps them. But I am not quite there yet."

The deacon sighed in disappointment. "Well, I understand your feelings. I am disappointed, and would be so happy seeing you taking part in meetings. Will you think about it and try it out some time soon?"

"I. . . maybe. I'd better get inside. Lizzie and Leora probably have supper pretty near ready by now."

"Okay. If that woman or anyone else comes back, let me know. And please, think about the peer meetings. They have helped other husbands learn to see their wives as true partners. Their marriages are even stronger."

Something held Wayne back. Something he didn't want to look too closely at. "I'll pray about it, deacon. I'll also talk to Lizzie about it."

"*Gutt*! I'll let you go now." Waving, Hannes walked out of the yard and toward his own farm.

Wayne walked into the house and smelled roast beef cooking. He closed his eyes and savored the scent. "Wife, that smells so *gutt*! I'm going to wash my hands and come back down."

"Okay. It will be ready soon." Lizzie bent over and checked the doneness of the meat and vegetables. "How is the dessert coming along?"

"I took it out of the oven five minutes ago and it will be cool enough by the time we finish supper."

"The biscuits will be ready before long. When the timer goes off, take them out, please." Lizzie swung around and began setting the table.

"Let me. "Wayne took the plates and silverware from Lizzie and began putting them at each place. "Well, Deacon King came down the road and saw that woman trying to get more information out of me. She still refused to leave even when I told her to go. It took the deacon and I to make her leave!"

Lizzie shook her head. "If I had known she would try to satisfy her curiosity like that, I would not have taken the main road coming home."

Wayne shook his head. "*Ja*, that might be a thought for

tomorrow. I cannot believe her nerve! You know she asked me about our lifestyle. Leora, I don't know if you know the answer to this. . . but what is a 'blog?' It sounds like something that's not very appetizing to eat."

Leora started chuckling, then her chuckles became full-on laughter. "*Daed*, it isn't a food. A blog is a diary that is kept on the internet. People write down their thoughts, their experiences and they try to expose people to new ways of thinking." At that last, Leora wished she could take it back. She knew her *daed* didn't like to look at new ways of thinking or doing things. "It's just for the English people, *daed*. They like to try different things."

"Hmmm. Hmmm. *Ja*, apparently. Well, she said she was going to 'tell the truth' about our family, how rude we are."

Leora started laughing again. "Oh, that's *gutt*! She was rude in the store and rude here! The timer went off. Grabbing the pot holders, she opened the oven and removed the biscuits. She tested the roast and veggies while the oven was open. "*Mamm*, it looks like the roast is just about done."

Lizzie took the fork from Leora and tested the meat. "*Ja*, maybe another five, ten minutes and I can take it out."

After supper, Wayne went out to his shop and carefully cleaned the surfaces and, holding his broom against his shoulder, he pushed the sawdust out into the yard. Next, he positioned the dustpan against the wall of the shop and began sweeping the sawdust in it. After tossing all the accumulated sawdust into the 55-gallon trash can, he put his cleaning items away and blew the lantern out, closed and locked the door.

***

For the next few months, things were calm for Wayne and Lizzie. He knew they needed the income she was earning and was grateful for her willingness to step up and help. At night, he saw how tired she was and, as his arm continued growing stronger, he would help dry dishes or straighten out the house along with her. One night, Wayne was deeply asleep when he began to dream. . .

"Mary, where were you when I came home? The house was empty!"

"Thomas, I was at the market, buying food. The lines were long today and it took longer than. . . ow! Stop hitting. . . ow!"

Thomas, not satisfied with his wife's answers, kept striking her, ignoring the presence of his children in the house.

Wayne, upstairs with his sisters and brothers, heard the fight as it began and went on. Grabbing the younger ones, he herded them into his and his older brother's room. Closing the door, he directed the younger children to sit quietly on the bed. All of them winced as they heard the repeated blows. As the younger children tried not to cry, Wayne put his finger against his lips. "Shhh. We don't want them to hear us."

"Wayne, *mamm* is telling the truth. I was with her." Anna, older than Wayne by four years, had just slipped into the room. "We were at the market and it was packed with community members and even tourists. It was taking a long time for people to pay for their purchases."

"We can't tell *daed*, Anna. He'll hit us." This was John, the oldest at seventeen.

"I'm scared!" Five-year-old Hannah sat on the bed, trying not to cry. Unconsciously, she stuffed her fingers in between her legs so she wouldn't wet her pants.

"Hannah, come with me right now!" Anna lifted her off the bed.

"I don't want to go out there!"

"Well, you don't want to wet yourself or the bed, do you?"

It was too late. Everyone heard the sound of liquid tinkling on the floor. Hannah, in her fear and distress, hadn't been able to hold her bladder until they got to the restroom. Hannah, totally humiliated, began sobbing loudly.

Anna set her down and quietly ran to Hannah's room for clean underwear and stockings. Along the way, she grabbed an old towel that she wet in the bathroom. "Hannah, did you get your dress or apron?" She checked quickly. "Boys, turn around." She helped Hannah remove her wet clothing, cleaned her up and helped her to put the clean items on.

It seemed to take a long time for Thomas to exhaust his store of anger against Mary. Soon, no more sounds issued forth from the first floor. Once Thomas slammed the front door, the house was virtually silent.

Wayne woke up, sweating. He hadn't had that dream in months! Please *Gott*, don't let it be starting again! Things have been going so well for Lizzie and me. Getting out of bed, he gazed at Lizzie's still, sleeping form. Remember Wayne, she has been truthful. She goes to work, takes her paychecks to the bank and comes home. Whenever she's not at work, she's here at home. Taking care of the house, as a good wife does. Wayne squeezed his eyes shut and kept reminding himself of these facts. Finally, his heart rate slowed down and he was able to get back into bed. Drawing Lizzie into his side, he allowed her warmth to comfort him. His eyes drifted shut and he slept dreamlessly for the rest of the night.

Lizzie noticed that, at times, Wayne was more quiet than usual. Yet, his mood was still loving, calm and good. She also monitored his progress at physical therapy and as he began to take on more and more of his carpentry tasks again. He was beginning to take on heavier carpentry tasks, although he still had to rely on area carpenters to help him with the heaviest tasks. Moving completed, heavy items was still beyond his physical ability. Vernon and Hannes King, along with other carpenters from Peace Valley, had helped him to move and deliver large items.

She wasn't aware that Wayne was experiencing dreams and flashbacks from his childhood again. She also didn't know that he had begun to watch her as she did her work at home. Thus, she was completely unaware that, when she left the house to go to the store, that Wayne had begun to time her. As far as she was concerned, things were still going normally and their marriage was only getting stronger. The only thing that had disappointed her was Wayne's continuing refusal to go to peer meetings with her. But she had decided to give Wayne room and time to make up his own mind about that. It wasn't until a few weeks later that she began to feel the change in Wayne's mood when she left for work or came home.

"Wayne? What's. . . what's wrong? You seem angry about something." Lizzie had just set her things down in the kitchen and was washing her hands before starting supper.

Wayne started. He hadn't wanted her to see his mood change. "Ahh, *nee*, it's nothing, wife. I'm just. . . disappointed in myself. I set a goal for my carpentry and I wasn't able to meet it." Wayne's voice trailed off and he looked away from Lizzie as he told the lie.

Lizzie wasn't sure she should accept that explanation. Something was wrong. Whatever it was, she could feel it just beyond reach. "Wayne? You know the therapist told you it would take a while. Your arm suffered so much damage."

"*Ja*, because I was angry when I was running that lumber through the router. It was my fault. I wasn't paying atten. . . forget it. I'll be in the shop, cleaning up." Wayne waved his hand in irritation at Lizzie and walked out.

Lizzie stared at the back door for several minutes after Wayne had walked out. Her hands bunched and pulled at the dish towel as she tried to figure out what was going on. *Nee!* His anger feels almost like. . . like what it was when he didn't want me to go to work! He was lying. I'm sure of it. She started as Leora hurried into the kitchen.

"*Mamm*? What's wrong? Your mind is somewhere else."

Lizzie grabbed Leora's arm. "Listen. I think your *daed* is starting to become angry about my working again. I don't know how to explain it. But when I came in, I noticed he was angry. I asked him and he made the excuse that he was disappointed that he wasn't able to do something with his work today. He lied." Lizzie's voice was quiet enough that only she and Leora could hear what was being said.

"*Mamm*, we need to get him to come to a peer group meeting. Or he's going to make it impossible for you to work!" Leora's voice was a quiet, though panicked murmur.

Lizzie nodded. "I will talk to Linda Yoder after meeting this

Sunday. We still need my—our—income. He's still not back to full strength." Lizzie looked out the kitchen window. "*Daed*'s coming back. Start the chicken. Roast it. I'll work on everything else." She and Leora split up and, by the time Wayne came into the kitchen, they were both busy working on supper preparations.

"Wife, are you working tomorrow?"

Lizzie's voice was purposely casual and relaxed. "*Ja*, I am. Annie has a big sale going so we can move some of the older quilts out. We have more coming in and need the room. Why?"

"I was just wondering. Don't you need to make anything in preparation for Sunday?"

"I'm starting the preparations for that tonight. I'm making the bread and biscuits. By the time we get cleaned up from supper tomorrow night, I'll be able to bake everything. Is there anything wrong?"

Wayne could find nothing. Forcing himself to stay relaxed and calm, he shook his head. "*Nee*. I was just wondering if you would have enough time to get everything done."

"Wayne. It'll be like any other Saturday. I'll be home before mid-afternoon. I know how long it will take to rise the dough and get supper started."

As the tense conversation went on between her parents,

Leora felt the knots of tension slowly tightening her neck, shoulders and back. Finally, she spoke. "*Daed*? I'd like to invite you to one of our peer group meetings next week. It's on Tuesday, and it will be at Deacon King's house."

Wayne started, then looked at Leora. Her light-green eyes were as clear as the creek running through the community. "I don't know, daughter. It depends on how much work I'm able to get done." Wayne didn't want to go to the meeting. He was convinced that the leaders were indoctrinating the women into wanting to work and defy their husbands.

"Is anyone helping you out with the heavier stuff?"

"Tuesday? *Ja*, Vernon and his *daed*. Although I really want to be able to tell everyone that I can handle the work just fine on my own."

"*Daed*, what has your therapist told you?"

Wayne allowed a small smile to escape. "Not to go too fast, to take my time."

"*Daed*, you don't want to have any setbacks. Everyone's helping you because they want to see you make a full recovery, in *Gott*'s own time." Leora's heart was pounding. She could feel that her *daed* was struggling to stay calm.

Wayne looked quickly at Leora's face. He saw only concern etched there. His eyes strayed to Lizzie's face and eyes. The concern was echoed in her expression. "*Ja*, I know. I'm just impatient." He swallowed. "And I still struggle with my beliefs about wives working outside the home."

Leora seized her chance. "That's why you need to attend this meeting. Try going to just one meeting. If you like what we talk about, what we discuss, you can decide later on to attend another one." And then more, until you see what we are talking about with sexism and sex discrimination.

"Just one? You aren't going to make me commit to attending every one of these meetings?"

"*Nee*. I know you have a lot of clients, now that your arm is getting better. Not everyone is able to go to every meeting. That's when members share what went on with those who couldn't be there."

"And. . . what, exactly, goes on in these meetings?"

Leora was so caught up in her enthusiasm that she missed the note in Wayne's voice. "We talk about how some of the women who want to help their families out struggle to get their husbands to agree to let them."

"Ahh. Well, I guess I can go to one meeting. See what it's like. But if I get bored. . ."

Leora looked at her *daed*, seeing his eyes seeming to twinkle. "You won't be. We talk about traditions and beliefs."

Wayne's voice grew stern. "Daughter, I hope your group isn't trying to assimilate English beliefs in this peer group you're in. If it is, you're going to have to leave it."

Leora's eyes widened and she glanced at her *mamm*. "*Nee, daed*! Never! The elders make sure of that. If we were trying to abandon Amish beliefs and faith, they wouldn't approve of this group."

"Then explain to me. What is the whole purpose of this group?"

RACHEL STOLTZFUS

CHAPTER SIX

Lizzie started to speak and stopped only when Leora raised her hand. As she did, she began preparing the chicken for roasting. "*Mamm*, I can answer. *Daed*, our order isn't Old Order anymore. Over the last few, what, decades, the elders have realized that and amended our *Ordnung* accordingly. Economic realities mean that married couples both work. Whether it's from home or outside the home, either the husband or wife has employment that enables them to bring needed earnings into the household so they can provide for the needs of their families. You saw that yourself."

"Yes, I saw that."

"When you had your accident, you weren't able to earn money because you couldn't do carpentry. *Mamm* went back to work and I continued to work. Your business has been kept going because other carpenters here offered their time and talent to meet your orders. If none of that had happened, where would we be today?" Leora allowed her *daed* to think about that for a few seconds, then continued. "*Mamm* has a skill and she wants to help us out. She knew that you needed to keep paying that bank loan or lose your equipment. That is what we talk about in our meetings. How we can continue to honor *Gott*, follow our *Ordnung* and still manage to adjust to today's realities."

Wayne felt a crushing weight of guilt smack into his chest and gut. "*Ja*. I understand. We would have lost everything. I still struggle with my beliefs and my past. I'll go to the meeting." He walked quietly out of the kitchen.

Lizzie and Leora looked at each other, twin expressions on their faces. Their eyes were wide and their mouths had fallen open. "Daughter, what just happened?"

Leora shrugged in confusion, shaking her head. "*Mamm*, I don't know! He was trying to give you a warning about working again. When I told him that our meetings are held in accordance with our *Ordnung*, he knew he couldn't say anything against the group." She chanced a quick look out the window. Wayne had just entered his shop. "I think he is struggling. I don't know much about his childhood. Can you share with me later on?"

"I will, what I know. He has never been open about discussing that part of his life. After supper, and after I prepare the doughs for the bread and biscuits, we'll go for a walk, you and I. You and Vernon have no plans?"

"Not tonight. He and his *daed* are working on a rush order and the customer wants it tomorrow."

"Like your *daed*, I hope he gets back up to full speed soon. This is so hard on so many. Let's get supper ready." With that, she began peeling the potatoes and preparing the two vegetables she had planned.

Leora began working on their dessert, making the crumble for the apple crisp her *mamm* had planned. Preparing the fresh apples, she added sugar and cinnamon to the sauce pan, poured in water and began boiling the peeled Granny Smith apples. After they had boiled to the tenderness she wanted, she poured the mixture of apples and sauce into the baking dish, then topped it off with the crumble and set that into the oven. "We have enough vanilla ice cream, right?"

"*Ja*, unless anyone ate it all. I just bought it the other day." Lizzie pulled the chicken out of the oven and set the biscuits inside. She pulled them out as Wayne returned to the warm kitchen. "Husband, it is hot in here. Why don't we sit on the back porch tonight and eat?"

"You mean buffet style?"

"*Ja*. I'm sure it's no hotter outside than it is inside. And the change of view will do us all good."

Wayne shrugged. "That's fine with me." He helped carry

the dishes out, setting them on the small picnic table he had made years before.

The next day went smoothly, with Lizzie and Leora leaving the house with no resistance from Wayne. He had planned that out, however, busying himself with a task he had saved for that day. "I will see you this afternoon! Have a *gutt* day!"

Leora and Lizzie waved at him from the buggy. While they were in the quilt shop, they were unaware that, an hour after the shop opened, Wayne had arrived at the small diner across the street. There, he occupied a table, drinking coffee and eating slice after slice of pie. As he ate and drank, he watched the entrance and windows of the quilt shop. He was able to see into the store, watching Lizzie in particular.

In the shop, Lizzie moved back and forth from displays and cabinets to the cash register, where she rang up sales. She would disappear to the back of the store, coming back to the front laden down with arms full of folded quilts.

Wayne remembered what Lizzie had said—that they were clearing out older merchandise to make room for new quilts. As he saw tourists and English people going into the shop, he frowned. He didn't want his Lizzie to be influenced by their practices or beliefs. Somehow, I have to make it to where she stays at home, working only from home. But that will have to wait, sadly, until I am fully recovered and can work without help. Shortly before lunch, Wayne left, going back home.

Lizzie and Leora never knew that he had been stalking Lizzie.

When Lizzie hurried into the house, she saw evidence that Wayne had been there all day long. Coffee cups and dishes sat in the sink, rinsed but not washed and dried. Looking out the kitchen window, she saw his shop door open, which told her he was at work inside. She hurried to prepare the dough for the bread and biscuits she was making for the next day's post-meeting lunch. After the biscuits had been formed and placed on baking sheets, she began working on a light supper, using ingredients she had used earlier in the week. Setting a formed meatloaf in the oven, she checked the bread dough and punched it back down, allowing it time for its second rising.

Leora came in and washed the dishes already in the sink. Once that was done, she worked on the potatoes and salad for supper. "Cookies for dessert?"

"*Ja*, I think so. It's hot and I don't want to eat too heavily. Another walk tonight after I bake?" Their walk the night before had been shortened by Wayne's demand that they be back before it got dark.

"*Ja*, that's fine. Until Vernon comes for me."

After supper, Lizzie and Leora walked out to the creek, speaking quietly. "What I remember, daughter, is that his *mamm* left his *daed* after being put through years of abuse. We don't know where she is or if she's even alive. She never came back."

"How did you learn she had been abused?"

"His nightmares. They don't happen as often as they used to, but he still does get them every month or two."

"*Mamm*, it sounds like he has some condition. 'Traumatic syndrome' or something. I'm not sure what it is."

"You mean, a mental condition? Are you sure?"

"I don't know and we need to get back before long. What I do know is that, when someone experiences something traumatic, it affects their emotions and sometimes their mental state. I'm thinking that's why *daed* is how he is. I'll go to the library next week and see what I can learn."

"Okay, *denki*. We had better get back. I need to cut the bread and place the biscuits in a basket for tomorrow."

"And we'd better pray that *daed* hasn't gotten any of it."

"That's why I had you make apple crisp. He loves your apple crisp." Lizzie hurried, not wanting to be late—or anger Wayne.

"I'll help with the bread before Vernon gets there." As it turned out, Leora had only a few minutes to help Lizzie prepare their contribution to the next day's lunch. Vernon got to the house as she was helping Lizzie to put the sliced bread into an airtight container.

Wayne answered the front door. "*Ach*, come on in! Before Leora comes out, can you tell me what Tuesday night's meeting will be about?"

Vernon was surprised. Looking closely at Wayne, he shrugged. "Truthfully, I don't know. Are you going?

"*Ja*, Leora finally convinced me to try one meeting. She knows how busy I am, even with help in the shop."

Vernon smiled. "We will be happy to have you. And rest assured. Everything we discuss is in accordance with the *Ordnung*. The elders make sure of that."

"*Gutt, gutt*. So, you talk about women and working outside the home, *ja*?"

"That's only a small part of it. We also discuss how women in our community can become true partners with their husbands, to help their families thrive."

Wayne nodded. It all sounds good. But we will see.

***

On Tuesday evening, Lizzie, Wayne and Leora drove their buggy to the King home, where the peer group was meeting. They sat in one large group in the living room, with the men sitting on one side and the women on the opposite side. After a silent prayer, the group got to work.

Standing, Eli Yoder addressed the attendees. "Tonight, we will talk about how the *Ordnung* has led to families believing that wives should not work outside the home, even when economic times are rough for everyone. Even though our economy has improved, some of our families are still feeling the effects of the Great Recession, making it difficult for them to earn enough money to pay for their bills and cover note payments. This hasn't been made very easy by the belief that wives should either not work at all or that they should only work from home, as bakers or quilters. I have some statistics here that Linda is passing out, showing that families where the wife works either from the home or away from the home do better. Their relationships are more supportive. The *kinder* thrive. But I have to caution everyone that this only works when couples agree to do this from the viewpoint that the wife is a helpmate to her husband." Eli opened his mouth to keep speaking.

Wayne raised his hand. "Eli, does this make the wife an equal partner with her husband?"

"*Ja*, it does. When couples begin to see each other as equals, they are able to accept the added responsibilities." Eli wasn't aware of the internal storm that his words had just stirred up in Wayne.

Deacon King spoke up. "Our husbands here are supposed to honor and love their wives and wives are to respect their husbands. When the wives work outside the home, they are still expected to contribute to the financial support of their family."

"So their earnings are to go into the family account?" Wayne wanted to be sure he understood all of this. "What about if the couple decides, say, that the wife can work from home?"

Lizzie, hearing this, groaned inwardly.

"Wayne, that's for individual couples to discuss and agree upon."

"I understand, deacon. But I still struggle with Lizzie working in The Quilt Place. The way I grew up, wives stayed at home. If they worked at all, they worked from home. I can handle that."

Eli intervened. "Wayne, do you see Lizzie as your equal?"

This question stopped Wayne cold. He realized just how much Lizzie had helped after his accident. But now that he was nearly back to normal, he wanted her to take a back seat again. His brow furrowed as he thought. "I. . . Eli, I know that she helped our family, along with Leora and so many of you, after my accident. But that wasn't the way I was raised."

"Okay. Do you think you can get to that point, seeing Lizzie as your equal in life and in your marriage?"

Wayne sighed gustily. He was uncomfortable. Changing his position, he tried to come up with an honest answer. "*Ja. . . nee*. Honestly, I'm not sure. She does a *wunderbaar* job in our home. Our *kinder* are strong, giving adults. They are capable and I give a lot of that credit to her. But. . ."

From that point, the meeting centered on how peer counselors could help struggling couples and families address sexism as it was expressed in family relationships.

Eli and Deacon King took Wayne aside and tried to help him solidify his position regarding Lizzie's role in their marriage. "Can you see yourself accepting that she is an equal to you?"

As Wayne heard those words, he remembered the afternoon he had realized his *mamm* had left. As he tried to think of Lizzie being his equal in her marriage, he saw the dark, silent and cold kitchen once again and his heart started pounding. His heart pounding soon became so intrusive that he lost his breath. Gripping his throat, Wayne staggered back. Shaking his head, he stumbled to the back door and outside. Under the large, spreading oak in the back yard, he rested his good hand against the rough bark, his fingers scraping down the bark with no regard for cutting himself. Forcing the thoughts out of his head, he dragged in one noisy breath then another. Soon, he was able to pull in slow, but raspy breaths. As he did so, he realized he was feeling light-headed and nauseated. He collapsed onto the grass just under the tree and pushed his head between his knees.

Deacon King found him this was several minutes later. "Wayne? Are you all right?"

"I'm getting there." Wayne found he needed to limit his words or risk losing his supper. He swallowed convulsively, forcing his stomach back down.

"I'm getting you a glass of water. I'll be right back." The deacon ran back into the house and was back quickly with the promised water. "Here." He forced the glass into Wayne's shaky hand.

Wayne took a small sip and closed his eyes, praying he wouldn't embarrass himself. As the water promised to stay down, he took a few more sips, then wiped his sweaty face with his shirt sleeves. "Whew. I didn't expect that reaction in there."

"What? You mean when we asked about Lizzie and being an equal... sorry, I'm sorry!"

Wayne had thrust his hand up, forcing the deacon to stop speaking. "Hannes, you know something of my childhood. My *mamm* left us when I was barely in my teens. That changed my life and that of my brothers and sisters."

"Wayne, I see now that it's difficult for you. I am going to suggest something and I would hope that you won't get even more upset."

"What?"

"Wayne, it's clear... that your childhood has... marked you. I ask you to please consider getting counseling. I mean therapeutic counseling. Being abandoned as you were was traumatic. And getting over it is not like getting over a rough case of the flu."

Wayne started to shake his head.

Seeing Wayne's nonverbal reaction, the deacon went on. "Wayne. The strength of your reaction in my house tells me that you still feel very strongly about a wife's proper role in the marriage relationship. And I am rightfully concerned about what that might cause you to do about that with Lizzie. I am going to the other elders and discussing today's events with them. Remember, our edict of several months ago still stands." Rising, he walked back into the house and rejoined the meeting.

Wayne sat outside for several minutes more, just trying to get over his upset and the new surprise that the deacon had just delivered. Squeezing his eyes shut, he contemplated the choices he had. Bare his soul to an English counselor. . . or risk the ban. Growling low under his breath, Wayne shook his head, realizing the nausea was now gone. Swigging the water back, he rose and walked into the house, determined to hide his true feelings.

Lizzie saw Wayne come back into the kitchen. Seeing the hardness in his normally gentle, chocolate-brown eyes, she stopped her rush toward him. "Wayne? Are you okay?"

"*Ja.*" He sat down with the men and listened, keeping his emotions under strict control. He was careful to allow only neutral expressions to cross his face as the men discussed equality for their wives, the *Ordnung* and sex discrimination.

CHAPTER SEVEN

Over the next several weeks, Wayne continued exercising strong control over his reactions and emotions. He didn't want Lizzie, Leora or any of the elders seeing what was going on his mind. Because the memories and insidious whispers had returned full-force and he was unable to stop them—or, he was unwilling to make them stop. Wayne had also returned to monitoring Lizzie's comings and goings, timing her when she left the house and came back. He had even begun to think about keeping track of the money she had in her wallet, just to make sure she wasn't stashing funds without letting him know.

Lizzie, meanwhile, was almost unaware of the lengths to which Wayne had begun to go as he tracked her whereabouts. She didn't know that, on Saturdays, he trailed her and Leora to the shop, sitting in the diner across the street, just watching her. Nor was she aware that he was monitoring her spending. But she was aware that his attitude had changed. He was harder. She wasn't able to feel the softer, loving side of his nature anymore. One day, as she was showing various quilts to an English tourist, she got a creepy feeling, like cold fingers brushing down the back of her neck. When she got that feeling at home, she began to wonder, looking around for Wayne.

***

The situation finally came to a frightening head one day when Wayne blocked Lizzie's and Leora's path out of the house as they tried to leave for the shop. "What are you going to do at work? After work?"

Lizzie froze, feeling her entire body slowing down and turning to sludge. Her voice refused to work at first. "W. . . Wayne, we're going to work! So we can earn money for the bills! Then, come home, fix supper and get things done here! Leora, let's go." Coming back into her body, Lizzie grabbed Leora's arm and turned her physically so they could run headlong out the back door.

His point made, Wayne stood sentry at the front door, just watching them drive fast out of the yard. His eyes mirrored his torture as the memories taunted him. Then. . .

"Wayne, what did you just do? You accused your own wife of plotting to hurt you and leave you when, in actuality, she has been working hard to keep your family and home from being taken away by the bank. You owe her a huge apology. She is plotting nothing!"

Hearing these soft words from *Gott*, Wayne fell to his knees, sobbing hard. He knew he had messed up in a major way.

On the way to work, Lizzie gave the reins to Leora so she could get her sobbing and tears back under control. "I'm sorry daughter."

"*Mamm*, if you need to, you and I can go stay with the Yoders. Jethro offered, just in case."

Lizzie was quiet for a few minutes, just thinking things through. Her silence also allowed her to get her emotions back under control. Sighing, she nodded. "*Ja*. Let us see how he is tonight. If we need to, please let Naomi know so she can tell Jethro. We need to pack a few necessities, just in case."

Leora nodded quietly. She knew already what was coming. "I'll tell her before we open."

Back at home, Wayne puttered around his carpentry shop. While he had made so much progress in therapy, he was still limited in what he could do with less than two arms. His injured arm was still weak, making everyday chores more difficult to accomplish. Yet, he knew he needed to get back to full strength soon so other carpenters could go back to their own shops full-time. As he cleaned and swept up, Wayne continued to be distracted by the memories of his past. Sweeping sawdust, he heard his *daed*'s voice echoing in his head. Get moving faster!

By the time I was your age, I could finish one entire row of planting or weeding in less than two hours! All the memories that assaulted Wayne had him sweating and gasping by the time he was done cleaning the shop before he began to get his newest order ready. Realizing how much his arm was throbbing, he grimaced and massaged it. Grabbing his large kerchief, he swiped it over his face and neck with his good hand. The voice of reason spoke in his head. Lizzie has done nothing wrong and she is not going to do anything. When she comes home, she will be with Leora and they are going to make a tasty supper for the three of us. Our house will be clean, warm and full of love. Even though Wayne tried to remind himself of these facts throughout that long, dragging day, the voices telling him that Lizzie was planning to leave him continued to torture him.

As he remembered his *mamm* leaving him and his siblings, he forgot one huge, vital fact: She left because she sensed, deep down, that her husband was getting perilously close to killing her. Wayne remembered that, as his *mamm* got ready to flee, she didn't make any plans to take any of her *kinder* with him. That was what made him the angriest—he and his siblings, older and younger, were left behind to face their *daed*'s anger. While he dished anger and abuse out on all of the children, the girls were in for a disproportionate share of physical and emotional abuse. That didn't mean the boys escaped the effects of the mistreatment. On the contrary, they were just as scarred as if they had been the ones to be struck or put down.

Wayne wiped streaming tears from his face as he remembered his older sisters being struck on their faces or where the bruises wouldn't show under their long sleeves. This usually happened when their efforts at cooking or cleaning fell short of their *daed*'s high expectations. Wayne was uncomfortably aware that, to this day, his sisters still experienced abuse within their marriages—and they couldn't escape.

Turning to another organizing chore, Wayne picked up chunks of lumber from the floor and, organizing them by size, he put them into safekeeping bins for use at a later time. This work didn't stress his arm as badly. Yet, the memories that continued to stream through his mind unabated resulted in an anger that he had never before felt or displayed. By the time he was done, the shop sparkled. Nodding once, he left, closing and locking the door. In the kitchen, he saw Lizzie moving around the kitchen, busy with supper. Looking all around, he didn't see Leora. "Where is she? Leora?"

Without turning, Lizzie knew that Wayne was angrier than he had ever been at any time in their marriage. Continuing to stir the sizzling meat, she spoke. "She's upstairs. Why?"

"I just wanted to make sure she was at home, like any other good Amish girl. I will be in my shop again. Call me when supper's ready." Turning back around, he stomped outside and went right back to his shop. He couldn't abide being in the same room as Lizzie. A small part of him felt unworthy of being near her.

***

Back in the kitchen, Lizzie inhaled deeply, biting her lip and forcing tears back. Turning the stove off, she hurried upstairs as soon as she was sure Wayne would stay in his shop. Knocking quietly on Leora's bedroom door, she spoke. "*Ja*. Pack enough for both of us. We will need to come up with a sufficient reason for leaving the house after supper."

"*Ja, mamm*. We can say that there's another meeting at Deacon King's house. That's in the opposite direction of the Yoder house. "

"*Gutt, ja*. That's what we will say. Hurry with the packing so you can help me. Your *daed* is in a real bad state tonight."

Forcing herself to swallow, Leora felt a nauseating lump of fear lodged in her throat. Nodding, she moved faster. Hiding their bags in her room, she hurried downstairs, barely beating her *daed* into the kitchen. She had only been cutting out the biscuits for a minute when Wayne came back inside.

"Supper isn't ready yet?" Wayne's angry growl was even more pronounced now.

"Another fifteen minutes, husband. Leora, how are you on the biscuits?"

"I just put them into the oven. I'll get the vegetables ready now."

"*Gutt*. I just need to chop the onions for salad and get the dressings on the table." Lizzie's voice was deceptively calm, trying to calm Leora down.

"Before I forget, our group is having a meeting for Mrs. Stoltzfus. We are raising funds for her. She was just. . ."

"Recently widowed. Go ahead, do your business and then come right home. I don't know why you couldn't have done this during the. . . oh, that's right. You work!" Wayne's voice was loud and sarcastic.

Lowering her hand below the level of the tabletop, Lizzie motioned Leora not to speak. "Husband, more than half of us work, so an evening meeting is necessary. And, until Mrs. Stoltzfus gets her emotions and grief back under control, she will have to do so as well."

Wayne growled again. "Just be home by dark. No respectable Amish woman is out after dark with no excuse, anyway."

After supper, Leora hurried upstairs and smuggled the duffle bags outside the house and into the buggy. "*Daed*, we're going now!" She refused to say when they would return—she didn't want to be forced to lie.

***

At the Yoder house, Jethro quickly let both women in. His *daed*, Eli Yoder, went to pick up Deacon King so they could go meet with Wayne.

***

Cocking his head at the unexpected knock at the door, Wayne swung it open, standing spread-legged in the doorway. "Deacon! Eli, what brings you here? Is something wrong?" Wayne felt a strong quiver of apprehension.

"Not in the way you think, Wayne. Can we come in?" The deacon had taken the lead.

"*Ja*, certainly." Wayne did his best to appear hospitable and untroubled. Yet his eyes told the whole stormy story. "Lemonade?"

"*Ja, denki*. Wayne, Eli came to pick me up. You were doing so well in accepting the reality of Lizzie's job outside the home. The Yoders got word today that you have taken some huge steps backward. Apparently, you tried to start an argument with your wife about the suitability of an Amishwoman working outside the home. You are still recovering and unable to take on the full weight of your carpentry orders. You aren't yet up to all of the demands of filling carpentry orders and it will be some time until you are. Lizzie's earnings are helping you keep your home. They are helping you pay down your note at the bank so you don't lose all the new carpentry tools and saws you had to buy. If you force her to quit now, you'll lose all of that and it will still be a long time until you can get back into the shop at full strength. Wayne, I'm a carpenter, so I know exactly the demands you face."

Feeling guilt and anger vying for supremacy in his emotions, Wayne shifted on his chair. He grimaced. "*Ja*, I know. I am making *gutt* progress in therapy. But it will take time. . . *ja*. Deacon, I can't help it. . . for a time, I am *gutt* with her working, then things happen. . . thoughts I. . . and I get angry all over again."

Eli listened closely, picking up on something Wayne refused to say. "Wayne, you mentioned thoughts. Can you tell me what they mean? What they are?"

Wayne jumped in his chair, startled at how quickly Eli had zeroed in on the subtext of his words. "*Nee*. . . I can't, just yet. My wife and daughter will be home soon, anyway. It's just beginning to get dark."

With a motion of his head, the deacon indicated to Eli that he would respond. "Wayne, we told Lizzie and Leora to go stay elsewhere temporarily until you are able to resolve whatever it is that you are struggling with. They will be coming home, *ja*. But not until we all know that they are no longer in danger of any physical manifestations of anger and your emotions."

Wayne reared up and out of his chair, knocking it over. His

entire posture communicated rage. "What? Where are they? I want them home with me, now, where they belong!"

Neither the deacon nor Eli responded to Wayne's shouts and roars. They just waited for him to get all the anger out of his system. Finally, Deacon King stood and, setting the chair back up, motioned to Wayne to sit back down. Once Wayne had reluctantly sat, he resumed speaking. "Wayne, if this room had a large mirror in it, you would be able to see the same thing we see. What Lizzie and Leora saw this morning and this afternoon. Your anger is out of control. It is dangerous to them right now. Eli and I have made arrangements with our families. We will stay here tonight with you to make sure you don't go out of control. You aren't going to know where they are staying because, right now, you are just too much of a danger to yourself and to them."

Wayne's mind was split into two sections. The rational part heard the deacon's words and agreed with him and Eli. The irrational part fought back. "*Nee!* I want you out of here! I will be fine. I just need to. . . get over the shock. Eli? Will you tell me where they are?" He forced his voice to sound more gentle even though he still wanted to shout at them.

"*Nee*, I am sorry. I won't. Besides, I don't even know where they are. I'm a messenger, that's all."

Thus began an odd, frightening chapter in Wayne's life. Over the next several days, Wayne ratcheted back and forth between denial and anger, swinging over to understanding the seriousness of his situation. Finally, the deacon resorted to staying at the Lapp home full time, getting to know the ghosts and demons of Wayne's tumultuous childhood. "So, when your *mamm* left, she left all of you behind? Even the youngest?"

Wayne felt as though his psyche had been turned inside-out and exposed to the whole world from a second-floor window. He spoke reluctantly about his childhood.

Deacon King had a basic understanding of psychology. Falling back on that, he began slowly pulling responses out of Wayne. As he did so, he began helping Wayne to understand his memories and responses to how his *daed* treated all of them. "Remember, I'm no expert in matters of the mind or heart. But, it seems to me that your childhood memories are coloring your ability to respond to this need in your family for Lizzie to work, and for Leora to work. *Ja*, they are your wife and daughter. And they are good, steady Amishwomen. But remember, she is also your partner, standing beside you, not kneeling at your feet. Tell me, what did your *daed* expect of your *mamm*?"

Reluctantly, Wayne remembered the shouting, insults and hitting. No wife of mine will be earning money! I don't care if she works in my house. She is to take care of my house and my *kinder* and that is all! Despite his mother's arguments that they needed the money she earned. Husband, our crop failed because there was no rain! How were we to feed and clothe the *kinder* and ourselves? That was followed by a resounding smack that Wayne felt in his entire being. Hearing his *mamm* landing on the floor, he gulped back tears, hating his weakness, but knowing he couldn't run out to protect her. . . next, he remembered walking into the still, cold kitchen that horrible day. Learning that his *mamm* had left, leaving all of them behind felt like the biggest betrayal he had ever experienced. "Deacon, he wanted her to stay at home, taking care of the house and all of us. She baked and got other wives to take the cookies, pies and cakes and sell them for her. Then, they brought her the money the items earned. She used this for the bills and to build her 'escape account.' I. . ." Wayne couldn't continue. His anger and grief closed his throat tight.

Deacon waited for a few minutes. "Wayne, have you ever heard the term, 'domestic violence?'" At the shake of Wayne's bent head, he continued. "This is when a spouse, sometimes but not always the husband, abuses the other spouse physically. Sometimes, they abuse emotionally, putting the other spouse down. Other times, they use money to control their spouse. And sometimes, they use. . . well, sexual means."

Wayne was angered. "Deacon, I don't do that!" He felt shame when he remembered how he was counseled by the elders several months earlier. "*Ja*, well, I was just. . ."

"*Nee*, Wayne. You were trying to exert your physical control over Lizzie and that was why she had to quit work.

Many of the wives saw the bruises you left on her face. They aren't stupid. They knew. And we found out. That is why the elders came to talk to you. Now, Lizzie and Leora are in a safe space. They will come home once they know that you aren't going to assault Lizzie or even Leora to force Lizzie to quit her job at the shop. *Ja*? Now, I strongly suspect. . . *nee*, I'm not going to sugarcoat this. He, that is your *daed*, abused your *mamm*. And you and your siblings by extension because you were forced to hear or witness all that. And now, because it is all you know, you use that as a measure against your family, even though you love them."

Wayne opened his mouth. Unable to speak, he closed it again, then the realization slammed into him, just as though he had been punched in the gut. He forced his breath out through pursed lips and closed his eyes. He's right. "I need to think about this, Deacon. I see what you are saying, and I see the connections I couldn't see before. But. . . I need time to think."

Deacon King nodded. "I will be in your shop, working on that dining room set. When you are ready, join me."

Inside the kitchen after the deacon had gone to his workshop, Wayne struggled with all his realizations. Seeing the parallels between his actions and those of his *daed*, he felt ashamed and dirty. For the first time, he began to wonder if everyone was right.

***

While Wayne was struggling with his past, Caleb began to experience pride in his own level of progress. He believed that, unlike Wayne, he had become truly "understanding" of Annie's need for creativity and to have something of her own. Caleb had been to the hospital to visit Wayne after Wayne's accident. During those visits, he didn't discuss the reasons that Wayne got so badly injured. Missing a huge opportunity, Caleb didn't realize the depth of Wayne's struggles with his abusive childhood.

At home, Caleb would remind himself that he was grateful that Annie only had to work half-days in the store now that Naomi was the full-time manager. When the money came in for the crops he sold, he put some of that back into the family's savings account to pay off a huge portion of his bank note. Driving his buggy back home, Caleb said a quiet prayer of thanksgiving and made plans to ready his fields for the next spring's crops.

That night, after supper and devotions, he and Annie sat down with their notebooks, book of accounts and receipts so they could see where they were financially. "So, now that my bank note is paid down so much, maybe you can. . ."

With a sinking heart and strong sadness, Annie sensed where Caleb's thoughts were going. She promptly dashed his hopes. "*Nee*, Caleb. You know this year's crops were good. If they hadn't been, you would have had to make a much smaller payment or use some of the money from my store to make a good payment. Thank *Gott* you had such a good crop this year! But what will happen next year? And the year after that? We don't know. Only *Gott* does, so we need to be ready just in case weather or some other reason has a bad effect on your crops next year. Caleb, I have been watching you as I go to work and come back home. I see that you have made so much progress! You are responding so well to my store, but don't make the mistake of thinking you have your thoughts and feelings under control."

Caleb was stunned and speechless when Annie spoke up. That was just what he had been doing. He thought he could let loose of the tight control he had been exerting over his reactions to Annie's store. He admitted privately to feeling sinful pride. Now, he felt shamed and frustrated. "Annie, I need time to pray and think." Retreating into his barn, Caleb sank to the bench, where he buried his head in his hands and prayed silently and fervently. "Gott, please help me! I allowed my pride to get in the way of my good judgment and I very nearly took something away from Annie that we clearly still need."

Son, Annie gave you a very good lesson. Use her store as a reminder that, even when things go well for you, you still need to rely on Me, just as you rely on her and her store to keep you afloat when things are bad.

***

It was several weeks later that Caleb bumped into Wayne in

town. By now, Wayne's fears and insecurities had fooled him into thinking that Lizzie would be leaving and that he had to make her quit her job at the quilting shop. Lizzie and Leora had been staying in hiding for some time now, and Wayne had to force himself to rely on the word of others that they were still in Peace Valley. "Caleb, we need to sit down and talk about my... situation..."

Caleb grimaced. He didn't want to be involved in the middle of another family's messy situation, but he also wanted to let Wayne know that he had been praying for him. "Okay, but I really need to get back. I have my helpers doing the weeding and I want to make sure they aren't weeding the corn out of my fields."

Wayne's chuckle was halfhearted. He could barely think of anyone else, for the loud clamor the warning voices had going in his head. "*Ja*, I know what you mean. Listen, can we go to get some coffee? But not here. I don't want anyone here overhearing us."

Caleb's brow wrinkled as he gave his old friend an odd look. "It'll have to be in a day or two, if you can wait. I really have to oversee these kids."

Wayne sighed loudly. "*Ja*, I suppose I can wait. Meet me at my place right after breakfast. We'll get something there and talk."

CHAPTER EIGHT

Two days later, Caleb drove into Wayne's yard. Seeing his friend standing on his porch, he nodded to him and waved him over. "Let's go! The morning is still young, but that town is a ways away."

Wayne jogged over to Caleb's buggy and clambered on. "*Denki*. Did your crew weed the weeds and not the crops the other day?"

"*Ja*, but barely. One of them was convinced that a starting corn plant was a weed. No matter that my older helper was telling him that it was a young corn plant, he was convinced it was a weed. It took me to tell him that Joshua was right."

Wayne grunted absentmindedly. "*Ja*, that's why I haven't hired anyone that young. Carpentry is dangerous and I just don't want anyone else hurt like I was."

"*Ja*, I understand. What were you doing, anyway?"

"Cutting out a special pattern with the router. I wasn't paying attention to how close my hand was to the blade."

"Aren't you normally more careful? Were you, what, distracted?"

Wayne didn't want to admit, even to one of his oldest friends, that he had been so angry at Lizzie and about their argument that he had completely ignored basic safety. "*Ja*, pretty much. I had. . . a lot on my mind and just let it intrude on my normal good sense."

Finally, they arrived in in a town that was about seven miles distant from Peace Valley. Wayne directed Caleb to a diner on an out-of-the-way side street. "The coffee and the food here are *gutt*. Well worth the drive."

Caleb nodded. "I'll have some coffee and a slice of pie."

"I'll have a full breakfast. My cooking is just bad."

Caleb chuckled. He felt uneasy—the anger coming off Wayne was almost palpable. "Where do you want to sit?"

"In the back." Sitting down, the two men placed their orders. As they waited, Wayne finally brought up what was on his mind. "Caleb, they're staying somewhere in Peace Valley, or so I'm told. And I've been told they won't come home until I get my anger under control and I'm 'less of a danger' to Lizzie.

But what they don't realize is that her job is the problem." As he rambled on, Wayne repeated this point several times, alarming Caleb slightly.

"Wayne, Annie told me something the other day. I will confess, I was becoming prideful about my success in viewing Annie, her store and need to own something of her own. Well, I had a *wunderbaar* year with the crops. I did well and made a large payment on my bank note. I made the mistake of telling Annie that, maybe, she could sell her store and be at home with me full-time. Well, Wayne, let me tell you. Annie set me straight fast. She reminded me that *Gott* gave us a good year with the crops this year, but that there is no guarantee for next year or any year afterward. She told me that I had been doing so well in accepting the reality of her store and working outside the home. Then, she told me not to make the mistake of thinking that I have my feelings and thoughts under control every day of the week.

"Wayne, I had to hear that. It was *Gott* speaking through. . ." Wayne stopped as the server brought their orders and more coffee. "Thank you, miss." He waited until the server was a good distance away. "It was *Gott* speaking through Annie, reminding me that I had allowed myself the sin of pride. I thought I could relax a little on my feelings about her working. After that, I went to my barn and prayed for a while."

Wayne was silent, quickly downing the scrambled eggs and

sausage on his plate. "Did she say anything else?"

"*Ja*, as a matter of fact. She told me that my beliefs that women should stay at home are sexist. That I need to start looking at her and other women in other ways, that they are capable of holding down jobs outside the home as well. . ."

"Sexist? *Nee*! It's the way of the world, the way *Gott* intended the world to be! Bah, whatever. I am working with the elders and trying to understand. But it's not easy!"

After listening to Wayne, Caleb began wondering if Annie was right after all. Trying to decide whether Wayne or the group of people that were protecting Lizzie and Leora were right, he got fed up. "Wayne, all of this thinking is just giving me a huge headache. I need to stop at the market and buy some repair tools anyway, so we'd better get back to Peace Valley. Are you done with your plate?"

"*Ja*. I'll pay for breakfast." Pulling several wrinkled bills out of his wallet, Wayne covered the tip and the bill. Leaving, he swung up into the buggy next to Caleb, allowing his dark thoughts to take him where they would.

Caleb looked at Wayne's downcast face. "How is your carpentry coming along these days? Are you finding that you're stronger now and taking on more of your work?"

Wayne roused from where his thoughts had taken him. "*Ja*, it is getting better. Slowly, but that's what my therapist warned me about. He said that I would want to move faster, but that I should respect the healing of my arm and hand."

"It has been weeks. No months! *Ja?*"

"*Ja.* Here it is, fall, and I am still not working on everything as I used to do. I still need help from other carpenters. But I am getting there. Last week, I made myself handle the broom with both hands. It hurt, but I did it. I also made myself pick up chunks of lumber with both hands so I could put them into saving bins. By the end of that, I was sweating and hurting. . . but I did it!"

"*Gutt* job! So, when will you be released to go back to working full-time?"

"Not soon enough! I am chafing! I guess this allows me to put everything into my stupid physical therapy. Who knows? I am determined to get back to normal and start my carpentry work as soon as they say I can do so. Then, Lizzie will be quitting her job. For *gutt.*"

At a certain tone in Wayne's voice, Caleb felt a chill that slithered down his spine. Even though he felt it, he chose to ignore it. "Are you working with the Yoders and the elders?"

Wayne let out a loud, guttural growl. "I am. I have to or risk losing everything. Including my membership here in Peace Valley."

That warning shiver skated along Caleb's nerves once

again. Again, he chose to disregard it. Dropping Wayne off at his home, he saw the woman who was cleaning Wayne's house coming out the front door. Before pulling out of the yard, he overheard her beginning to speak to Wayne. "Mr. Lapp, it's taking me longer, not shorter, to clean your house every week. I am going to have to bring one of my girls with me so I can finish in a reasonable amount of time."

Caleb was now well out of the yard and down the road, so he barely heard Wayne's response. What he did hear was the anger in Wayne's voice. Turning and looking back, he saw the woman running toward her buggy and jumping in, fear outlining her posture and movements. Again, that feeling of fear scraped Caleb's nerve endings. Now, he wondered if he should pay attention to the warnings it was giving. Arriving at home, feeling preoccupied, he found Annie, busily working in the house.

"Husband, Linda Yoder came by today. She, Eli and the deacon will be able to come over starting next week so we can start working together. I said that, because of your farming schedule, we'd have to meet in the evenings or on Saturdays. She was agreeable."

Caleb was silent for several minutes, just thinking. At first, he wanted to refuse, but remembered his own concern with several of Wayne's statements. "*Ja*, that's fine. Do you know if they are still working with Wayne and Lizzie?"

"*Ja*, to my knowledge, they are. Of course, with Lizzie and Leora staying elsewhere, they have to meet in a neutral place They go to the bishop's house to work on the intervention sessions. Why?"

Caleb decided to speak up, but instead of voicing all of his concerns, he minimized them to Annie. "I spent a little time with Wayne today. He still seems pretty angry that Lizzie has gone back to the quilt store."

"Well, of course, she has! After nearly chopping his arm off, he can't work! It's only with the blessing of the other carpenters and Lizzie's work that they haven't lost their home!"

This reminds Caleb of the precariousness of their own situation. "*Ja*. . . it's only *Gott*'s blessings that allow us to live as we do."

Caleb's tone of voice captured Annie's attention. Knowing him as she did, she knew something was wrong.

Picking up a cookie, Caleb thought. "His anger at not being able to work is normal. I get that, he wants to get back to making things and earning money again. But he sees to forget that, if Lizzie hadn't gone back to work. . ."

"They would have lost a lot, Caleb. She was frightened when she and Leora left their house. Apparently, Wayne threatened her again."

Caleb tossed the cookie into the trash. "He could be banned! Annie, I know I'm not always thrilled about your store. But I am working on getting used to it and accepting your ownership."

"But Wayne? He's not accepting the necessity of Lizzie working?"

Caleb was reluctant to tell on Wayne, but honesty compelled him to speak. ". . . *Nee*. He isn't. As soon as he's cleared to work, he plans to make her quit working."

"Caleb, you need to tell the bishop! Lizzie and Leora can't go home until he realizes that we women can work outside the home without violating the *Ordnung*."

Caleb didn't want to argue with Annie. "I'll be in the barn. I need to think." Before he lost his temper, Caleb left the house.

***

Driving to the deacon's house, Caleb and Annie met with the Kings and Yoders. After thinking about what he heard from Wayne, Caleb decided it was past time to speak up. "I am just worried that Lizzie is going to go back home from wherever she is. . . and he's still got a lot of anger toward her and their situation."

"We will intervene with Wayne. Thank you for telling us this because you are right. They can't go home until Wayne has felt with his feelings and realizes that it is okay for our women to work. Speaking of which, Annie, how has Caleb been treating you in respect to your store?"

Annie was honest. She forced Caleb to own up to his feelings. "*Ja*, I fell into pridefulness and she called me on it. Ever since then, I have been remembering to work on my own attitude daily."

"Is it still a still a struggle? Do you still feel like you have to force Annie to sell and stay at home full-time?" This was Eli speaking.

"At times, *ja*."

"Annie, has he been calmer? What about threats?"

"*Ja*, he is calmer. Less anger, no threats, although he does admit to frustration. He goes to the barn when he feels that happening."

"*Gutt, gutt!*" The meeting went on, with everyone discussing sexism and misogyny. The meeting ended with Deacon King reminding Caleb that Annie was no longer tied to the house, caring for a large family. "Most of your *kinder* have grown up, married and have homes of their own."

Caleb nodded slowly. He was beginning to understand. "So, what everyone has been saying is that, if couples agree together that the wife can or should work, it's within our *Ordnung*. It's okay for wives to work outside the house. I'm beginning to see that. But, if husbands need their wives at home, what then?"

Eli leaned forward, wanting to respond. "This is why married couples are to discuss their individual situations among themselves. They are to decide what their family's needs dictate. Caleb, what are your family's needs?"

"We rely on my farming and her store. Before we became involved with your group, I wanted her to sell it. Every time, Annie has reminded me that, in bad farming years, the proceeds from her store have allowed us to keep our heads above water. In good farming years, the profits from her store go into savings, against emergencies. And I do have to admit, she has been open to making changes to meet me halfway. She stopped working full-time. She works part-time now after making Naomi the manager."

After conferring with each other, the peer group decided on five more sessions before assessing their progress once again. Caleb was pleasantly surprised. He decided to ask again about Wayne. "What will happen to him if he doesn't begin working with you?"

"Nothing, really. But if he goes after Lizzie or Leora, then he knows full well what could happen. I do want to ask you not to allow him to work on your mind again."

Caleb readily agreed, still feeling spooked. "I know I will probably bump into him and I will just say I have too much work. But there is something. . . strange going on with him. I don't know what it is, but it feels like his anger comes from deep within."

Eli and Linda looked at each other, then at Deacon King. "Hannes, I think we've been given an excellent direction on Wayne. Caleb, *denki*. We will be able to work much better with Wayne now that we know this."

***

At this time, Wayne decided to try and find where Lizzie and Leora were staying. He also withheld some of the truth about his own situation, then followed Lizzie back to where she was staying.

Eli was ready for that and, seeing Wayne trailing far behind them, he took Lizzie and Leora to the bishop's house.

Wayne, seeing Lizzie stepping out of the buggy with Leora, broke off his pursuit. Feeling the familiar anger bubbling close to the surface, he went into the shop and gathered several small pieces of lumber. Outside, he began flinging them, with his healing arm, at the oak tree. Screaming at the top of his lungs, he threw every scrap until he was physically exhausted. Collapsing to his knees under the tree, he closed his eyes. Then, he heard the smallest voice.

"Why do you try to control everything? Deep down, you know you need Lizzie's help. She loves you and your *kinder*.

She isn't going to leave you. If she had bad intent, she would have done so long ago. Don't you want a much more mutual, relaxed relationship with her, where you can focus on your love for her? Or do you want to control her through fear of your temper and fists?

"Wayne, I want you to tell the peer group what happened when you were a boy. This is why you are acting as you are. And, if you don't get yourself off that path, you are going to lose everything and everyone."

Raising his head, Wayne looked around. He knows it was *Gott* speaking to him, but he wanted to be sure nobody was around. The voice returns. "Wayne, you can be a big help to help, women and the elders here. You don't need to let anyone know that I am talking to you or that you are the source of the help. Go talk to the bishop and tell him everything. You need healing in order to get past your anger."

"Lord? If this is you, am I losing my mind? Or are you really talking to me?"

"I am really talking to you. Yes, you are struggling, but that's because you went through such a horrific time as a young boy. If you hadn't had your *daed*'s actions and attitudes ad an example, you would not struggle with the thought of equality for Lizzie or your daughters. Think about your sisters. Have they married men who welcomed their financial help? Or are they in bad, abusive marriages?"

"They are all in bad marriages. Their husbands don't even allow them to sell their baking or quilts from their homes." Wayne rolled to his knees just in case he vomited from the memories. After this encounter with *Gott*, Wayne became much more introspective. He committed himself anew to working with the peer group even though he still struggled with the idea of equality for Lizzie and Leora. He also went to talk to the bishop, telling him of his abusive childhood.

Sitting with Wayne in the sparkling kitchen of his home, the bishop nodded once. "At a glance, Wayne, I think you need to speak to a mental health specialist. Continue working with me, the peer group and elders. Lizzie and Leora are fully committed to coming home to you when it is safe and you won't be at risk of losing your temper and beating either one of them. *Nee*, I won't tell you where they are,"

Wiping tears from his face, Wayne gave a broken chuckle. "*Ja*, I understand." As long as his therapy was kept confidential, he agreed to begin working with a counselor. This began several days later. After a few months, Wayne began to respond differently to situations that, before used to enrage him.

Both Lizzie and Leora noticed this during peer counseling sessions.

Wayne noticed that Caleb was avoiding him. Catching up to him after Sunday services, he asked Caleb to join him for lunch.

After several minutes of discussion, Caleb agreed reluctantly that he had been avoiding him. "I didn't want to set you off. The last time we got together, some of the things you said scared me. I don't want to be banned. I want to keep my family and friends around me."

Wayne stayed quiet for several long seconds, thinking. "Caleb, let me tell you something in confidence. I am in therapy to deal with the memories of my childhood. My *daed* was abusive to my *mamm*. To my brothers, sisters and me. I know now that *mamm* left because he abused her so much. He didn't even allow her to work from home, baking to earn extra. . . *nee*, no, not 'extra' money. To help our family financially. *Ja*, I'm still angry with her for not at least taking the youngest *kinder*. But that's in the past. I am realizing that now. I don't want to lose my family or friends either. I know in my heart that Lizzie doesn't have bad intentions for me."

After this conversation, the two men resumed their friendship, which helps Wayne to make even more progress in therapy. He overheard one of the Peace Valley women talking about Lizzie's absence from the Lapp home. This brought back old fears; he began to skip peer sessions. However, he kept up with his therapy, knowing he would be banned if he started to skip them.

***

The elders and peer counselors sat in Bishop Kurtz' home, discussing Wayne's non-attendance at peer meetings. "I am not surprised. I have seen the anger returning to his face again. I'm going to go visit with him and let him know what I am seeing."

***

While the elders and peer counselors were meeting, Caleb and Wayne were at the market, buying items they needed. Again, the same gossipy Amish woman was at the market at the same time. She wasn't able to let go of the titillating topic of Lizzie not living with her husband—Wayne and Caleb overheard her.

"*Nee*, she's still not there! She probably separated from him for one reason or another. . . and Leora is with her as well. She's still working at The Quilt Place, probably earning up enough money to move to another Amish community. Anna, I have to admit that Wayne scares me, with those dark, angry moods of his. . ."

Caleb looked at Wayne, seeing the dark flush of embarrassment on his cheeks. "Here, watch my stuff. I'll be right back." Caleb's long strides ate up the distance between them and the gossipy woman. Taking her elbow firmly, Caleb got her attention. "Ruth, anyone in this market and clear into the next three counties can hear everything you are saying. And what you are saying is no more than worthless gossip. Shut your mouth."

Ruth's mouth opened as she understood Caleb's words. Flushing, she clamped her lips shut and turned away from Caleb.

The two men paid for their items and left. "Let's go to the diner and get some coffee. My treat." He tried to find out what Wayne was thinking, but Wayne had shut himself down. He only said, "Deep down, I knew it. She wants to leave me. That's why she's back at the shop."

Despite Caleb's best efforts, Wayne continued stubbornly believing that Lizzie was about to leave their marriage. "She only went back to the store because you were so badly hurt! She knew you needed money coming in for your bills."

Obstinately, Wayne shook his head. He continued believing he was about to lose his wife.

Throwing his hands in the air, Caleb gave up. "Just promise me one thing: That you will talk to me before you do anything."

Standing, Wayne barely nodded before he left. That day, he began surreptitiously trailing the peer counselors, trying to find where Lizzie and Leora were staying. He also began to plan their murders. He visited Caleb, trusting the strength of their friendship, detailing his plans for his wife and daughter. "Will you help me out?"

Caleb wanted to run away from Wayne. Stilling his face, he continued looking at his old friend. "Wayne, what happened to the man who was starting to accept that women are equal to men?"

"*Nee*. It's only a ploy so they can hoodwink their good husbands until they decide it's time to abandon them! She's not going to leave with everything I've worked for." Wayne conveniently forgot that Lizzie didn't have access to anything in their home because she was living elsewhere. "Caleb, I'm working again. I won't have to rely on her ever again."

Sighing, Caleb decided to agree to work with Wayne, if it was the only way he could stop two tragedies. "*Ja*, I'll help." After Wayne went back home, Caleb hurried to the bishop's home. "Bishop, he's about to kill Lizzie and Leora. He wants me to help him. And that's what he told me. He also said he knows where they are living."

Bishop Kurtz scrubbed his hands over his face. "Keep meeting with him and pretend to go along with his plans. We will meet any time you call me. Just leave a message if I don't answer. Let me know what he is coming up with. And, if he tells you when he plans to kill them, let me know right away! Call me when you are away from him."

Caleb nodded frantically, feeling slightly better. He didn't like the idea of continuing to meet with Wayne, but he knew that he had to, to protect Leora and Lizzie.

***

The two men were sitting in Wayne's shop, discussing his plans for Lizzie and Leora. "So, I was thinking that I could, oh, poison them somehow. What do you think?" As he stared sightlessly at Caleb, the madness glittered in his eyes,

Looking anywhere but into Wayne's eyes, Caleb sighed, hating this. "Well, why not just. . . force their buggy off the road?" He swallowed hard, trying to keep his lunch from coming up as he pretended to plan with Wayne.

Rubbing his hand over his whiskery chin, Wayne considered. "Maybe. But. . . no. They are always with one counselor or another. Ah! I see what you're saying! I could also take one or both of those blamed counselors, too! Ha! You're brilliant, Caleb!"

After every session, Caleb went home, feeling as though he had wallowed in a pig pen. As he arranged with Bishop Kurtz, he called him after every meeting.

Annie noticed that Caleb was oddly preoccupied and tense. When she asked him what was wrong, he pretended that it was just his worries about their crops. "It's been weeks since we've had a good, soaking rain. And I need to pay that note off before Christmas."

Annie was skeptical, but knew she had to accept Caleb's explanation.

***

The bishop rocked on his front porch as he thought. "This situation with Wayne is beyond our ability to resolve safely. We are going to have to involve the English law enforcement system. I'm glad I already got the go-ahead from the other elders."

Leafing through the notes he took from Caleb's calls, he rose and went to the barn, where he hitched his horses to his buggy. Placing the notebook at his feet, he drove quickly to town. Once in the sheriff's office, he spoke to the clerk. "*Ja*, I need to speak with the sheriff on an urgent matter. *Ja*, I will wait." He took a seat and waited patiently.

Sheriff John Mathis shook hands with the bishop, then took him back to his office.

"Sheriff, I am Bishop Joseph Kurtz from the Peace Valley community. You know we don't like to involve the English in our matters, but today, it is necessary." Joseph continued, explaining Wayne's plans for his wife and daughter.

"You say one of your church members is talking to Mr. Lapp and getting the specifics from him? I hate asking this, but if you could get him to continue. . . We need for this to be as specific as possible." The bishop agreed and the two men exchanged phone numbers.

That afternoon, the sheriff called the bishop. "Mr. Kurtz, I want to bring a female deputy into this. Several of your community members are involved in a peer counseling effort. I want my deputy to meet with them so they can begin trusting her."

***

The peer counseling group moved its meetings into the English community so they could meet the sheriff and his deputy. Deputy Johanna Drew spent several days gaining the trust of the men and women—as progressive as most of them were, they still carried an instinctive distrust of the English. Johanna began by discussing the roadblocks women faced as they struggled against sexism and misogyny. Finding the work slow going, she invited Linda Yoder to have coffee with her. "What have you found to be the most difficult in creating a place of equality in a male-dominated society?"

It took Linda some time to realize she could trust the deputy, so her initial responses were spare and guarded. "I find that I have to struggle to get the men of Peace Valley to accept that I am just as capable with numbers, working with people and even business administration as they are. In fact, it took several months—for my husband to accept that I have a better head at organization and drawing people together than he does. It was hard for him to let go and just let me do the work."

Finally, the peer group has accepted Johanna. The elder's wives, Annie, Lizzie and Leora began to work with her. During one of these meetings, Johanna gently informed them of Wayne's plans for Lizzie and Leora.

Panicking, Lizzie stood and began pacing around the room. "I have to leave, right now! Leora, you're coming with me. We will stay away until Wayne gets himself back under control."

"Wait, Lizzie! We are making sure he can't get to you We have plainclothes officers—that is, deputies in everyday dress—trailing you so he can't get close to you. Don't tell me where you're staying. Keep that between you and the group here. But I told you this because you need to be watchful—just in case."

Shortly after, Annie found out what role Caleb had been playing in keeping the sheriff's department informed of Wayne's activities. Bishop Kurtz' wife sat down with her, telling her Caleb had been meeting with the bishop, telling him what Wayne was planning. "Please, do not say anything to him. We need him to keep providing information until we can stop Wayne and get him the help he needs." Lizzie, Leora and Naomi overheard this conversation. Realizing this, the bishop's wife brought them into the group. "Ladies, whatever you do, do not reveal Caleb's role. He is doing everything he can to protect the community, Lizzie and Leora."

Annie finally understood why Caleb had been so tense. "Can I tell him you told me? In absolute confidence?"

"*Ja*, but nobody else. In fact, Lizzie, Leora, you should go only to meetings and work. No frolics or other gatherings. We don't want you close to Wayne. We pray that this ends peacefully and soon."

***

Caleb learned that Wayne had developed a solid plan for attacking Lizzie and Leora. Hurrying, he went to the bishop's and gave them an update. "He will be attaching her at the next Meeting Sunday. In two weeks. That is at our house, bishop! He'll use his bare hands."

Joseph Kurtz paled. Thinking of violence made him ill. "*Denki*. I will call the sheriff. We will be including you, Naomi and Annie in our discussions because meeting takes place at your house."

Within a few days, the plan fell into place. "Visiting Amish" would attend the meeting. The "visitors" would be deputies, dressed as Amish men and women. "He will attack after the service ends, probably during lunch."

Heading to the safe house, the bishop brought Leora and Lizzie into the plan. "Carry out your usual serving roles, but stay far away from each other. The Millers know what is happening and are going to do everything to make sure you are safe. The peer counselors will be watching. When Wayne makes his move, one of the women will get you, Lizzie, inside.

Leora, you stay inside. The 'visitors' will detain Wayne and transport him to a mental hospital."

***

On Meeting Sunday, Wayne struggled with his emotions during the service. Staring hard at Lizzie, he saw how neat she was, with every hair in place under her prayer covering. He noticed the same about Leora. For a few seconds, he doubted his fears. Then, his temporary madness roared back. Flexing his newly recovered hand, Wayne checked its strength.

After the elderly community members ate, the men took their seats. As arranged, Leora stayed inside, preparing platters while Lizzie helped to serve.

Seeing Wayne, Lizzie plastered a smile to her face and served everyone. Looking around, she saw Wayne set his glass down and walk purposefully toward her. Again, she smiled.

As he neared her, Wayne reached his hands out toward Lizzie's neck and. . . he was pulled back from her by the "visitors." Several women had pulled Lizzie away and into the house.

EPILOGUE

Several weeks later, Wayne had come back to himself. Hospitalized and receiving medication and therapy, he slowly began to see that Lizzie wasn't going to leave. Eagerly, he awaited her visit—he wanted to apologize to her for doubting her and planning to kill her.

"Keep your jobs. I see now that you were trying to keep us from going under. We can both work."

"Am I your equal partner, or am I still below you?"

"Equal partner, for sure. You know what you are doing, keeping our house running. What has been happening with my orders?"

Lizzie updated him and showed him the bank book and list of orders completed and paid for. Before she left, she turned and smiled tenderly at Wayne. "I love you, my life partner."

THE END.

AMISH LOVE SAVES ALL

Violence. Redemption. Love.

In the wake of Wayne Lapp's brush with tragedy, the Amish community of Peace Valley has made it clear that women are allowed to work and earn money outside the home. Yet still, some resist. An Amish widow faces pressure from her beau to close her small touring company, the only income that sustains herself and her small children. Another Amish teen a similar choice when her boyfriend insists she leave her job in a local diner in order to "be a good Amish woman." And when this pressure shifts to violence, can the residents of Peace Valley, working together, truly move past antiquated views of a woman's place in order to save themselves?

CHAPTER ONE

Naomi Miller leaned against the kitchen wall, shoving her hands into her neat, blonde bun, displacing the round ball of long hair. Tears streamed down her cheeks as she grieved for her best friend, Leora Lapp, who had been forced to watch her dat go into a mental hospital after trying to kill Leora and her mam, Lizzie. "Gott, why? They have done nothing to deserve this! Please, Lord, watch over all three of them and help Mister Lapp finally heal from all of his memories."

Finished with her quiet prayer, Naomi pulled her hair covering from her head and shuffled to the kitchen table, grabbing a napkin. She scrubbed her face clean of tears, and then blew her nose. *It wouldn't do for Dat or Mam to see me reacting so, or they won't let me continue working on the peer group.* Releasing a long, shaky sigh, Naomi exerted control over her emotions just as her mam came into the house.

"Naomi, what's wrong?" Annie's concern was evident on

her round face.

"Nothing, Mam. I just came from seeing Leora."

"Ach, with her dat in the mental hospital, ja. How were she and her mam?"

"Upset." Naomi's voice quivered as she forced control over her vocalization. Exhaling slowly, she forced the sobs back again.

"Of course. Please let them know that I am so sorry for what happened." Annie glanced outside the large kitchen window, allowing the late-fall scenery to calm her spirit. "And you, my daughter. I know you're more upset than you are letting on. Go outside and take a walk. Your dat won't be home for a while—he'll be late for supper. I just got word from Deacon King."

"Oh? What is he doing?"

"He is working on presentation materials for our young teen couples. Go. Calm yourself down and come back in later. You do know that if he sees you so affected, he will take you off the peer committee."

"Ja, I know. We knew what was going to happen with the Lapps, but it was still a shock. Lizzie has to be so torn apart!"

"Ja, daughter, she is. But the English sheriff explained to her and Leora that a mental health placement is best for them *and* Wayne. That, when he is discharged, he will be stabilized on medications and better able to control his moods and reactions to stresses."

Seeing it from that viewpoint, Naomi felt better. "And Lizzie was already working in the store, so it's not like she would have had to come back in, hoping there would be an opening waiting for her."

"Exactly. If you want to stay on the committee, child, you need to start looking for the silver linings. Go. Walk, then help me with supper."

Naomi's smile was much more heartfelt now. Grabbing her cape, she swung it over her shoulders and waved goodbye to Annie. "I'll be back soon."

Walking outside in the crisp fall air, Naomi thought about everything she and her mam had just discussed. *Ja, Lizzie and Leora were frightened and upset. They are going to miss Wayne. But it's better for them to miss him, knowing he's finally getting the help he's needed for so many years. And they are both working at the store, earning the money they need. I'll ask Mam to find out if they will need help with Wayne's carpentry orders. I am sure they hate having to ask once again.* Her thoughts veered back to the time, nearly a year ago, when Wayne had seriously injured his arm in a carpentry accident. The community's carpenters had lent their expertise and efforts in helping Wayne to keep up with his orders so he wouldn't lose customers and all of his tools. Shivering slightly in the chill breeze, she decided it was time to go back inside.

"Mam, what do you need me to do?"

"Hmmm, please make the dessert. Peach pie, I think. Then, take vegetables from the pantry so we can have them with the chicken."

"Should I make the potatoes?"

"Nee. I'm working on them now."

Looking down, Naomi saw that her mam had cut several potatoes into small chunks, along with most of an onion. "Mmm! Potatoes Anna!"

Annie smiled, her round face beaming. "Ja, I figured we could use some comfort-type foods. I know this whole thing has *ferhoodled* your dat because they have been friends for so long. What does Jethro say?"

Working on the piecrust, Naomi shook her head. "I don't know yet. All this happened after we went out last. I'm sure I'll hear from him and his parents about this. I do know they were really worried about Wayne. Then, when we learned he was planning to try and kill Lizzie and Leora, Mister and Missus Yoder felt so horrible, feeling like they had failed the whole Lapp family."

"But they didn't fail them." Annie worked on the chicken and potatoes, deftly stirring the potatoes as she placed the chicken into the roaster. "If Wayne had been more direct about what was happening in his mind, we could have gotten to him and gotten help to him more quickly."

"I'm just grateful that we were able to do what we did." Naomi turned the peaches into the pie plate, on top of the piecrust. Sprinkling cinnamon on the peaches, she continued. "I was very surprised that the English sheriff and deputies were able to get to him as quickly as they did."

Naomi shivered before she could stifle the automatic reaction. Looking quickly at her mam, she smiled slightly when she realized Annie had caught her reaction. "Sorry."

"Why? We all saw something frightening. It's better to deal with it now than have it affect us for weeks down the road, ja?"

"Ja. I just don't want you and Dat to take me off the committee. That's all."

"So, you still want to work on it?" At Naomi's emphatic nod, Annie continued. "You can. As long as you are honest with your dat and me about how you feel about what we witness. This past Sunday was…horrible for all of us. We love the Lapps. Realizing that Wayne had fallen apart as much as he did frightened even the elders and the Yoders. I'm sure Jethro's parents will tell you that."

Now, it was Naomi's turn to gaze outside the large, bay window. Seeing the leaves falling off the trees, she allowed the sight to help calm her spirit. "Ja, I'm sure. Mrs. Yoder looked…well, more than concerned." As the sky darkened, Naomi's mind went back to the lunch in their back yard. Seeing Wayne approaching Lizzie, a look of determination on his craggy face, had chilled Naomi. Shaking her head, she reminded herself of one thing: *We all knew what he had planned. And thank Gott that we had the assistance of the sheriff's department!* Remembering these two things, Naomi was able to calm herself down. "We had a lot of help. I'm keeping that in mind as I get over this. Mam, would you mind terribly if I went to visit Leora and Lizzie after supper?"

"Nee, as long as your dat has no objection. If you do go, don't be too long. And please, pass on our prayers and good wishes for them and Wayne."

"Ja, I will." Naomi worked in silence. Taking jars of vegetables out of the pantry, she brought them into the kitchen. "Beans and peas, I think. I know they're both green, but we have so much of them!"

"That's fine. They are your dat's favorite… Oh! There he is!"

Caleb walked into the kitchen, removing his black felt hat. Holding his cupped hands over his mouth, he blew into them, trying to warm them up. "It's getting cold out there!"

"Husband, I'm glad you're home! What did you and Deacon King get done?"

"Some teaching materials that go along with our Ordnung. We've found that so many of our married couples and courting couples either believe the Ordnung doesn't allow our married women and teen women to work outside the home, or even that some of the men in the community are actually using the Ordnung to force their wives to stay at home, even as they know the Ordnung doesn't forbid wives working outside the home."

"I'm not surprised." Annie turned to check the chicken's progress, missing the way Caleb looked around the house.

"Ja, I truly thought our Ordnung would cause you to be brought before the community. Now that I know it doesn't, I am fine with your ownership of the Quilt Shop. And with Naomi managing it so you can work half-time."

Annie closed the oven door and wheeled around to face Caleb. Her eyes were wide. She had never heard that calm tone of voice coming from him in connection with her store. "Caleb! You're serious!"

"Of course! Seeing what happened with the Lapps opened my eyes to the dangers."

Annie quieted down quickly at that. "Are you saying…he may still be…?"

"Nee. But when he comes home, he will be watched closely. Deacon King and the bishop are determined that this kind of thing won't happen again, ever."

***

As the Millers were recovering from the events of the weekend, John Andrews, whose family had moved to Peace Valley several years earlier, smiled, thinking of his girlfriend, Beth Zook. John had a hard time adjusting to his new community—as conservatively as the Peace Valley community thought, it was much more advanced than his Old Order Amish community.

John's smile slowly disappeared as he thought of Beth's consistent refusal to quit her job at the diner on the edge of Peace Valley. He rolled his eyes, thinking of her objections. *She says that she and her mam need the money they both earn. I am sure she could quit and, with a little budgeting, they would still be just fine. I am just going to have to continue working on her until she sees things my way.* John conveniently forgot that "working on her" included smacking Beth with a closed fist. As a farmer, he had become unusually strong, which he was willing to use against Beth's disobedience to his wishes. *I just have to strike her where marks won't show. Say, on her arms or her ribs. Soon, though, she will agree with me. I wonder what Mister Lapp did to convince* his *wife to quit her job…but why did she go back to that quilt shop? Does she care that she violates the Ordnung?* John was aware of the differences between the Ordnung from his old community—which was probably slightly more advanced than when he, his dat and mam had left—and that of Peace Valley. Still, he chose to discount the fact that he was thinking of the Ordnung that existed for his former community rather than that of his new home because it was something he was more comfortable with.

"John! Have you finished repairing the harvester?" John's dat, Big John, came into the barn on short legs.

"Ja, just a few minutes ago. I think it will be gut for next autumn."

"Gut. Come into the house for supper. I want to have devotions early so I can get to bed early."

"Ja. I will. I was thinking I could spend some time with a…friend."

"Hmm." Big John glared out at his son from under bushy, graying eyebrows. "Tomorrow's a working day. Ja, go on ahead, but be back here at a reasonable hour!"

John had grown up with those strict rules all his life, so he was quite comfortable with them. "Ja, Dat. I will." Hurrying inside, he barely greeted his mam, instead rushing upstairs to wash his hands and face. Coming back downstairs, he stood behind his chair, waiting until Big John was ready to give the silent prayer of thanks.

Mrs. Andrews silently and quickly served her husband and son their plates. Her husband had made it crystal clear at the beginning of their marriage that he expected this level of service at every meal. She was the last to sit and start eating. Out of long habit, she averted her eyes from both her son and husband, whose table manners were atrocious.

"Oh, wife, son is going out after devotions to spend a little time this evening with a friend. And he has promised he will be at home early, so we can start early tomorrow morning. As you know, John, though we may have harvested all our crops, the work still continues!"

"Ja, Dat. I will be home early and up at my usual time." John's voice, when he responded to his dat, was uncharacteristically modest.

"Gut, son." Big John continued to shovel large forkfuls of food into his mouth, barely giving himself time to chew and swallow.

"Hmmm. Apple pie. I was hoping for shoofly pie."

"I'm sorry, husband. I plan to serve that another night this week."

Big John sighed. "Okay, as long as you stick to that promise." He slowed down his chewing, fixing his gaze on his wife, Emma's, face.

Emma continued to get more and more nervous. Soon, she couldn't eat her pie because her stomach was twisted in knots. She knew she would pay for this later in the week.

"Mam? Aren't you going to finish your pie?"

"Nee. I must have eaten so much I didn't leave room for dessert."

"Can I have it?"

"Ja, go ahead." Emma got up and began gathering her cooking dishes around the sink. She wanted to finish early so they would be on time for devotions.

John greedily grabbed the plate and finished his mom's pie in three quick bites.

"Wife, finish the dishes and clean the kitchen. We will have devotions in here and I want our setting to be appropriate for our discussion of Bible passages." Big John stood and, without thanking Emma for the meal, belched and went to relax in the living room.

As Emma worked to wash dishes and clean her kitchen, she stifled tears, wondering how her life had gone so wrong. Her dat had been strict with her and her sisters. But he had never been abusive toward them or their mam. Meeting Big John, she had been impressed with his ability to run a farm and coax the plants to grow. *Ja, we have had our rough years when, no matter his farming skills, weather conditions made it impossible for the crops to grow.*

After devotions, John left quickly to stop at Beth's parents' house. Standing at the door, waiting for someone to answer, he anticipated convincing her to quit her serving job. His smile creased his face as he anticipated her responses.

"Beth! I was hoping we could go for a buggy ride tonight."

Beth Zook gave a shy smile to John. Shaking her head, she said, "Nee. I am coming down sick and I'm responsible for taking care of mam. She's sick as well. And we both have to be well enough to go to work on Wednesday." She began to shut the door.

"I can take my chances," John spoke as he pressed his hand aggressively against the door.

Beth sneezed and coughed. "I'm sorry, John. I would love to go driving with you, but I'm running a fever. I can't leave mam."

John hated to be thwarted. Scowling, he allowed his hand to fall. Perceiving her refusal as deliberate disobedience, he allowed his hand to fist behind his back. Lashing it out fast, his fist connected hard with Beth's ribs.

CHAPTER TWO

Beth gasped and bit back her cry of pain. As she felt pain shooting from her ribs to her spine, she thought yet again about the peace she would have if she only had the courage to break up with him. "John! I'm sorry, but I can't go out. I have a fever and Mam does too. We need to recover. Please leave." Working up her courage, Beth stepped back and quickly shut the door. After making sure it was securely locked, Beth leaned weakly against the solid wood and allowed tears of pain and frustration to trickle down her pale cheeks.

"Beth? Daughter? Who was at the door?" Beth's mam was coming slowly downstairs.

Beth quickly wiped her tears away. Pulling a fresh tissue from the small package on the table, she blew her nose. "It was John, Mam. He wanted me to go riding with him, but I told him we are both ill. Do you need anything? Water?"

"I am getting some ibuprofen for my fever. You should take some as well. I do feel better, thankfully."

"Ja, I will take some, thank you." Beth's hand snuck under her crocheted shawl as she felt her painful ribs. She knew she would have a nasty bruise soon. Slowly, she moved with her mam to the kitchen, where she took their glasses out of the cabinet. "I'm just grateful tomorrow's our day off so we can continue recovering."

"I know. We can't afford to take very many days off. But the owner won't allow us to work sick, either. I do wish..."

"What, Mam?"

"That we either got sick leave, or that I had confidence in my baking so I could work from home and earn the income we need. There's nothing I can say about Amos...Gott wanted him, so he's gone."

Four years earlier, Amos Zook had died after suffering from congestive heart failure for several years. "Mam, his heart just gave out. He was so tired at the end. I'm sure that, while he didn't want to leave us, he was also relieved. I would be, if I had been in his situation. And, about your baking...you bake beautifully. You could get the high prices some of our other bakers get for their products. I know it."

"Maybe. I just remember what Amos' mom said when she tasted my shoofly pie the first time. She said it didn't have very much flavor. When I tasted it, I wondered what she was talking about."

"What? She really must have loved a strong molasses taste or even the brown sugar taste. Any time I've tasted it, I loved the flavors."

"Ach. Well, she was the only fly in the ointment when it came to Amos and me. Well, other than his heart. But we knew as soon as we got his diagnosis that it would be just a matter of time."

This time, Beth couldn't hold her tears back. She missed her dat so much! Plus, her ribs were really sore and she felt horrible. "I'm sorry, Mam. I just miss Dat and I feel so sick."

"Let's go to bed, girl. That's the best thing for us right now—sleep."

The two women trudged slowly up the stairs so they wouldn't stimulate more coughing. In her bedroom, Beth removed her robe and lifted her gown. Looking at her ribs, she grimaced, seeing the bruise already beginning to bloom. She remembered how kind and gentle John had been at first—even if he seemed moody or angry at unpredictable times. His moods had served to keep her off balance. Of course, now she knew this. *If I could only predict when he's going to be in one of his moods!*

Sitting on her bed and sliding under the covers, Beth leaned against her pillow. She remembered the first time John struck her. They were coming home after the singing. It was supposed to be a celebration. They had been seeing each other—or "courting," as John still called it—for one year. Beth noticed he had been almost angry most of the evening. He wouldn't talk about it. But he said he wanted to spend more time with her after leaving the singing. She told him that she needed to be home right away because she was going...*wait!* Beth finally made the mental connection.

Every time she had work hours scheduled, he would get moody. It was her work the whole time! Her mind slowly took her back to that first time John had hit her. She had told him she had early working hours the next day, and he didn't like that. "I'm supposed to be your focus!" He practically screamed in her face. Then, his fist hit her arm, hard. She nearly fell out of his buggy. He grabbed her before she fell, and she was grateful...she thought. But he hit her again—this time in her stomach.

Beth came home and threw up almost in the hallway. She told her mam that she ate something that disagreed with her. *My Gott! He's serious! He doesn't want me to work.* She wasn't an able enough quilter, so she couldn't do that from home. She wished she had the courage to stop seeing him. Resting her hot forehead on her fisted palms, Beth began crying quietly.

The next day, her temperature was normal. Aside from some weakness, she felt normal again. "Mam, how do you feel?"

"Much better, denki! I just feel weak. Breakfast will help with that now that we can eat. Eggs and oatmeal, I think, with toast. Coffee?"

"Ja! I am so hungry!" But Beth was only able to eat a portion of what she normally ate. "I am so full. Are we ready to go now? We have to clock in soon."

"Ja. Let's just wash and dry the dishes. Why are you moving so carefully?"

Beth had been favoring her left side after being punched so hard the night before. "I don't know. Maybe I sneezed or coughed so hard that I pulled something." She now felt free to place her hand against her bruised ribs.

"Just be careful in the diner. You don't want to stress that any more."

"Nee!" Beth dried the dishes as her mam washed and rinsed them.

As they drove to the diner, Beth froze just slightly; she saw John in his dat's wagon. Turning away from the sight, she prayed he wouldn't see her. She knew she couldn't say anything to her mam. *I'll figure out a way of getting him out of my life. For gut.* Glancing in the direction John had been traveling, she let out a silent breath—he hadn't spotted them.

"Mam? When Dat got upset at you, how did he express it?" She held her breath, hoping her mam wouldn't figure out what had been happening.

"Did you and John have a disagreement? This is common with couples who are getting to know each other." Her mam seemed to be thinking back to her own courting days. "Well, our first disagreement was over whether I would work. He wanted me to stay at home and take care of the house and kinder. But he told me that, if we needed for me to work, he wouldn't stand in my way. In fact, after he took sick, he was the one who found out about the cook's position at the diner. He told me about it. 'You'd be perfect for it. Your roasts, chicken and vegetables top anyone else's in the community. And your desserts!' While I didn't feel very confident about my shoofly pie, he did. This was right before he had to stop working as a farrier. So the timing was just right. I applied and got the job." Her voice softened as she seemed to remember taking the job and, over the next year, seeing her husband's condition worsen. "He died a year later."

"I... I remember." Beth's voice was choked. "He loved you so much. And he supported my working as well. Do you think he did so because he could no longer work?"

"Partly, ja. But he was always somewhat forward thinking. While he would have preferred for me to stay at home, it didn't bother him that I liked working."

Beth remembered the scene at the Miller's several weeks earlier. "Ja. I thinking of the Lapps. Mister Lapp nearly killed Missus Lapp. Didn't he go into some kind of mental health place?"

Mrs. Zook thought for a few seconds. "Ja, something operated by both the Amish and Mennonites. At least he won't be made to give up his faith."

She shifted her position on the buggy seat, trying to ease the pain in her ribs. *I hope they aren't broken. He hit me hard enough.* As the morning wore on, it became harder and harder for Beth to hide her pain. Finally, just before she took her lunch, the diner's owner called her into her office. "Beth, you're obviously in pain. What's going on?"

Beth couldn't lie without being called out on it. Shifting on the kitchen chair in the small office, she opened and closed her mouth before speaking. "I...was hit in my ribs last night. My boyfriend." She flushed with shame. "Please don't tell my mam!"

The owner, an older, kindly Mennonite woman, opened her eyes in shock. "Beth! You need to be seen by the doctor! I'll send you—"

"I'll go, but please, Ann, don't tell Mam!"

"Beth, I'll keep your secret on one condition. *You* tell your mam." She waited until Beth nodded slowly. "Now, go. I'll call my doctor. He's the soul of discretion. Oh, and you need to make it clear to your boyfriend that physical violence against women is wrong, period. Promise?"

"Ja. Thank you. Can I come to work tomorrow? We need the money for bills."

"Only if you don't have broken ribs and can hold heavy trays of dishes." Ann stood. "Now, I have daughters of my own. Unpin your dress. I want to see the damage for myself."

Beth looked with longing at the door, just wanting to escape. With reluctance, she unpinned her dress and opened it, exposing the large, ugly bruise to Ann's view.

"Oh, my! You will be very fortunate if you don't have at least one broken rib."

Beth swallowed hard, trying not to cry. "What will you tell my mam? She'll see that I'm not here."

"That I sent you to run an errand for me. I'm not lying." Ann quickly phoned her doctor's office. When the receptionist said that the office had two cancellations, she spoke. "I'm sending my employee, Beth Zook. She needs her ribs X-rayed. They may be broken."

"Do you want us to send the bill to you?"

"Ja, please." Hanging up, she smiled softly at Beth. "Okay,

they have a cancellation and can see you in twenty minutes. Doctor Stone's office. You know where it is?"

Beth thought. "Ja, over on Second, right?" She finished pinning her dress up.

"Ja. That's the one. When you're done, come back and give me the report. If you don't have broken ribs, you can work the rest of today and this week. Otherwise…"

Not for the first time, Beth felt a strong anger toward John. "Denki." Turning, she hurried out.

***

At the doctor's office, she was carefully examined. As the doctor ran her fingers over Beth's ribs, she flinched. Finally, she was taken to the X-ray department.

"Okay, Miss Zook. No broken bones, but you definitely have some strong bruising there. Take ibuprofen every four to six hours and apply an ice pack. How did this happen?"

Beth's lips were paper-dry. Licking them, she inhaled carefully. Looking at the middle-aged doctor, she noticed her blue eyes were alert and sharp. She decided to tell the truth. "My boyfriend got mad at me last night. He…"

"Hit you. Do you know that whether a couple is married or not, that qualifies as violence? And it's wrong. I don't want to pry, but what made him mad?"

"He doesn't want me to keep working at the diner. I'm a server there. My mam is a cook."

"Wait a minute...Zook. Your dad was Amos, right?"

Beth's chin wobbled as she nodded. "Ja."

"I remember now. So, you and your mother need to work to bring money in. Have you explained this to your boyfriend?"

"Many times. He doesn't care. He doesn't believe that women need to be working outside the home. I could quilt, I guess, but I earn more money faster by working as a server."

The doctor sighed. "You know that I need to report this to the state of Pennsylvania, right? I won't use names. But I'm required by state law to report every case of violence against a family member or an intimate partner."

"We have never been—"

"Intimate? That doesn't matter. I still have to report it. You can work, but I want you to tell your mother what happened."

Beth nodded. "I will." *Just not right away.*

***

Naomi sat in the back of her mother's store with Eli Yoder. "I want to see women be free to work outside the home. You know, sometimes their family circumstances make that necessary. Someone like Missus Hershberger for instance. Amy was widowed two years ago in that accident, remember?" At Eli's nod, she continued. "The only way she can make money for her and her kinder is to operate a corn maze in the fall and sell baked goods, hot chocolate or lemonade to the English tourists. Now that she's seeing Andy Stoltzfus, he's starting to give her trouble about quitting what she's doing. Has anyone invited him to our meetings? He needs to know that because Amy is singlehandedly supporting her kinder, she can't be away from her home for several hours every day. This is the only way she has to provide for them."

Eli nodded thoughtfully. Occasionally, he scribbled notes to himself. "I know who he is. He's pretty traditional Amish, and I think he needs to be at our meetings. I'll go and explain Missus Hershberger's situation to him and invite him to start taking part in our meetings. I happened upon them last week as she was leaving the market. He was trying to argue with her so she would quit. He just doesn't see that she has very little beyond what she earns from the tourists. He doesn't like that she and her kinder are exposed to them five days a week. He raised his voice at her and was waving his arms around. Bishop Kurtz and Deacon King are meeting with him now."

***

In his barn, Andy Stoltzfus wore a look of confusion as he

talked with Deacon King and Bishop Kurtz. "But allowing her to work is an abomination! Even worse, she is exposing her kinder to all of those English tourists, and who knows what ideas they are giving to Amy and her children?"

"We need to worry much less about that than the very real possibility that Amy and her children would have no home if you were to be successful at making her quit giving tours of her farm. You do realize that since her husband's untimely death three years ago, she is the only form of support for her family, right?"

Andy could do little more than allow his mouth to hang open. "Uhhh...well, to tell you the truth, the only thing I was thinking of is the Ordnung."

"Okay, our Ordnung, as you know isn't written. It's all oral. But, if you think about the section governing families and work, there is nothing that says wives and young, unmarried women can't work outside the home. Amy works at her home, bringing honest money in from tourists. She follows all our rules. Nothing in the Ordnung says she and her kinder can't be around the English. She has assistants who work with her and they help with her children. The youngest ones don't even see the tourists. So what is your worry, really?"

"Just...that she's violating the Ordnung in some way." Andy's large Adam's apple bobbed as he swallowed hard.

"Hannes, I'll speak." Bishop Kurtz knew just what he

wanted to say. "You say 'In some way.' But you can't say in what way, specifically. We have a peer counseling organization in Peace Valley. This group is made up of elders and Amish men and women who want to help people whose confusion and fear about women working have led to relationship issues. Now, you and Missus Hershberger aren't married, but it isn't unreasonable to think that won't happen under different circumstances.

If you rip away Amy's only form of income, she won't be very happy with you. She will begin to feel you are responsible for her loss of income…and of her home. While she and her departed husband had some money in savings before he was killed, she knows that money won't last indefinitely. Therefore, given the young ages of her children, she has chosen to work *from home*, giving tours of an Amish farm to visitors who come to Peace Valley. Before she started, she came to see me with her idea and I explained to her exactly what she needed to do to start her home business and stay in complete compliance with the Ordnung. Did she tell you this?" The bishop was well aware that Amy had not explained her discussion with him.

"Nee…well, no."

"And…why would that be?"

Andy couldn't speak. His throat had frozen, not allowing words to come out.

After waiting for several seconds, the bishop spoke. "Is it because you never gave her an opportunity to explain what she did beforehand?"

"Guhhh… Well, maybe. I was just…"

"Ja, 'concerned about the Ordnung.' Andy, from this point forward, why don't you allow the elders to do their work?"

Andy flushed, feeling shamed. Not wanting the elders to see his emotions, he looked at the ground and scuffed one shoe along the ground. "Ja, I will."

The deacon broke back in. "Andy, before we leave, I want to get one piece of information from you and make an offer to you."

Andy nodded quickly.

"Do you intend to propose marriage to Amy Hershberger in the future?"

"Well, I do, ja. But… I want to make sure it's right for both of us."

"Okay. You do that. Stop putting pressure on her. She can't leave her home to work and she doesn't want to bake or quilt. Finally, we have that group. I want to offer several sessions to you. Come to six of our meetings, try them out, and see what you learn."

"Hmmm. That's all? Ja, sure." Andy didn't seem to be aware of what he was committing to.

"There is one more thing. You know now that she has no other form of income. What she's doing complies with the Ordnung of our community. Please, Andy, stop pressuring her to quit. You say want to continue your relationship with her. If she feels any additional pressure from you, she will stop courting with you. Do you understand?"

Andy seemed to take a long time processing what the deacon was telling him. Slowly, he nodded. "Ja, ja, sure. Whatever."

Here, the bishop spoke. "Are you agreeing just so we'll get off your back? Or because you truly understand that Missus Hershberger has no income other than what she brings in from the tourists?"

"Bishop, please forgive me. But you are making me feel guilty for looking out for the safety of Amy's soul…"

"Ach! Now, I get it! You were only looking out for her soul! Hannes, that's funny…I thought that was *our* role."

"Same here! Andy, if you have any concerns about anyone, you are to discuss them with that person one time. If they don't change what they are doing, then you come to us and let us begin working with them. It's for the bishop and me, along with our two ministers, to look out for the souls of everyone in Peace Valley. Understood? I'm concerned about your soul, too, if you are going to try and badger a young widow out of her sole source of income."

CHAPTER THREE

Andy flushed. Looking out his barn door, he sighed heavily. "Okay, ja. Whatever. I'll stop. I just don't like that she's hobnobbing with the English."

"Andy, remember that she came to us. She asked us what would be permissible to do in starting her tourism business. She wanted to be sure that she wasn't in violation of our Ordnung. I believe you've lived here from birth, meaning you know our Ordnung quite well, ja?"

"Ja, Bishop, I really gotta get back to work."

"Okay, we'll go now. But I want to see you at our next meeting. They are set up for people such as you, who have trouble understanding that the women in our community have the right to decide how they are going to make a living. As long as it doesn't violate state law, federal law or our Ordnung, we are fine with their choices. There are some men, however, who believe they need to dictate how and what women can do. It looks like you fall into that group. If you want your relationship with Amy Hershberger to go well, you'll back off and let her earn her money. Hannes? We should leave now." Clapping his hat back on his head, Joseph strode out of the barn before he said something he knew he'd regret.

***

At her farm, Amy Hershberger was finishing her baking, knowing that what she earned this weekend would allow her to pay off a big bill. "Anna, what are your brothers doing?"

"Just playing outside. They're in the yard." Anna, at seven, was Amy's assistant. She had been assigned the responsibility of checking out the door occasionally, and she took that seriously. "Mama, Mister Stoltzfus is coming into the yard!"

Amy squeezed her tired eyes closed. She didn't need this now! Sighing, she spoke. "Get your brothers inside and go into the far room downstairs. If you hear anything strange, you go to the phone house and call 911."

"Ja, Mama." Running, Anna hurried to comply.

At the loud knock on the door, Amy started. Covering the dough with a clean towel, she sighed. "Ja? Andy, I am very busy right now. I can't—"

"Amy, open the door. I just want to ask you some

questions."

Hearing the back door open, then clap shut, Amy sighed again. "We can talk through the screen here. I need to get back to my bak—"

"Amy, have I been trying to force you to quit your business?" Andy was tense and he paced back and forth.

"Well...ja, you have. I don't have very much savings left after my husband's funeral and his medical bills."

"Why did you choose to start a tourism business catering to the English?"

"Because it allows me to earn money without having to leave my house. I don't have to get daycare for my kinder. I can take care of them while I work."

"And do they interact with your customers?"

Amy knew this next answer was critical. "Only in directing them as to the parts of the farm they can go to. They know not to allow people into the house. They help people who get lost in the corn maze."

Andy stopped pacing around. Looking into the far distance, he considered. Looking at his boots, he seemed to make a decision. "Amy, did you know that the elders visited me today?"

Amy was stunned. "Nee! I didn't." She wasn't about to ask

why because she'd been thinking of breaking things off with Andy before they went much further.

Looking at her with expectation, Andy waited. He waited some more. Finally, realizing that Amy wasn't going to ask, he spoke. "They were counseling me that what you do doesn't violate the Ordnung. That you went to speak to the bishop before starting this business of yours."

"Ja, I did. I wanted to be sure that it wouldn't violate anything. I don't want to put myself or my children at risk of having to leave here."

"And? What did they say?" Andy's shoulders and neck were tense.

"That, as long as I showed the tourists how a typical Amish family lives—kind of an educational tour—I would be okay. I couldn't allow them into the house. The barn would be okay, but I'm not too comfortable with that. So, I make baked goods, snacks and seasonal beverages they can enjoy at the end of their tours. At night, I work on small Amish dolls. I buy small, wood toys for the boys. After going through the corn maze, tourists can enjoy snacks and either lemonade or hot chocolate. Andy, I really have to get back—"

"Let me in." This was said in a low growl.

"Nee, Andy. Go away." As Amy gave this order, she gasped. Bishop Kurtz was coming into her yard. She said nothing else, not wanting to let Andy know what was going on.

"Please. I just want to discuss this."

"Andy! I thought you were going to get back to work after the deacon and I left your barn!" The bishop's tone was friendly, but his blue eyes were glacial.

Andy, noticing the bishop's temper, began to perspire even though the outdoor air was cool. "I came by to...uh...discuss this issue with Amy."

"Missus Hershberger, do you want him here right now?"

"Honestly, no. I have a lot of baking still to finish, then supper to make. The kinder have their homework and baths, then bedtime because it's a school night."

"Your next tour is this weekend, right? My wife and I were wondering if we could help you out."

Amy's slender face lit up. "Ja, denki! We could always use the help!"

"We'll be here bright and early. You think of what you want us to do and we'll take care of it. Andy? I believe you were leaving with me."

Andy was frustrated. With that direct order, he had no choice but to obey. Hearing the door close and lock, he sighed. He was displeased. All he wanted to do was get to a point where Amy had no choice but to agree to marry him.

"Andy, you could see she was busy—flour all over the front of her dress and apron. She was baking. She had her kinder home because school has ended for the day. Still, there's little Anna can do yet to help her with the baking. Their help comes more on tourism days. What was your purpose for this visit? And understand that I am aware you need to get back to your…chores."

Andy was trapped. "I just wanted to…to hint at the possibility of marriage."

"In the afternoon, before harvest season has ended? How long have you been courting her?"

"Nigh on two months? Something like that."

"First of all, Andy, you are rushing things. This should be the 'getting to know you' stage of your courtship. Second, she didn't look very loving toward you. She looked frustrated. Dare I say, angry."

Andy lost all discretion here. He couldn't lose her! "Bishop, I figured that if she lost this chance, she would…" Gulping, he stopped speaking abruptly.

"She would, what? Agree, out of desperation, to marry you?" Totally frustrated himself, the bishop threw his black hat onto the grass. Striding over to pick it up before the stiff breeze could blow it away, he turned to look at Andy. "You are trying to manipulate her situation. Harm her financially." Closing his eyes, the bishop breathed in and exhaled deeply, trying to regain control of his emotions. "Understand this. All during her husband's stay in the hospital, I came to regard her as a daughter. So did my wife, along with many of us here. If they were to know what you were trying to do, they would make you leave and never let you return!

The talk that the deacon and I had with you earlier today still holds. I am going to add one more thing to that: Stay away from Amy Hershberger until you understand that she has the right to choose how she will support her family. She has no husband. And second, if she does decide to remarry, she can choose whom to marry. By trying to manipulate her financially, you are abusing her. And I have to warn you, Mister Stoltzfus, that if you continue to do so, we will be forced to discuss your actions with you. Even more, if you still don't stop, you could face the Meidung. You don't want that. Please go home right now, Andy. Go home. I'm going to be watching from the yard. Don't come back."

Feeling as though he were no higher than a slug, Andy trudged to his buggy. Climbing in, he obeyed the bishop's order and went home.

In Amy's yard, the bishop waited until he was sure that Andy had gone home. Wheeling about, he returned to Amy's house, knocking at the front door.

Seeing Anna on the other side of the screen, the bishop smiled. "Hello, Anna! I need to speak with your mam."

"Okay, but she's baking. She says she's very busy."

"Ja, I know she is. I want to discuss that with her."

"I hope you're not going to tell her she can't do this anymore. My brothers and I, we enjoy helping the tourists."

She is a smart little one. "I know. You'll be able to continue helping them. May I speak with your mam?"

Anna sighed. "Come in." She unlocked the screen door, looking outside and all around the yard."

"He's gone, Anna. I made him leave."

Anna sighed, closing her eyes in relief. "Denki. Mam wasn't happy with his visit today. Mama! The bishop is here!"

"Oh! I hope…" Amy came into the living room wiping her hands on a dishtowel. She now had a smudge of flour on her forehead.

"Mama, bend down." Plucking the dishtowel from her mam, Anna scrubbed the flour off her face. "You had flour on your face."

Amy flushed slightly. "Denki. Tell your brothers supper will be ready soon. Do your homework. Bishop, come into the kitchen."

The bishop followed her. "I am sorry for disturbing you once again, Amy. I thought I should stop by after we had our talk with Mister Stoltzfus." Looking around, he made sure Anna wasn't in listening range.

"Let me." Amy moved quietly to the hallway. Listening, she heard the three kinder beginning their homework. "They're doing their homework. What happened in your meeting?"

"Have you ever heard the term 'sexism'?"

"Ja, I have. And I do feel that what Andy has been doing is sexist. He wants to manipulate my ability to earn, take it away from me along with my right to make decisions on behalf of my children, so he can make me marry him."

The bishop was temporarily speechless. "My! You are direct. Gut! He did say that, after courting you for two short months, he is thinking of asking you to marry him."

Amy's fair skin went even paler, making her look like a brown-haired ghost. "What? Nee! I've been getting to know him and he is not what I want in a husband. He's trying to manipulate me. That's not very loving."

"Has he told you he loves you?"

Amy nodded. "He's tried. I've told him that love takes much longer to develop. I was married to the most wonderful man placed on God's earth. God decided he needed Matt. I am blessed with Matt's kinder and I take my responsibility toward them seriously. If I meet the right Amish man and we grow to love each other, I will marry him if he asks."

The bishop closed his eyes, giving thanks. "I am so relieved to hear what you said. Ja, he is trying to manipulate you. He has personally brought complaints to the elders about your business, even after we have told him that you discussed your ideas with us. For that reason, all of the elders and our wives are going to be here every weekend, helping you with the tours. Just let us know where you need us and what you want us to do. I am praying that he will get the message that way."

Amy was relieved. Anna and Joshua were seven and six, barely old enough to help her out. At five, Matt, Jr. was just too young, so she kept him with her as she worked with the tourists.

"And another thing… You won't have to pay any of us for our work. Our pay will be seeing your Amish tour become a huge success. Because, if you decide not to remarry, you'll need to establish some form of reliable income for you and your kinder. The more you can put into the bank, the better."

Amy's smile was grateful. "Denki. I hope he will get the message. But, bishop, somehow he may take his sweet time doing so."

"You just let any of us know if he's becoming a pest. Does your fence have a locking door?"

"Nee."

"I'll look around for one, bring it over and install it. Thankfully, you have a six-foot fence around your property."

"Bishop, why are you looking out for me like this?"

"Amy, all through the struggles after your husband's accident, we all came to see you as our daughter. We all feel a responsibility toward you and your kinder. Now, I think I remember who might have a fence gate. I'm going to go check and, if so, bring it back and install it." Jumping up, he left and went on his errand. Amy had finished her baking and was busy making supper for her and the children when he returned.

"Gut news! I found two gates and they will fit! Both lock. I picked up locks as well. You'll have to add two keys to your ring of keys. After I install them, make sure they are locked every time you leave and at night"

Amy's smile was grateful. "I will, denki!" Thinking, she pulled a plate out and filled it with cookies. Seeing the bishop working in the backyard, she sent Joshua out. "Tell him I have a plate of cookies for him and his wife."

After the bishop had left, Amy gratefully locked both gates. She felt somehow more secure now. Andy couldn't get into the house, unless he was able to climb a high fence.

CHAPTER FOUR

That Sunday was a Meeting Sunday. Arriving at the Lapp house for the service, Amy and Anna took the lunchmeats and pickles into the kitchen. Making sure all three of her children were with her, Amy found a seat in the meeting room. "Joshua and Matt, go sit with the boys and behave. I can watch you."

Several minutes later, Amy was confused when the boys came running back. "Why? You're supposed to be—"

"Sc-c-ary man ca-ame." Matt had begun to stutter shortly after his dat's death. Andy's intensity didn't help his speech.

Sighing, Amy looked around. She saw the deacon's wife, Lovina King, smiling at her. She shrugged, a "what can I do?" gesture.

Lovina sat next to her and began to speak. "As soon as Andy went to the men's area, Matt and Joshua scuttled over to you. I believe our kinder can sense the gut and the bad in people."

"Ja, Matt has always been wary of him. I want to thank you for agreeing to help us when tourists come to my farm on weekends. It will be such a big help."

"We're happy to do so, child."

In the men's section, Andy stewed quietly. He had seen Matt and Joshua hurry over to Amy when he came in and sat in back of them. He just wanted to be sure that they were listening to God's word! Boys needed a firm hand and male leadership. Stealing a glance Amy's way, he sighed, seeing her in quiet conversation with the deacon's wife. She appeared calm, her hands resting naturally on the boys' shoulders. Really, she was spoiling them. She should have made them return. If the deacon's wife weren't sitting next to her, he would have already gone over to her and made the boys return with him. He looked expectantly at the elders, hoping they would see what was wrong with the boys sitting in the women's section. He watched for several seconds as the elders conversed quietly. He watched their gazes sweep over the women's section, and he held his breath. But…nothing. Why didn't they see the violation? He would be discussing that with the bishop after service.

Amy listened closely as Lovina King told her about an upcoming peer group meeting. "I would have to bring the kinder."

"Ja, they are welcome! We have teen girls who supervise them while we discuss the day's topic."

"Would they be sensitive to Matt's stuttering?"

"Of course. I'll make sure of that. Is he still stuttering badly?"

"It's not as bad as right after their dat died. Only when he feels stress or is scared does it come back out. The doctor said just to work with him on breathing and spacing his words. We've even been told to allow him to sing."

"Gut! What kinds of songs?"

"Children's songs and I've chosen a few simple ones from the Ausbund. It seems to help him."

"I'll pass that on to the girls. Maybe a sing-along would help him feel welcome. During lunch, I'd like to speak with you…alone."

Amy nodded. Not looking at Andy, she knew it was about him.

At lunch, the Peace Valley women trooped out of the kitchen, bearing food and beverages for the elderly, then the men, and then the kinder to eat. When the women could finally sit down to eat, Amy was starving. Feeling Lovina King and Linda Yoder joining her, she smiled.

"Keep smiling. Andy Stoltzfus looks like a grim thundercloud. And he's coming this way. Whatever he demands, refuse it." This was Linda Yoder.

"Amy, I need to talk with you. Come." Andy's voice was a menacing growl.

"Nee, I'm finally enjoying my lunch," she started as Andy clamped his hand painfully on one shoulder. "Take your hand off me. Now."

Andy, seeing the women's gazes trained on his hand, slowly removed it, letting it fall at his side. "Why didn't you send your sons back to the men's section? That was a violation. I would have supervised them for you, gladly."

Amy had had enough. Setting her fork down, she stood, facing Andy. "Andy Stoltzfus, I am a woman of twenty-eight. I believe I can make decisions for my own kinder and do quite well at it. I chose to allow them to stay with me after Matt told me that you had sat behind them."

"What? Did he stutter in that cute way of his?"

Amy gasped at the cruelty of his words. She was speechless.

"Your boys are being raised by just a woman. They need a gut, strong man in their lives if they are going to be upstanding Amish men."

"Excuse me! Ja, I am widowed. But I am following my

husband's wishes in how they are raised—"

"Mister Stoltzfus, maybe you should go back with the men," Lovina's voice was low, but had a thread of steel running through it.

"Andy, I'm more than, what did you say? 'Just a woman?' I am their mam. I look out for their physical, spiritual and emotional needs. I will not be seeing you again, from today onward. I cannot be courted by someone so overbearing."

Andy's high color suddenly faded to the color of old canvas. "What? Are you breaking up with me? I'm the best thing that ever—" As the bishop clamped his hand hard on Andy's shoulder and neck, he startled.

"Nee, Mister Stoltzfus, you are not the best thing that ever happened to her. She married that man. Sadly, Gott took him, or she would still be married to him. Now, go. We will be by later on to discuss this issue with you."

Andy stalked away, diminished and embarrassed. Amy let out a long, shaky sigh. "Denki, bishop. I had already decided on a parting of the ways. When he said that, I was—"

"Sickened? Did I hear him say that you are 'just a woman'?"

"Ja, you did."

"Okay. We'll have a meeting with him about his actions and attitude this afternoon. Missus King? Missus Yoder? Will you be assisting Amy this afternoon?"

"Ja, we will follow her to her house and discuss her options with her there."

"Gut, because it looks like Andy just started a round of gossip." Raising his voice, the bishop spoke. "Everyone! It won't be easy forgetting what you just saw and heard here. Ja, Missus Hershberger just had a parting of the ways with Andy Stoltzfus. He brought it on himself. Now, you know that gossip is deadly…and a violation of our community's Ordnung. You can't forget it, but you can resolve that you are not going to tear down reputations by besmirching gut names. Amy, tell me if you hear that the gossip has continued."

Sitting quietly in the corner with her mam, Beth Zook marveled. "Mam, she was so strong! She didn't take any of his nonsense."

"Nee, she didn't… I hope you will take this as a lesson in what to do with John Andrews."

Beth, who had just taken a healthy sip of iced tea, gasped, choking on the drink. Flapping her hands in the air, she tried to get her breath.

Mrs. Zook whacked Beth on the back until her daughter could breathe. "Are you okay?"

"Ja, but you…surprised me."

***

"Let's go inside if you're finished. I'll ask Lizzie if we can talk privately," Lovina said.

Having gotten permission from Lizzie, Lovina led Amy into the house and a small bedroom on the first floor. "Amy, now that we know you want to be a part of our peer group, I need to ask you to be very careful. What happened earlier is likely to have angered Andy greatly."

"That's partly why I made the break publicly. If I had waited until I was at home, I could have been in danger."

Lovina, about to speak, paused. "Have you picked up on something? Or has he done something?"

"I've felt a...danger coming from him for the past few weeks. Matt began to stutter again. He had almost completely stopped. At about the same time that I realized something could happen, he began stuttering again. I listened to that."

So, he's never hit you?"

"Nee, thank Gott. If he had, I would have called Sheriff Mathis. I know how he helped with Wayne Lapp. I know we aren't supposed to involve the English in our lives, but I am responsible for my children. I'm the only—" Amy stopped speaking as she fought a sudden urge to cry.

"You would have done the right thing. It's my

understanding that the elders are driving out later today to speak with Andy."

"That does make me feel better. If he knows he's facing the ban, he may behave himself and stay away from me."

"Okay, before Lizzie needs her room back, let me just tell you that we talk about sexism in our group meetings, and what it is and how it affects us. We also talk about ways to combat it peacefully—in fact, I think we are going to use your words and actions today to demonstrate what to do and say."

Amy blushed. "Denki. But I don't want—"

"You don't want to be the center of attention. Ja, I understand."

***

Later that afternoon, the bishop, deacon and both ministers pulled into Andy Stoltzfus' yard. Jumping out of the buggy, the bishop strode to the front door and knocked.

Inside, Andy heard the knock he'd been dreading. With a deep sigh, he got up and slowly walked to the door, opening it. "Come in." He swung the door wide, though he was much more inclined to slam it shut in their faces.

The bishop, as had been agreed upon beforehand, started. "Andy, what was that at the Lapp's house? Are you aware that not even three months ago, Wayne Lapp was bent on murdering both his wife and daughter because they wouldn't quit their jobs?"

Andy had been over the entire embarrassing episode on his way home and as he waited for his visitors. Seeing his mam coming into the living room, he waved her off. "It's nothing, Mam."

"Wait a minute, Andy. I'm sure she saw the whole thing, right, Missus Stoltzfus?"

"Ja. It was…embarrassing."

"Well? You embarrassed your parents. What do you have to say?"

"I have been courting Amy Hershberger for two months now. I feel a connection to her, but I worry that her chosen…*profession* could get—"

"Stop. I believe Deacon King already spoke to you about that. Amy spoke to us. Her farm tour harms nothing and nobody. She's at home, taking care of her kinder and she is paying her bills independently."

"But I could take all that off her…"

CHAPTER FIVE

"If she wanted you to do so. She made it clear today that she does not want that. Ja?"

Seeing the discomfort of both Andy and his mam, the bishop quietly told Mrs. Stoltzfus that, if she wanted, she could leave the room.

She was happy to do so, seeming embarrassed by the discussion.

Andy's eyes filled. "I...didn't expect her to do that today. I mean, I know there has been a little strain—"

Here, the deacon took over. "Andy, I would say she was feeling more than a 'little' embarrassed or upset. You inferred, in two sentences, that as 'just a woman,' she is incapable of making decisions for and acting for her children's needs. Do you remember when Matt Hershberger died?"

"Ja. It was…a year ago?"

"More like two. Her kinder were three, four and five. Shortly after she buried him, she came to all of us with her farm tour idea. She had everything written out, down to the budget numbers. 'I don't want to be dependent on the community,' she told us. 'I want to be able to provide for the needs of my kinder and me, all on my own.' You know why?"

Andy didn't and he shrugged.

"She knew there was no guarantee she'd meet someone, either here or from another Amish community, willing and able to become an instant dat. So, not wanting to completely deplete their savings account, she conceived of the idea of her tour. Everything she planned falls well within our Ordnung.

"Now, let's talk about your attitude toward women. Then we will discuss, in detail, what kinds of consequences you could face from this—especially if you don't leave her alone. 'Just a woman.' Do you truly believe that she isn't equal to us men?"

Andy knew he had to be honest, even though his beliefs would bring anger upon him. Sighing, he stood tall. "Ja. I believe all men are superior to women. We are bigger and stronger. They need us even if they don't know it or admit to it. Amy could have quilted and earned money by taking the quilts to that quilting shop. She could have baked and sold her items on the bakery stands around here. But a *tour*?"

"Andy, who conceives the child and gives birth to it? The dat? Or the mam?"

Andy choked. "The, uh, the mam."

"Andy, childbirth doesn't tickle. It hurts something powerful. I had to assist at the birth of one of my kinder and I never saw my wife go through more pain. She tried to bear it in dignity, but I could see and feel that she was hurting. Now, who takes care of the kinder more? Mam? Or Dat?"

"Mam. As she should. Dat is in the fields, shoeing horses or making furniture." Andy spoke his beliefs proudly at first, then, feeling the keen disappointment coming off the other men, he began to feel small. But he had to stand for himself. Who else was there to rescue Amy and her kinder?

"Hannes, I'll speak. We're at that point anyway. Andy, as bishop, I am responsible for the spiritual wellbeing of people in our community. You saw Amy and decided to begin courting her. From what we understand, at first, for a few weeks, it went well. Shortly after, you began pressuring her to give up her tours. You told her that she was violating the Ordnung. Were you present for the meetings that were held for the most recent change?"

Andy didn't know what to say here. Obviously, he hadn't been there! He said as much.

"Ja, the Ordnung was last updated when you were a schoolboy. I was there. My dat was there. We made the change to employment of district wives for one reason—because, back then, a recession was making life hard for many of our families. The women came to us, telling us that their families were struggling to make it on only one income. Previously, we had given families leeway so the women could work within the home. But beginning with that time, we had to make changes so that women might work *outside* the home. To be able to do this, wives had to be in agreement with their husbands that their earnings would be used only for the needs of the family. If they decided to work at our market, the diner next to Peace Valley, or the Quilt Place, wherever. And that's the way it's been since then. So, how would Amy have been in violation of the Ordnung, in its present form?"

Andy couldn't answer, so he only shrugged.

One of the ministers spoke up. You have two choices...no, three, here. Keep on as you did today and face the Meidung. Take part in peer group meetings, or one-on-one sessions, and learn about how *outdated* your attitude about women truly is."

The deacon began speaking again. "Amy didn't care for your beliefs today. Because of that and because of how you've been treating her, she'd had enough and she decided to break your relationship off. I noticed how you were looking at her boys before services began."

Andy's look was confused. They hadn't been looking at him! Or had they? "Andy, very little slips past these old eyes. You weren't happy how, when you sat behind them, Joshua and Matt left the men's section and sat with their mam. I saw—"

Andy remembered what he'd been thinking. "I thought that they should not have been sitting in the women's section. She coddles them. I would have set them straight." At that brag, Andy stood at his full height.

"Why do you think they left the men's section? Right after you sat behind them?"

Andy shrugged, completely lost. "Why" had nothing to do with it. The only thing he saw was deliberate disobedience. But, looking at the bishop's question, he waited to answer. "I dunno."

"Andy, kinder, just like animals, have an uncanny ability to detect bad in others…"

"Me? In *me*? I'm the best thing that has ever happened to Amy Hershberger!"

"How? Why?"

Andy's laughter was incredulous. Closing his eyes, he reminded himself to treat the old man with respect. "Sir, she lost her husband two years ago. She hasn't had any man around other than me. I have been working to show the boys just how they are supposed to act. Like men."

"When you courted her, you met her family, right?" After Andy's emphatic nod, Bishop Kurtz continued speaking. "She has brothers. Their relationship is loving and supportive, which means they have spent many days and hours around their nephews. You aren't the only man influencing them. When you sat behind Joshua and Matt, I was watching them. They were minding their mam, sitting still. Then you sat behind them and they noticed it. I saw a look of…panic on Matt's face. Joshua grabbed his hand and they ran to Amy. Children, like animals, are able to sense the gut—and bad—in people.

"If you want to be a part of Amy's life, you must give her the room she needs to make her own choices. She is—"

"But bishop, she needs a man around to ensure that she does make the best decisions possible. She's a woman. She can't do that."

The bishop's breath whooshed out of his chest when he heard that. "Repeat that? Nee, never mind. Did you actually just say that because she's 'just a woman,' she can't make gut decisions? Did you?"

Andy swallowed and closed his eyes in dismay and self-anger. *Had he really said that?* Thinking back a few seconds, he realized he'd given voice to very private thoughts. "Ja."

The deacon stepped up. "Okay. That makes it necessary for

me to tell you this: You are not to spend any time with her. Wait a minute. She broke your relationship off. I forgot! Ja, you are definitely not allowed to be around her or her kinder. And this brings us to the next reason for our visit. You are running the risk of receiving the Meidung. You don't want the pain or embarrassment of that. You have been attempting to live pridefully, trying to convince Missus Hershberger that you are the only hope she has. And that isn't true. The elders and I have all decided that you have to stay away from her, beginning with this afternoon. She wants nothing more to do with you. Not now, not next month. And not ever. She is moving ahead with her life, making a living and raising her children. You are to return to your farm. And, beginning this week, take part in weekly peer group meetings, where we discuss the role of women in Amish communities. Not just the traditional roles we've always given them, but those they feel they have the potential to hold."

Andy, looking steadily at the ground, sighed. He looked up slowly, into the deacon's eyes. "And if I don't?"

"You're one step closer to a banning meeting. You aren't going to learn how to view the women here any differently until you attend meetings."

Reluctantly, Andy began to accept the inevitable. He sighed and shuffled his feet, took his hat off and put it back on. "I got farming, deacon."

"Ja. And we all have farming, farrier work and carpentry to do. We all go to the meetings, too."

"What if I can't learn to see women differently?"

"Then, first, all your relationships are going to fail. No woman wants to feel like she isn't listened to. They don't want to be overpowered. Next, as the bishop said, you're running the risk of the Meidung. We don't want to see that happen. We all prayed before coming here today, asking Gott to give us his guidance."

Andy gave a loud sigh that sounded like a groan. "How long do these meetings last? What happens in them?"

"We try not to go longer than an hour and a half per meeting. We pray, and then we discuss women's roles and how they relate to our Ordnung. Not the Ordnung of any other community, just ours. Then we talk about why it's so hard for us men to 'let' them go to work, whether they leave the house to do so or they work within the home."

"And I have to do this to avoid the possibility of the ban?" Andy's voice was skeptical.

"Ja. Exactly."

Andy modulated his facial expression, looked out over the horizon and, again, removed and put his hat back on. Sighing, he nodded. "Okay. Only because I don't want to put my mam and dat through the pain and shame of a ban."

The ministers looked at each other. "Gut decision. We will leave so you can have time with your family. I believe they may be driving up."

Andy groaned. That was all he needed.

"We'll get our horses and buggies. You let your mam know that company's here." Boarding the buggies, the elders left the Stoltzfus yard. Down the road, behind a copse of trees, they stopped. "What sense did you get from him?" the deacon asked.

"He's doing it only to avoid the ban. I'm glad you didn't tell him he'd have to go to twelve sessions, minimum."

The deacon chuckled slightly. "Me, too. It nearly came out. Ja, he needs a minimum of twelve sessions."

Back at the Stoltzfus farm, Andy was taking some grief from his brothers. "Why were all the elders here? Normally, when they all come to someone's house it means it ain't good news!"

"Amy Hershberger told me she wouldn't be seeing me anymore. I've been trying to convince her that she shouldn't be running that tour thing on her farm because of the exposure to the English every weekend. Then I asked her why her boys ran from the men's section over to her at today's service. She answered and I told her she needs a man around who'll influence her boys right, that she's just a woman." Hearing the lighter footsteps of his sisters, Andy squeezed his eyes shut. He knew they'd heard him...

"Andy Stoltzfus! What were you thinking? Or *were* you thinking? You don't say things like that to any woman! She has been widowed for two years. She's all on her own. I love you, little brother, but I'm also happy she broke things off with you. There's a lot about us you don't know...and if you ever want to marry a gut woman, you'd better get to know what we think and how we feel."

"But that's how dat is..."

"Nee. He isn't. He's decisive. He knows what he wants after he's thought something through. But look at Mam. She's quiet, but she's also strong and she doesn't put up with nonsense from any of us. Including Dat. Let's go for a walk. Mike, tell my parents I went for a walk with Andy, please." Gripping Andy's forearm, she pulled him off the porch and toward a small stand of trees not far from the house. "Tell me."

CHAPTER SIX

Sighing, Andy tried to think where to start. "I met Amy years ago. I was going to ask her to let me court her, but Matt Hershberger asked her first."

"Okay, do you think she would have waited for you? Or that Matt would have been her first choice? And think carefully, brother."

"Ah… I don't know. All I know is that when I first noticed Amy, she was the most beautiful girl I'd ever seen. After Matt started courting her, I dated around but not seriously. Oh, I met a few I thought would make a wonderful wife, but…they weren't Amy. Then she and Matt married."

"Is that why you've never married? Because Amy was gone?"

"Ja, I guess."

"And now that she has had to become so independent, and

she is refusing to stop her farm tour…is she still attractive to you?"

Andy didn't even need to consider. "Ja, always."

Becky, Andy's sister, sighed. "Andy, when you meet someone and make them a part of your life, you accept the gut and the bad of them. Obviously, if the 'bad' is something like killing or cheating, you can't do that. But why is supporting her family by herself such a bad thing?" Becky asked her question in just the way she had for a reason.

Andy sensed a trap but wasn't sure why. So he answered instinctively. "It isn't!"

"Okay. Then why were you after her to quit her farm tours?"

The trap still hadn't snapped shut. Andy blundered right into it. "Because she is exposing herself and her kinder to the English! She's not using gut judgment. It's up to me to show her that and make the decisions for her."

"Had you asked her to marry you?"

"Nee. Although we had been courting for two months already."

"Oh! Two months! Is that enough for the two of you to really know and trust each other?"

"I know her heart, ja. She is a good woman."

"A good woman who is exposing her kinder to unsuitable Englischers?" SNAP! The trap shut.

Andy realized too late that he couldn't respond back.

"Andy. Were you going to ask her to marry you in this year's wedding season?" Becky waited.

"Well, ja."

"After dating two months? That's awful fast. And why would you marry someone who you believe is influencing her kinder wrong?"

Again, Andy couldn't answer. Then he came up with his answer. "I was going to make her quit and tell her I'd be the support for all of us."

Becky wasn't a violent woman. But in that moment, she wanted to smack Andy upside the head. "Andy!" Her voice came out as a strangled scream. "You're not making a lick of sense!"

"Why? I make sense to me!"

"Nee, you don't! You're forcing your will and decisions on a woman who has had to learn to be very independent very quickly. If I were her, and you were courting me, I would feel very crowded in, like I couldn't breathe without asking for your permission."

"But—"

"But what? What don't you understand?"

"What is this about 'feeling crowded in' or 'being unable to breathe without asking for permission'? I never did that!"

"Oh?" Becky's eyes roved over the stand of trees as they approached. Breathing deeply, she allowed the serenity of the scene to calm her down. "So, when you kept telling her that she was 'just a woman' who couldn't make decisions…no, wait, Andy. When you told her that she needed a gut man in her life to teach her boys how to be gut men, you weren't pressuring her. When you approached her at today's meeting, telling her to make your boys go sit with you, you weren't pressuring her."

Andy ground his teeth and squeezed his eyes shut. "But she is just a woman! She doesn't know how bad the world can be!"

"Yet an accident took Matt, her husband. Where do her parents live?"

"They're…passed on, I believe."

"And where do her siblings live?"

"I dunno. Here?"

"One brother and his family live here. The rest live in settlements in other states. And she makes sure all three of her kinder get to spend a lot of time with her brother, his wife and their kinder. So they do get that male influence."

"Oh. I didn't know that."

Becky flopped onto the ground. "Oh, Andy. It seems there's so much you don't know. Like how to view women in today's world, whether it's Amish or not. Are you aware that, even in our community, women can work outside the home, if she and her husband agree to that? Amy Hershberger is widowed, so that decision was all hers. It was the choice between working and doing what she is able to do best, or having her and her kinder lose their home. Would you want that to happen?"

"Nee!"

"I'm sorry, but it doesn't sound like that to me. She has to stay at home with her kinder. If she works as a server or in the quilt shop or even at the market, she has to get someone to watch them or take them with her to wherever she's working. And I don't think there are any bosses out there who would welcome a woman's three young kinder in the job every day. She would get fired. So it does sound like you want her to fail. No, Andy, don't answer. Think about what I just said."

Feeling confused and defeated, Andy flopped down next to Becky. Did he want Amy to fail? "I don't think I do. No, I don't."

"You sound sure of yourself. Andy, be honest. Making her quit work before she even agrees to marry you means she is at risk of becoming homeless. There is only so much community support here in Peace Valley. Other families here have to pay their bills and obligations and they can't support her indefinitely. She knows that. So, she looked at all her options.

"She knew that the interest and demand from English tourists was out there. They want to learn about the Amish and our lifestyle. Knowing Amy, she wasn't going to start this without telling the elders what she had in mind. If they had told her 'no,' she would have had to settle on another form of earning money. I believe she's still paying off a large hospital bill. Her farm belonged to her parents, so she doesn't have to worry about that. Repairs, ja, and she has to worry about food and medical care for her and her kinder. Clothing, she can make, but she has to buy four pairs of shoes, fabric to make their clothes, and felt and straw hats for Matt and Joshua. That's not cheap, Andy.

"Nee, don't say anything. I want you to think about what we discussed. Learn something from it. I'm not happy with what you've been doing to her. I love you, but I'm relieved that she finally had enough and broke off your courting relationship. For the success of any future courting relationships, you need to figure out why you see women as 'less than men' before you get involved with anyone else. Ever. I'm going back to the house." Rising quickly, Becky walked home before she said anything she knew she'd regret.

Andy remained behind, shook to his core. Questions roiled his mind. *Did I really do that to her? Make her feel pressure?*

Why is thinking about our women as "just women" so bad? I've been single because I didn't want to marry anyone unless it was Amy. I can't see myself with anyone other than her, so I guess I'll just stay single. He sighed, feeling lower than he'd felt in years. *Maybe the elders were right. Maybe I should get involved in those peer classes.*

The following Wednesday, Andy walked reluctantly into the Yoder house behind Jethro. "Denki for inviting me." At the offer of coffee, he nodded, thinking he'd need it to keep from dozing off.

"We're going to get started with prayer first, then start discussing our planned topic for today. Go ahead and join the other men." Eli waved in the direction of the large living room.

Andy hid his shock at some of the faces he saw and recognized. He was also surprised at how many people were there. Glancing over into the women's section, his eyes swept over the number of women in attendance. As he spotted Amy, his gaze stopped.

Amy, seeing Andy going to the men's section, allowed her true feelings to come out in her expression—her eyes narrowed in anger and the corners of her mouth tightened.

Andy, seeing this, sighed. Dropping his gaze to the ground, he walked slowly to an empty spot on one of the benches. He prepared for a boring hour and a half.

"So, now that we've prayed for understanding, let's get started. Many of you are here because you struggle with the idea of women being equal to men. I'm not going to get biblical about this, mainly because I don't have the required understanding of the Bible." A wave of laughter followed Eli's words. "Instead, we're going to look at what our wives, daughters and mothers actually already do, beyond taking care of kinder, keeping the house, cooking and gardening. I'm going to point to several of the women and ask them to give us a list. Linda will write down responses on this easel." Eli pointed to several women in succession. As he did, they listed everything they did beyond "traditional women's chores."

"Accounting, working in the Quilt Place, feeding and watering our livestock, negotiating loan payments with the bank... Leora, anything else?"

Amy responded. "Advertising my farm tour, budgeting for the household and my business, hiring farm workers to keep the farm going, finding an English worker to create a new corn maze every year, directing helpers every weekend so tours go smoothly. I think that's it."

Most people present shook their heads in admiration of everything Amy was able to accomplish.

"Manage my mother's quilting store, advertise in the *Amish Quarterly*, set up weekly schedules and write out paychecks that Mam signs. Help with the peer group and meetings here,"

Naomi said.

"Work in the diner just outside Peace Valley so I can help Mam with expenses," said Beth Zook. Her voice was low and shaky.

Every woman or girl that Eli pointed his pencil at came back with a list of chores or tasks they did that were not considered to be "traditional." Some managed the livestock for their fathers; others were responsible for hiring helpers during planting and harvesting; one wife singlehandedly ran the dairy for the farm she and her husband owned—he was busy full-time with the crops and couldn't turn his attention to the cows.

"Okay, I think we've all gotten an eye-opening view into what our women do. Ja, some work outside the home like Lizzie, Leora, Annie and Naomi. Sometimes, it's out of sheer necessity. Other times, it's because the women and their husbands have realized that they have a gift for business or for connecting with the public.

"This isn't to say that the traditional Amish businesses that are run from home are wrong or outmoded. They aren't. If that's what works for families here, then that's what those families should do. Amy, I'm going to use your situation as an example, if you don't mind." At Amy's nod, Eli continued. "Amy was widowed two years ago. Her oldest child is seven and the youngest is five. Any traditional job she could find to support her family and farm would not be sufficient. She would have to find childcare because her mam and dat have died. She has one brother here; the rest of her siblings live out of state. What about quilting or baking? I'm sure Amy considered them."

"Ja, I did. I don't bake well enough to sell what I'd need to keep our household running. I've never been interested in quilting. It's too much sitting still for me."

"That means that her farm tour, which is pretty popular, is the best option for her. She's able to buy food and supplies, pay her late husband's outstanding medical bills and maintain repairs to the house. She buys shoes, fabric, notions and hats for her and her kinder. Amy, do your earnings get you through the month or year?"

Amy sighed. "I'm getting there. With a lot of support from people here, prayer and hard work, my earnings are going up. Eventually, I would like to hire a few teens to manage each of the stations and I could manage them. Right now, that's just not in my budget. I do get through the month, but just barely."

Hearing this, Andy swallowed a rush of shame. He really hadn't cared to consider her situation.

Eli let Amy's words sink in for a few seconds, and then he continued. "Why is it so hard for us men to see our women as capable of making decisions and running businesses and farms? Naomi, please tell us how it was when you first started managing the Quilt Place."

Naomi smiled and shook her head. "Challenging. It would have been worse if Mam hadn't exposed me from the beginning to the running of the shop. She did so much all by herself. But, when she decided to take her hours to half time, she needed someone to manage. So, I learned about managing the books, keeping the time sheets, making the deposits at the bank, writing checks for employees and to pay for supplies. I thank Gott that Mam was there to teach me and supervise while I learned."

"Do you mind telling everyone why your mam decided to step back?"

Looking at her mam, then at her dat, Naomi sighed. "Okay. Dat had a very hard time with how Mam owns the shop. He wanted her to sell it. But she knows that farming isn't predictable. A year can start out gut, and then one or two weather events can destroy the crops. That's happened to Dat, as well as other farmers here. She wanted the shop's earnings to be available in bad farming years so she and Dat could keep up with payment obligations, or if we had another emergency, we would have money available to handle it."

Naomi grew emotional at this point. "Before he got involved in our peer group, Dat believed that women should not work outside the home, much less own a store. He tried to intimidate Mam into selling, and the elders got word of it. They came to talk to him and made it clear that if he didn't stop intimidating Mam, he'd be banned. I was already involved in the peer group, so I convinced him to try it out."

Many of the men who were there for the first time had come under promise of bad consequences if they didn't stop trying to keep their wives or fiancées from doing what they needed or wanted to do to earn money. Hearing Naomi's soft, emotional words, most of them felt ashamed.

"Denki, Naomi. Lizzie, how is Wayne doing?"

CHAPTER SEVEN

Lizzie sighed. "He has gut days and bad. Right now, the bad days outnumber the gut ones. We go to see him one day a week, and he's trying to understand why it's not bad for us to be 'out there,' working around other people. I was able to make quilts at home, and then sell them on consignment in Annie's store. That helped us while Wayne was laid up with his arm injury. It also helped that every carpenter here stepped up and helped fill all his orders—and they're continuing to do so!"

"Lizzie, if you don't mind, would you reveal just why Wayne is in the Mennonite-Amish mental health hospital?"

"Ja, because I think it's a lesson to everyone here, whether they are man or woman. My gut husband experienced years of child abuse at the hands of his dat. He witnessed his dat beating his mam. His mam escaped, leaving all the youngest kinder with their dat, probably because she sensed he was about to kill her. Once she left, his dat's only outlet for his anger and abuse was…the kinder. "That's what he grew up knowing, so I don't blame him for what he believes. He is working hard to change that, but it will be a while before he can safely come home. The psychiatrist and psychologist have told Leora and me that he suffers from something called PTSD. It means post-traumatic stress disorder. He can be fine one minute, and the next, something will happen around him and it's as if he's back in a moment where he's being abused or hearing his mam being beaten.

"Ladies, he did beat me. The elders came to talk to him, and for a while he really tried. But, the last time he went backward he was in the market, and he overheard shameless gossip about why Leora and I were not living in our home. And all his fears and those old ghosts came back. That's when he began planning how he would kill us. He completely lost his grip on reality then. I'm not making any excuses for him. He was wrong, and now he's paying for that." Lizzie sat down, her heart pounding.

The room was so quiet that a mouse could have twittered and it would have sounded loud. Linda Yoder stood and approached the front of the room. "Lizzie, denki for telling us such a hard story. I do have one question that everyone here should know the answer to, so they can put Wayne's situation into perspective. Why was his dat so abusive of his mam?"

Again, the silence descended into the room. Andy felt it and his gaze centered on Lizzie, who stood once again.

"I understand this only secondhand from Wayne. His dat came from a very conservative Amish sect and believed that no woman should get the opportunity to earn money, even by working from home. His wife was desperate to earn what she needed to escape, so with the few extra dollars she had, she bought baking supplies. Other wives in the community sold her goods for her and then took the money to her. She was able to hide it from Wayne's dat. Also, he believed that women should not speak up unless spoken to. He was raising his daughters in the same way. Wayne told me that he knew their dat abused his sisters as well. And that they are abused to this day by—" Lizzie couldn't continue. She collapsed onto the bench and Leora wrapped her arm around her shoulders.

Linda grabbed a box of facial tissues and gave them to Leora. "I'm sorry for bringing up something so painful, Lizzie, but it's important that everyone here know just how far sexism can be taken." She turned toward the entire group, men and women. "Because that's what women are facing, is sexism. That simply means that men and society believe that women should take care of 'women's chores' only. That they aren't good enough, smart enough or strong enough to own, run or manage a business. Ladies, since you were all fourteen years old, you helped your mothers or your fathers to run their own home-based businesses, right? And you learned what you needed by being exposed to what your parents did. That was gut training for your own lives as married women, ja?"I want us to take a break now. We have coffee, lemonade and cookies ready for everyone. Men, think about what the women have said here. We'll come back in ten minutes for the last half of our session."

The group broke up, moving to the kitchen for the mentioned snacks. Andy toyed with sneaking out, but seeing Bishop Kurtz's eyes trained on him, he sighed, gave up on his idea and grabbed a fresh cup of coffee. Sitting on the bench again, he thought. Realizing it was too noisy, he decided to go outside. "Bishop, I'll be in the back yard. I need to think for a few minutes."

"I think I'll join you."

Andy sighed yet again. Plopping himself onto the back porch swing, he sipped the hot coffee. *I can see where Amy had to make the decisions she needed to make. I made some bad mistakes there. Ja, Lizzie needed to find a gut job so she could keep the household running. I see that. But this thing about 'if women want to work outside the home, they should be allowed'? I don't know. . .* He turned his head at Deacon King's call. Slipping back into the kitchen, he poured another cup of coffee.

Eli approached the front of the room. "Men, I want you to think about where your beliefs come from. Your parents? Conservative Amish communities? Or even English communities? Because the English struggle with this, too. Right now, there is a conservative strain in government. I agree with much of that, but not the parts that say a woman shouldn't earn a salary equal to a man's. Using Annie's words, she wanted to have the protection of the store supporting them if Caleb, like other farmers, had a bad farming year. He can't control the weather. It took him some time, but Caleb now supports his wife's store, knowing that it's a protection for their family as well as a way for Annie to have her own creative outlet.

"Another new member here is Beth Zook. She came by herself for this meeting. She is struggling with her own beau, but I won't get into the particulars. She and her mam work in the diner just outside Peace Valley. Her dat died, so it's up to her and her mam to earn what they need, as cook and server, to keep their home from being taken by the bank. *They have no choice. They have to work.* Quilting or baking wouldn't meet their financial needs. Beth, may I reveal just a little more information?"

Beth nodded slowly.

"Thank you. Beth's beau is pressuring her to quit her job. He tells her she shouldn't need to do any work at all. Now, his dat and mam came from a very conservative Amish sect out of state. We know where John gets his beliefs. We are working to get him to join our group and see why his beliefs and demands of Beth won't work. And I don't want anyone gossiping about

Beth's situation. If I hear of anyone doing so, I'll inform Bishop Kurtz."

Linda stepped up again. "Today's discussion question is, "Is it right for men to tell women whether they can work, or where they can work?" Break up into groups of four, please, and discuss that question. One person should be group recorder and write down everyone's beliefs. We'll discuss them in…twenty-five minutes."

The noise level in the room went up. Eli opened the back door while Linda opened the front, allowing some of the sound to escape.

Andy found himself in a group with Deacon King and Jethro Yoder. When the group's recorder pointed at him, he sighed. "I believed it was right for me to tell women where and when they could work. After hearing some of the situations here, I realized that I didn't know enough of each family's situation to judge."

"Who are we to judge?" This was Deacon King.

Andy's mouth opened and closed as he struggled with that. "Ahh, well, we are on this earth to make sure that women are safe. To make sure they use good judgment in the—"

"Wait," Jethro said. "We have pretty smart women who live and work here. I trust their judgment just fine. If my dat were to die, I would grieve him and miss him. But I would know that

Mam could keep our home and business running. She was encouraged and taught by her parents. Andy, I've helped Amy out with her farm tour. I saw a confident young woman making decisions and directing volunteers where they needed to be. The tour ran smoothly, with tourists moving from one station to another, fully enjoying themselves. Before they left, Amy made sure they enjoyed snacks. And, by the end of the day, she had entertained and taught over fifty tourists by my own estimate. She does that every weekend, and in between she prepares for the upcoming tour, which takes planning and coordination. She knows what she is doing. Ja, she is 'barely breaking even.' But she isn't relying on the generosity of the families here, is she?

"Ahh, nee. But shouldn't someone, a male, be guiding her decisions, to make sure—?"

"Ach, the 'judgment' question again. Andy, if your dat were to pass away today, would you trust your mam to keep the house and farm running?" Deacon King sat back, waiting patiently.

The question and topic hit Andy hard in the gut. Breathing deeply, he took a swallow of coffee and considered. "While she would need some help with some farming aspects, I believe she could keep everything running. But—"

"Nee, Andy. Leave judgment out of it. She has been running your household for, what, thirty, forty years, right? I'm sure your dat handed all that over to her. Consider the household and budget to be a small business. How long has it been since she's made a mistake that affected how the house functions? Or does she go running to your dat for every decision?"

Andy allowed his gaze to go outside. Seeing the leaves falling off the trees, he felt calm once again. "I can't think of a time when she's made a poor decision. The only time she and Dat confer on a decision is when they have to talk about a large expenditure. You see, they make decisions together for bigger money expenditures."

"Okay, can you see your household being operated like a small business, with your mam as the boss?"

Closing his eyes, Andy tried to imagine this. "I don't know. Maybe."

"Andy, can you see someone like Annie Miller, opening her own business outside the family home? Running it successfully with the goal of having it be a protection against a bad farming or carpentry year?" Jethro looked into Andy's confused gaze. "I know this is a strange new way for you to think. But you need to change how you view women and your relationship to them."
"Clearly, if I am not to keep fouling up my approaches to them," Andy growled.

"Andy, do you know where your views on women come from? Because I've always seen your mam as quite independent. And I never got the impression that your dat didn't want her to do anything, like work in the market or another business selling retail goods." Deacon King leaned forward, his coffee cup in between his knees.

"Nee. Dat has always encouraged Mam to do what she felt she needed to do." Andy paused, thinking back. "I remember…back when I was, maybe eight, ten years old, I met a boy. We were only friends for a short time. Mam and Dat let me spend the afternoons at his house before it was time for chores. After a while, I began to pick up on his dat's attitude toward women and girls. 'You're stupid. You can't do nothing right. Don't expect to be allowed to work outside the home because girls and women don't have the judgment to even work at the market without messin' up.'"

"But, Andy, if your dat didn't have those beliefs, how would it make sense for you to assume them? He would have had more of an influence on your thinking."

"Ja, that's why I can't understand why I think that way."

"Andy." Eli dropped into their group. "How does your dat express himself toward your sisters?"

"Protective. He is protective."

"Okay. And? Anything else?"

"Wait." A dim memory began surfacing. "I remember that

my oldest sister said she wanted to work a shop. Dat was reluctant, for some reason. Being that I was only twelve, I had to be upstairs in bed. But I had heard their discussion before I went upstairs, so I snuck over to the top of the stairs and listened to my sister and Dat. She wanted to work in an English store that specialized in selling Amish creations. 'I can do this, Dat. It'll allow me to save money so that Ben and I can start our married life out on the right foot.' Then my dat disagreed. He said that my sister didn't have the head for numbers and books. 'You'd do better makin' quilts here at home and selling them. Or baking and spending a day or two selling to other Amish and to the tourists.'

"My sister was hurt, and she asked him why he didn't believe in her. Well, that slowed my dat down and he told her he did believe in her. 'But I've always just seen you as soft and more suited for the home arts.' In the end, my sister didn't apply for that position. She does quilt and she does a great job at it. Her work is in demand and what she earns is a nice supplement to Ben's carpentry work."

"What did your dat say about your other sisters?" Eli was astounded.

"He had no objection to their working in that store. When Annie opened her quilt shop, they worked there for a year or two before they began having babies."

Eli thoughtfully pulled at his beard. "You know, putting

myself in your oldest sister's shoes, I would be hurt. What was her reaction when your younger sisters were able to get the permission she sought?"

"Angry and hurt, ja. She loves Dat, but that has put a strain in their relationship. And she has forgiven him...but has never forgotten what he said and decided."

Deacon King broke in. "And this had its effect on how you see Amy Hershberger?"

Andy had clearly never thought about it from that point of view. "Huh?" He took his hat off and scratched his full head of hair. "Huh! I never saw it that way."

"Think carefully and answer as honestly as you can. Why do you believe that Amy could use bad judgment? Or that she's made a mistake with her choice?" Eli watched Andy closely.

Andy did as Eli directed. He took his time and thought of both women's situations. He compared both women to each other. He thought about the decisions his sister had made and realized she had made very few significant ones. Nor had Amy. "Uh, well, they are both gentle in their personalities. Soft, you know? But strong. They both have a core of strength that, with their faith, gets them through the tough times. I guess—nee, I know—that I mistook that gentle personality as being too soft to survive out in the world. Hearin' that Amy is able to direct others during tours so every one of them is successful surprised me. It shouldn't. She's able to make a decision and stick to it. A lot like my sister."

"And about the risk of bad judgment?" Eli wasn't going to let him wiggle out of that one.

"Bad judgment… I still have a hard time believing that having tours every weekend and allowing English tourists to be around her kinder is good."

"Okay, let's go with that. Do you distrust the English?"

"Some, ja. I don't know that they wouldn't try to hurt the children."

"Amy has thought of that and taken precautions. Do you trust her ability to protect them?"

"Oh, ja!"

"Then, if she can protect them, having tourists around shouldn't be an issue, especially now that so many of us are volunteering to help her during her tours. It's that many more extra pairs of eyes to supervise the kinder, ja?"

Andy couldn't deny that. "True." A question occurred to him. "Do you think she'd let me volunteer?"

CHAPTER EIGHT

Deacon King leaned forward. "Let me ask her. But after Sunday's meeting, she was pretty mad. I wouldn't get my hopes up. I think you've burned your bridges pretty thoroughly with her."

Andy had known that instinctively, but hearing the words still hurt. He drew in a big breath, trying to minimize their impact. "Ja, I got it."

The group work came to an end and each group's recorder reported the results of their discussion of the question. "Okay, it looks like some of the men here still believe that women shouldn't work outside the home, even if the wife has the ability and aptitude to do so. Men, we still have some work to do. Those of you who still have this belief, please raise your hands. Ja, you'll identify yourselves, but we are going to at least understand that this belief comes from a sexist view of the women here. That way, when the question comes up in your families, you're better prepared to give your wives or fiancées the benefit of the doubt." The meeting ended and the participants went home.

Andy went home with questions swirling around in his head. That night, after supper, he asked his dat whether he truly believed women should work outside the home if they had the desire and ability to do so.

"Ja, now I do. I regret saying what I said to your sister. I thought I was protecting her and doing the best thing possible for her. I've watched her operate her quilting business over the years. She has done a great job, setting rates, ordering, making her quilts and receiving payment. There was only one customer who cheated her out of what she was owed. Your sister figured out what mistakes she made and hasn't made them again. Ja, she is a gut business woman. Today, I would say that if she wants to work in a store or office, she should do so, as long as her husband agrees. If she wants to start her own business, she should, with his agreement."

"Dat, I made a similar mistake with Amy. Only now…"

"Son, I saw what happened. Ja, she's a woman, but she is making that farm tour business work. I hear she has volunteers helping her out now."

"Ja. It is working and the volunteers are a big help for her."

"You miss her, ja?"

"Ja. But I was stupid. She won't want to go out with me again because I didn't trust that she had the ability to make the decisions and carry them out."

"Son, I am sorry. Like me, that's your burden to bear. Keep that in mind as you look around for another young woman to court."

"Dat, I don't think…"

"What?"

"I always imagined myself courting and eventually marrying Amy. Then, she married Matt Hershberger and I was ready to be single all my life. None of the other women here—"

"Stop. Don't be stupid. There is a young woman here or in another community that is right for you. Allow yourself time to grieve, then start noticing who's out there."

"But, dat—"

"Andy! You acted poorly around her and tried to order her around. You learned your lesson. Now, get yourself out of the muck and resolve to do better next time. You going to those peer group meetings?"

I went to this one. It was…okay. Not sure if I'll go to more."

"Well, I'm going. And you'll be with me."

Andy stared at his dat, his jaw fully dropped.

***

While Andy was having his discussion with his dat, Eli and Deacon King were discussing him. "Eli, you think he's learned that he has sexist ways of thinking?"

"It's occurred to him. If he's smart, he'll allow himself to figure out how to change that so that when he meets someone new, he won't blow that relationship."

Hannes stared at Eli. "You know, you sounded just like an Englischer there."

Eli chuckled. "Ja, remember, my family and I spent some years living in an English town. I picked up on some of the lingo."

Hannes' laugh came out as a bark. He shook his head. "Apparently! Were you able to maintain your Amish lifestyle and beliefs?"

"Ja, we were. I was there with my mam and dat. He had to work in a factory to earn the money he needed to pay off a bank loan. Once he was able to do that, he took the rest of his savings and we moved here and found our home."

"Back to Andy Stoltzfus. I think he'll learn more readily. Losing Amy was a real shock to him. John Andrews, on the other hand…"

"Ach! From what I've learned from Beth, his beliefs are rooted in extremely conservative thinking. When we have time, I think we should have a conversation with John's mam. I'll bring Lovina along with me so she might feel more comfortable."

"When do you have time?" Eli was thinking of his schedule for the next two weeks."

"No time like the present. Do you have any time tomorrow?"

"I have three shoeing appointments tomorrow. One early, the other two mid-afternoon and early evening. You?"

"I have to go to the lumber store and pick up a large order along with some other supplies. I want to take care of that early as well. What time do you anticipate being back home after your early appointment?"

"Probably around nine in the morning."

"Perfect. Go with me to the lumber store, we'll unload the wagon and store everything in my shop. Then we'll go to the Andrews farm."

"I like that. But no appointment?"

"Nee. I don't want to give her time to think of potential answers to anything we might ask. Our group has become well-known here."

"Ja, it has. Okay, I'll wait for you and we'll go from your house."

***

It was almost ten the next morning when Hannes and Eli finished unloading the lumber and supplies in Hannes' carpentry shop. Lovina was with them as they discussed what they would ask Mrs. Andrews.

Hannes began. "I met with Beth Zook a week or two ago. She had a bruise on the side of her face that John had given her. We talked about it. He had ordered her to quit her job serving at the diner and she told him why she couldn't. He took it personally, thinking that she was defying him."

"She is taking part in our peer meetings and says they are helping her."

"She doesn't speak out much or volunteer any information," Lovina said. "I get the sense she's frightened of him. She's also desperate because she has to keep her job so she and her mam won't lose everything. I spoke with her privately and she seemed more comfortable with that. She was actually able to admit that she was thinking of breaking off with John. She even said that she'd rather be an old maid than marry John if this is how he's going to treat her."

Eli listened, soaking everything in. "Has she met his parents?"

"Ja. She says his mam is like a scared little mouse. She says nothing without deferring to her husband. That makes me wonder—"

"Getting his approval before saying anything, along with being so fearful could be a sign that he has abused her. But until we see for ourselves, we should not assume," Hannes pointed out. He went on, seeming to mutter to himself. "It makes me wonder too, but until she is ready to say anything, there is little…but maybe…could it happen?"

Eli sent a puzzled glance over to Lovina, who smiled and shook her head. "That's how he does his best thinking. He figures things out by talking to himself. It's actually very effective for him."

"We'll have a discussion with Missus Andrews, and then decide who would be best able to work with her and her husband. It may be one of us, or maybe one of the elders and his wife, depending on how Mister Andrews responds." Eli rubbed his whiskery chin, thinking.

***

Arriving at the Andrews place, Deacon King knocked on the front door and they waited.

Inside, Big John waved his wife back to her kitchen work. "I'll get it. You get back to your work." Swinging the door open, Big John's surprise caused his jaw to drop. "Deacon!

Missus King. If we would have known you were coming, we would have had a pie ready! Come in! Enter!" Big John's voice was energetic, but Eli's finely trained ears picked up on the thin thread of anger running underneath.

"Denki! I need to introduce Eli Yoder to you as well. We have some business to discuss with you…and your wife." Hannes gave Big John no room in which to refuse to allow his wife to participate in the meeting.

"Okay, come in. Emma, make a pot of coffee, now! Do we have any pie left from yesterday?"

Emma's voice was whispery-quiet. "Ja, I'll make coffee. We have some pie left. Please, sit."

The guests sat, and after enjoying a few bites of the pie, they came to the reason for their visit. "We need to speak to the two of you individually. It's about the peer community group and its work here. We're trying to reach out to every family in Peace Valley."

"John, if you'll come outside with the deacon and me, we can get started so you can get back to your own work. I know your time is valuable." Eli rose.

"It's not necessary for my wife to speak up. I speak for her," John said.

Hannes tipped his head to the side. "Why is that?"

"Women don't have the judgment to speak about some matters. It's for their husbands to communicate for them."

Seated, Emma Andrews flushed and crouched over as she heard what her husband said.

Lovina rose and faced John directly. "I'll take my chances. Being 'a woman,' I may be able to pick up on what Emma says."

John understood Lovina's message. Flushing and scuffing the floor, he shrugged, mumbling. "Okay, whatever."

Outside, the men sipped their hot coffee gratefully. The mornings were becoming chilled, and hot beverages were more and more comfortable.

"So, what's this meeting for?" John was off-balance. He didn't like this feeling, and he sought to get information so he could regain control of the situation.

"We simply want to learn about your family. Who's the head of the home and how family decisions are made. What are your beliefs about family roles? Kinder? Your wife?" Deacon King purposely asked about John's wife at the last because he wanted him to think that her position wasn't as important as the other family members' roles were.

Big John was in his element. Feeling comfortable, he settled himself comfortably on his seat, gripping his coffee mug between weathered hands. "Oh, that's easy! Our family follows conservative, traditional Amish beliefs. The husband and dat is the head of the household. He makes the decisions and everyone follows his decisions and directions. Our kinder know their place in our family and they do what I tell them. I raised my sons to be strong men, respectful of Gott and ready to be the heads of their own households when they married. I'm still teaching that to John, my youngest. He's learning well."

Eli and Hannes waited for John to mention Emma.

"John, what about Missus Andrews? What's your wife's role?" Eli deliberately didn't ask whether she took part in the decision-making process.

"We discuss things important to the family. *I* make *all* the decisions and she goes along."

"She has no input? She doesn't tell you what she thinks or give you her opinions?"

"What opinions? She doesn't need them. What's important is my opinion on any given question. She's supposed to obey me, and that's all."

Hearing these words, Eli suppressed a sudden shiver. *I feel sorry for the womenfolk in this family.* Swallowing his coffee, Eli wet his mouth. "Has she ever worked outside your home? Say, at the market or the diner, as a server?"

"What! Nee, no way! Women don't have any business, workin' away from the family home. It's for their husbands to earn the family's income. Period! Is that what this meeting's for? You want my wife to be able to go traipsing out there and work?"

"Nee, John, and you know better," said the deacon. "We are visiting every family to find out what the dynamics are. If any families are interested in adding extra income through the wife, we help them achieve that goal. If not, then that's fine."

John sat back again, relaxing. "Okay. Just so you know, Emma isn't allowed to work out there. She has plenty to keep her occupied in our house."

Inside the house, Lovina worked gently to get Emma Andrews to explain how things ran in her household. "Do you get to make any of the decisions, say about a big expenditure?"

"Oh, nee!" Emma's voice was still whispery-quiet, but she was more comfortable around Lovina. "John doesn't believe wives have any business making decisions."

"Well, what about working, maybe from home? Quilting or baking, and then selling your work to earn money for the household?"

"Nee. I'd have loved to quilt and sell them to tourists. John told me nee."

"Was that all he said, or did he say or do anything else?"

Lovina felt her heart hammering in her chest as she waited for Emma to respond.

Emma waited for several seconds to answer. "He got…so angry at me. He was yellin', hollerin' and picking things up because he wanted to throw them at me. But the kinder were all in the kitchen with us, so he couldn't."

"Oh, my! I need to know this. Has he ever hit you or thrown things at you before?"

At this question, Emma's eyes filled with tears. "Ach, I'm sorry!" She looked quickly toward the closed back door, not wanting John to see her crying. Inhaling quickly, she regained control of her emotions. "Ja. He has hit me in the past. That seems to have stopped now that it's only John at home with us. Now, all he does is yell, order me around and throw things when John is gone."

"You grew up in the same conservative community as John, ja?"

"Ja."

"Did your mam work, either baking and selling her cakes and cookies or by making and selling quilts?"

"Ja, my dat actually said she could. He knew that as a farmer, he was never assured of a good farming year, and he knew they could put the money from her quilts back as emergency savings. And I expected I would be able to do that when I married John."

CHAPTER NINE

"But it never happened, did it? What happened in bad farming years for your husband?"

"A lot of worry—anger and worry from him. Strict budgeting. I got very gut at... Would you like to go out to the front and walk?"

Lovina immediately agreed because she knew Emma was going to tell her something important.

Outside, Emma continued. "I got very gut at pinching pennies and dollars in good harvest years. I hid the money and when the harvests were bad, I had that money to fall back on. I used a lot of coupons and made less-expensive meals. Still, sometimes we fell behind on bank loans. One year, the bank repossessed one of John's farming tools. He was so mad. He blamed me, telling me that I should have somehow been able to come up with extra money in the budget. Missus King, that beating was bad. I ended up in the emergency room, with a broken rib and a broken nose."

Lovina shook her head, feeling sick. She felt blessed, having Hannes as her husband. "Emma, you can call me Lovina. I want to offer you the opportunity to take a place in our peer group meetings."

"Nee, oh, he won't let me go! He never lets me use the buggy unless he's with me!"

Lovina was stunned. It took a few minutes for her tongue and throat to work again. "You mean you can't go out by yourself, without him being with you? Does he go shopping with you? What about quilting frolics?

"He goes shopping with me, but only when he can spare the time from farming. And frolics? I haven't been to one since I got married. John believes that women should not be anywhere their husbands are not."

"Emma, he's putting a very strict interpretation on our Ordnung. There's nothing in there that says wives or girlfriends can't work, and nothing that says wives can't enjoy participating in a quilting frolic. He's…he's abusing you when he hits you and even when he yells at you. When he doesn't allow you to attend social events or go shopping by yourself, he's isolating you. This is so you can't gain strength to resist him. And, by not allowing you to work, he is abusing you financially and telling you that you aren't gut enough or smart enough to hold down a job."

Emma was only able to open her mouth. Nothing came out. Then, "But. . . John, he loves—"

"Maybe. But he isn't showing that in a very gut way. Emma, too many of our men here are stuck in what is called a sexist way of thinking."

"'Sexist?'" Emma was shocked, and she began to feel angry. "Missus King, are you talking of...matters that better belong in the bedroom?"

"Nee! Sexism only means that men think that women aren't good enough to make significant family decisions, hold jobs, earn money or even make decisions about whether they will go to a quilting frolic. For all of your marriage, John has ruled you, telling you how things would be—because he believes you aren't smart enough or even good enough to do so."

Emma, who had been ready to order Lovina to leave her husband's house, closed her mouth. Sitting back on the porch swing, she pulled her shawl more closely around her shoulders. "Oh. But I am good enough! I run the household, even though I let him think he does. I budget the money and even squeeze out money here and there for emergencies."

Lovina nodded emphatically, nearly dislodging her head covering. "Ja, gut! Gut! I *knew* you had it in you! I would really like to see you at our next peer meeting. My husband and Eli

Yoder are trying to convince your husband to attend as well."

Emma pursed her lips, pushing them out from her teeth. Shaking her head, her still-beautiful eyes grew sad again. "Nee. He will never agree to attend a meeting where the topic goes in direct disagreement with his beliefs."

"Hannes and I will pick you up, then. At the least, you can learn what we are struggling against. And you can get some new knowledge about how to regain some of the equality in your marriage to John. Simple things, like salting away a few pennies, quarters and dollars, against financial emergencies, allowing him to think he is the one running the household. You don't have to be obvious about it. Continue agreeing with him—but, where and when you can, quietly do what *you* know to be right. If he tells you not to buy fabric to make new clothes, but you know you can't repair your existing clothes anymore, buy the fabric anyway. Store it away while he's working in the fields. And, while he's working, sew your new clothes. If you make a new shirt for him, tell him you had fabric left over from a year or so ago. If you take part in a community meeting where someone is facing the Meidung, you don't have to vote in agreement with him, when you know the person's actions don't rise to that level. Vote differently."

Emma was silent, thinking about everything Lovina had just advised her to do. "I need time to think. This Sunday is a Meeting Sunday, ja?" At Lovina's nod, she sighed. "I will tell you what my decision is. At lunch. When is your next meeting?"

"Next Thursday. Emma, there is one very important reason I want you to participate. Your son, John Junior, has been dating Beth Zook. And—"

"She is such a sweet girl. It's just too bad that to keep their home she and her mam have to work so hard at the diner."

"You understand. Gut! Because your son has been pressuring her to leave that job. I suspect she has told him that she has to work so she and her mam don't lose what they have—their home and everything in it. Money must be a constant struggle for them. I strayed off topic. I'm sorry. In trying to convince her to quit her serving job, your son has used physical pressure. In the same way your husband has threatened and hit you, John Junior has hit Beth."

Emma gasped, feeling physical pain. "Nee! No!" She gasped again, knowing her voice could carry. With difficulty, she moderated her tone. Then, she thought back to several incidents where John Junior had taken the same attitudes and actions as his dat. Weeping, she pulled a facial tissue from her apron. "It's true. I know that. I have seen him using the same actions that John, my husband, has used against me. Yelling. He has also thrown objects at me, trying to intimidate me. And my husband has said nothing to him."

Lovina was afraid for Emma and Beth. "Listen, we need to

finish quickly. Beth is already a group member. She's learning so much! That's why I want you to participate as well."

"I'll think about it and let you know Sunday at lunch."

"Denki. I hear the men inside. We'd better get inside ourselves." Lovina rose and delicately helped Emma to rise. She felt protective toward the older woman, instinctively seeing her as more delicate. *Nee, Lovina. If she has survived John's treatment this long, she is much stronger than you think.*

"Wife, why were you outside?" John felt suspicious, feeling that something was up.

"We wanted to enjoy the fall air as we talked about the Ordnung."

Lovina had stayed quiet on purpose, wanting Emma to give direction. "Ja, John, I learned so much from her. Now that I know you grew up and met in a conservative district, I understand your position. Are we done? I need to start dinner and begin preparations for supper. I also need to make more progress on that quilt for my customer."

"We're finished. Eli?"

"Let's go. John, Emma, denki for opening your home to us." Clapping his felt hat on his head, Eli led the way out. He had a lot to say. In the buggy, he leaned forward, looking across Lovina to Hannes. "Let's go to that diner first. The one where Beth works. We need to talk, and I didn't want to be around

John or Emma."

"Ja, we can go for a while." Hannes changed the horses' direction, making their new destination the diner.

"Lovina, what did you learn?" Eli was curious.

"He beats and intimidates her and has never allowed her to make a decision about their household. He doesn't even allow her to go shopping by herself or go to a quilting frolic! Because he doesn't believe Emma should be anywhere he isn't." Lovina's voice quivered, betraying her anger.

Drawing in a deep, calming breath, her gaze moved from bare trees to quiet farms as they approached them. Feeling calmer, she spoke again. "But she has a core of strength even he hasn't seen. She allows him to think he makes all the household decisions. She has, somehow, found a way of squeezing out a little money from the shopping budget and putting it away for emergencies. And she's thinking about coming to our meetings. She'll let me know after meeting on Sunday."

"Oh, my, it is bad there. Eli, do you think we'll have to hide Emma for her protection?" Hannes was worried.

"I don't know. Lovina, John is still refusing to attend the meetings, which makes me wonder if their son will." Eli finished speaking as they pulled into the diner's parking lot.

Inside, Hannes sat next to Lovina while Eli sat opposite them. "Gut morning, Miss Zook! We would like three coffees and, for me, a slice of your mother's apple pie. Lovina, Eli?"

Lovina ordered cookies and Eli, peach pie.

Beth hurried off to get their orders.

"Miss Zook, we have a small piece of gut news. Missus Andrews may agree to attend our meetings. She will let us know on Sunday."

Beth sagged in relief. "My boss gave me a short break. May I join you?"

"Please do! Lovina, why don't you explain what you learned?"

"Beth, just like John has been treating you, his dat treats his mam. She has managed, somehow, to survive all these years of intimidation and mistreatment. She also allows him to think that he makes every decision for their household. What this does about your decision regarding staying with John Junior, I don't know. But we felt you should know."

"That it comes from what he's seen and experienced. Ja. His anger has been out of proportion to the situation, many times. That will make my decision much easier to make. I don't want to live as Missus Andrews has for all these years. Before my dat died, I remember seeing him treating my mam with love and tenderness. He treated me and my brothers and sisters with love. Ja, when we were bad or did wrong, he was angry. But he never abused us. We would get one swat on our fannies and that was it. If he and Mam argued, they settled it like adults. And they made up. That's what I remember, and that's what I want when I meet the right man. I thought John would be the right man. But, it appears he isn't."

Lovina put her hand on Beth's forearm and hand. "Beth, my girl, I regard you almost as one of my own daughters. I feel protective toward you. Don't take too long in making your decision."

Beth sighed. Lovina's hand on hers felt gut. "Ja. His anger has been growing. When he...hit me the last time, I thought he had broken my ribs. I hurt for days! Mam took me to the healer and she gave me some herbs for the pain. I'm better now—no pain at all."

"Excellent. Now, if John's mam joins our group, we will be teaching her about sexism and how it affects the women here." The discussion continued for several minutes until the group paid and went home.

***

While the peer members were meeting with John's dat, mam and Beth, John Junior was working. As he did so, he ruminated on the distance he sensed between him and Beth. As he considered it, he grew angrier and angrier, thinking of what he could do to teach Beth a lesson. He was especially angry that he still hadn't been successful in forcing Beth to quit her job. *She's supposed to quit, stay home and do what good Amish women do! They aren't supposed to work outside the home. They aren't allowed to!* Unable to come up with a workable solution, he decided to talk to his dat about it. *He's been able to make Mam do what she's supposed to do for all these years. He'll have the answers.*

That night, after supper, John asked his dat if they could talk about something. "I need some answers and guidance, Dat. I figured you would be the best person to guide me."

John Sr. smiled. These words stroked his ego. "Certainly. Let's go to the barn. Wife! Make more coffee, now!" John snapped his fingers.

CHAPTER TEN

Emma scurried to obey her husband. Then, knowing that her husband and son wanted to talk in the barn, she filled a large Thermos. Once they left, she closed her eyes in relief. *Finally, a few minutes free of orders!*

In the barn, Big John turned to his son. "What's on your mind?"

"Dat, I have seen how you handle Mam and my sisters. I admire you for it, for standing true to the Ordnung we lived under in Ohio. I have been ordering Beth Zook to quit her job at the diner, but she has refused. I've used some of your...*methods* to try and convince her, but still, she holds onto her job. I need your guidance, dat."

"Sit, son, sit. It's clear to me that you are the one child willing to hold true to what Gott has told us. I am going to explain to you just how I have gotten your mam and even your sisters to obey me when I tell them something. You see, I reinforce my orders to them with physical action when they are…what's a gut word? *Resistant* to what I tell them to do. Years ago, before we had to leave Ohio, your mam expressed a desire to work to bring additional money in for our family. I was stunned! She didn't think I was earning enough, and she wanted even more! I told her nee, of course. She told me that all she wanted to do was bake and sell the goods for extra money for food. 'We have four kinder and maybe more, if Gott wills it. If I can earn a little more, I can buy more groceries. Or I can quilt.' I told her nee again. That I was the head of the household and my earnings were perfectly sufficient. She seemed to accept my decision as law. 'Seemed to,' John, because not three years later, she brought up the same bad idea. 'Husband, the weather wasn't kind to the crops this year. The harvest was—' and that's when I delivered my reinforcement, son. I backhanded her when she wouldn't stop crying about 'we need money.'

"Unfortunately, I hit her hard enough that she had a big bruise on the side of her face. She had to stay home from Sunday meetings for about a month. I learned after that to hit her only hard enough to get my decision across to her. Or I hit her where the marks wouldn't show."

"Dat, I confess, I… I did the same to Beth when she refused to quit her job at the diner. But she is still working!"

"Ach, she is a stubborn woman, ain't? Then, that's when

you deliver such a harsh physical punishment that she *can't* work—for weeks. She gets fired, and you get your wish. If she dies after you deliver your punishment…oh, well. You had to teach her a lesson."

As John was telling his son how he kept his wife and daughters under his control, Vernon King happened to be walking by. Hearing the ugly topic under discussion, Vernon stopped and listened. When he heard Big John tell his son to deliver a "harsh physical punishment," that was when he got scared. When he heard John brush off the possibility of Beth's death, he tiptoed away as quietly as he could. When he was a good distance from the barn, he ran home.

***

"Dat! We have to talk." Vernon bent over, gasping and trying to get his breath back.

"Son, what is it? You look scared!"

"Dat, I just overheard John Andrews—the dat—telling his son how to get Beth Zook under control." More gasps. "He said…he told John to beat Beth up so badly that she wouldn't be able to work for weeks. 'She gets fired,' he said. Then he said, 'If she dies after you deliver your punishment, oh well'!"

Hannes sat down, his legs refusing to hold him up. "Son, sit down here. This coffee should still be warm. Here." He shoved the thermos over to Vernon.

Vernon drank deeply of the still-warm coffee. "Dat, what are we going to do?"

"Tell Eli Yoder and the other elders. Then, you and I are going to go talk to Sheriff Mathis. We cannot allow this to be carried out. We would be condoning murder. Let's go tell your mam where we're going and why." Locking the shop, Hannes and Vernon hurried into the house.

"Lovina! There you are. Vernon and I have to go meet with Eli and the elders. Vernon, tell your mam what you just told me."

Vernon repeated what he had heard.

Lovina went pale and her eyes widened. "Oh my, no! Ja, go. I'll go to the diner. Beth and her mam may be working. I'll warn them both."

"I'll hitch the second buggy for you. Be careful! If you see either of the Andrews men, steer clear of them."

"Ja, Hannes, I will." Lovina took Hannes' and Vernon's hands and squeezed them. "*You* be careful."

***

In town, Hannes and Vernon, along with Eli and the other elders, jumped out of his buggy and strode into the sheriff's office. "Ja, we need to speak with Sheriff Mathis, if he's available."

The deputy behind the desk was wide-eyed. It was rare for the Amish to request a meeting with law enforcement. "I'll go see if he's available. Take a seat, please."

The men only had to wait a minute. Sheriff Mathis came out quickly. "Hannes, Joseph, I take it today's visit isn't social. Would you all come into my office?"

In the closed office, the Amish visitors sat or stood. "Sheriff, my son, Vernon, overheard something. Vernon?"

Again, Vernon repeated his words. "I think they're serious, sir."

"It sounds like it. Joseph, what do you think? I know you don't encourage violence or the use of weapons. Handle this situation the same way we handled the Lapp situation?"

Looking at the elders and Eli, everyone nodded. "Ja, we all think that's best."

***

Sheriff Mathis visited Joseph Kurtz at his home. "Joseph, have you heard of anything that tells you where John Andrews will be spending time with Miss Zook?"

"We spoke with Beth. She told us that she has agreed to a meeting with John. It will take place this coming Saturday night. She says that John likes to stop at a popular picnic spot, with tables. You know which one?"

"There's several. Is there one in particular your community members patronize?"

"It's the one about a mile-and-a-half away from the Andrews home, off state road twenty-three. It's just south of town."

"Oh, yes, I know which one you're talking about. Okay. What time do they generally get together?"

"She said he'll pick her up at about seven, after she's had time for supper with her mam and time to clean the kitchen."

"I'll have my deputies positioned close by, but not visible. You know, we're going to have to alert Beth's mother."

"Really? I was praying we wouldn't. She and Beth have been through so much since her husband died."

"We have to. Once we move in and grab Beth, we're going to take her straight back home. When she sees people she doesn't recognize, she's going to get worried. And if John is able to do any harm to Beth, she may need medical attention. Again, her mother will have to know so we can take her to where Beth is being treated."

A knock sounded at the door. "Let me answer that. It's Eli, his son Jethro and the other elders." Loping to the door, Joseph answered it. "Come in. John Mathis is here and we are starting to work on particulars."

"I think that would be an excellent idea." The sheriff had spoken up. "Beth and her mother are going to be shaken up and they'll need all the emotional support they can get. Is Beth's mother seeing anyone?"

"Not that we know of. She's been so busy with work, just trying to survive."

"Agh, poor woman! It just irks me when men think they can order women around to puff up their own egos." The sheriff grumbled as he thought about Beth's situation.

Finally, the plan was approved. "Okay, everyone, Sheriff Mathis will run this just as he did the situation with Wayne Lapp. His deputies will be dressed like us. Sheriff, we need to know how many men and how many women, and their approximate sizes so we can loan you Amish clothing. We will meet at the picnic grounds close to the Andrews home. Beth knows this, so she will suggest it to John."

The sheriff took over. "We want to move in as soon as it looks like Andrews is going to get violent. Allow my deputies and me to take care of that. You stay in the background. It's much safer that way."

"Would it be helpful if one or two of the wives approach Beth when it looks like things are going to get, well, difficult?"

Eli really wanted to help.

"No, that will only put them at risk of physical harm, especially if John knows he has been outed."

"'Outed?' What does that mean?" One of the ministers was confused about the term.

"I'm sorry. That just means that he's been found out and we're going to stop him. He will be even angrier and may try to take his anger out on Beth. We don't want that. It could also put other women in harm's way. This guy sounds like he's not afraid of hitting a woman to make his point or get his own way."

"Sheriff, what will happen to John's dat? And his mam?"

"Well, since Vernon reported that he overheard John's father plotting to harm Beth, we will send uniformed deputies to their home to arrest him. Is his wife participating in your meetings?"

"Not yet. We're working to make that happen, and she told us she would let us know at our next Sunday meeting. She really fears him. Whatever he orders her to do, she does."

***

Over the next few days, the elders met with Eli, Vernon, Jethro and the sheriff's office. Amish clothing changed hands and the final plan came together. "We'll meet at the picnic grounds at five p.m. I want a few of your community members to be there, doing something like a quiet celebration or something."

"Maybe we can make it look like a group meeting before it gets too cold. You know, in the next month, it will get seriously cold before winter starts."

***

Finally, the day arrived. Various people in Peace Valley and outside the Amish community woke up knowing that at the end of the day lives would change.

John woke up, and after breakfast he went with his dat to clean up the fields after the harvest. "Dat, was it a gut harvest?"

"It could have been better, son. Much better. But, with Gott's guidance, we will get through this winter. Let's begin cleaning up the chaff and the stalks left behind." Four hours later, sweaty and dirt-covered, the men came back into the house. "Wife! We're going to clean up. I want dinner in thirty minutes!"

"Ja, husband. It will be ready. I've been working on it." Emma scurried around, brewing coffee and heating vegetables. The beef potpie bubbled in the oven. Emma stirred some potatoes on the stove, checking them for doneness. She had already set the dessert on the counter, where it cooled.

Upstairs, Big John finished wiping the caked dust off, washed his face and combed his hair back. He put on clean clothing. Walking into his son's room, he saw that John Junior was doing the same. "Son, where are you taking Beth tonight?"

"She wants to go to the picnic grounds and just enjoy the evening, she said. What she doesn't know is that I am giving her my final ultimatum. She quits her job, and she goes home uninjured. If not…" John's voice was quiet, but not quiet enough.

Emma had quietly come upstairs, planning to tell the men that dinner was ready. Overhearing John's voice, she stopped in the hallway. Knowing what he meant, she covered her mouth and wheeled back around. As small as she was, her steps didn't make much sound. Still, she was cautious, avoiding parts of stairs that she knew creaked. Wringing her hands and pacing, she wanted to do something, but knew she couldn't. *But maybe…* She was jolted out of her musings by the noisy footsteps of her husband and son. "Dinner's ready." She was nervous, not wanting them to see that she knew what they had been talking about.

Neither man noticed Emma's nervousness. Instead, they dug into their meals, eating silently after their prayer. "What's for dessert?" Big John wiped his face and whiskers clean of his lunch, waiting.

"Apple crisp with ice cream. Here you go." Emma's hand

trembled slightly as she handed them their bowls. "More coffee?"

"Ja." John wolfed down his apple crisp and indicated he wanted a second serving. He waited as Emma hurried to comply. "Son, we should get back outside. It's a bit cool out there today."

"Ja, but it'll feel gut." Without thanking his mam for the delicious dinner, John walked out with his dat.

***

After picking Beth up at her house, John drove her to the picnic area. Lifting the small basket she had prepared, he took it to the nearest table.

Beth glanced around, half-hoping to see signs that help was close by. She closed her eyes briefly when she saw the Yoders and Millers at the far end of the picnic area. "This looks gut. I'll spread the tablecloth so our food stays clean." She quickly snapped the oval tablecloth out and spread it over the concrete table. Removing the jars of spreads, bread, cheese and sliced meats, she invited John to sit.

John made a thick, hearty sandwich for himself. "Mmm, this is gut. So, have you made a decision? When will you quit working at that diner?"

Beth sighed. She had hoped to delay this part of the evening.

"John, can we enjoy our meal for a few minutes, then talk about that?"

John looked deeply at Beth. "I would like an answer. Tonight." His voice deepened."

"Ja, I know. I will let you know, but I just want to enjoy a little supper and time with you first."

John couldn't see anything wrong with that. "Okay. This time." After finishing two large sandwiches, he dug into half of the cookies Beth had packed. Without thanking her, he burped loudly, and then took a large slurp of coffee. "Well?"

Beth took her time. Wiping her mouth and setting her napkin down, she sighed. "John, Mam and I are by ourselves. Other than the small amount of savings Dat was able to set aside for us, we have nothing. Mam needs my earnings to keep us in the house so the bank doesn't foreclose on it. Oh!"

John had slammed his meaty hand on the table in anger. "You know what I want! You know I want a wife who stays at home and doesn't work. She should only take care of the house and our kinder!" Rising, he moved around to Beth's side of the picnic bench. Grabbing her by the arm, he pulled her up and tried to pull her away from the table.

Beth tried not to resist. Still, her foot caught on the high, concrete foot of the bench. As John tugged at her arm, she tried to free her foot. Her leg and foot twisted painfully as he pulled on her arm. Nearly horizontal, she was unable to balance so she could pull her foot free. Feeling her leg twisting, she heard a sharp snap as the bone broke. "Ach, John, you hurt me! Let me go, now!" Beth's voice was shrill.

Hearing Beth's exclamation, the deputies surrounded the couple. They had moved closer as John grabbed Beth's arm. He hadn't noticed their presence.

"John Andrews, let her go!" One of the deputies stood close behind John, handcuffs in his hand.

John, turning, didn't recognize the faces. "Who are you? This is a private matter."

"Not when you hurt her, it isn't. Deputy, cuff him." Sheriff Mathis read John his Miranda rights. "We need a second set of cuffs. He's too big for one set."

Beth, lying on the picnic table by now, breathed deeply, trying to stave off nausea. She was angry. "John, we are not a couple anymore. I am not leaving the diner and I am not marrying you!"

"What? I'm your only—"

"Nee! I'd rather stay single!"

"Take this disgusting weakling away." The sheriff's voice was disgusted.

***

Weeks later, the peer group had made headway, signing up several new couples shaken by Beth Zook's beating. The group's main focus continued to be discussing and teaching sexism and its effects on Amish families.

THE END.

THANK YOU FOR READING!

I hope you enjoyed reading it as much as I loved writing it! If so, look for my other books at your favorite online booksellers in ebook for paperback format.

In the meantime, you can learn a bit more about my free digital starter library in the next chapter. And if you've missed any of books, check out Also by Rachel Stoltzfus and pick up any books you've missed at your favorite online booksellers :)

Best,

Rachel

A WORD FROM RACHEL

Building a relationship with my readers and sharing my love of Amish books is the very best thing about writing. For those who choose to hear from me via email, I send out alerts with details on new releases from myself and occasional alerts from Christian authors like my sister-in-law, Ruth Price, who also writes Amish fiction.

And if you sign up for my reader club, you'll get to read all of these books on me (in ebook format):

1. A digital copy of **Amish Country Tours**, retailing at $2.99. This is the first of the Amish Country Tours series. About the book, one reader, Angel exclaims: " Loved it, loved it, loved it!!! Another sweet story from Rachel Stoltzfus."

2. A digital copy of **Winter Storms**, retailing at $2.99.

This is the first of the Winter of Faith series. About the book, Deborah Spencer raves: " I LOVED this book! Though there were central characters (and a love story), the book focuses more on the community and how it comes together to deal with the difficulties of a truly horrible winter."

3. A digital copy of **Amish Cinderella 1-2**. This is the first full book of the Amish Fairy Tales series and retails at 99c. About the book, one reader, Jianna Sandoval, explains: " Knowing well the classic "Cinderella" or rather, "Ashputtle", story by the Grimm brothers, I've do far enjoyed the creativity the author has come up with to match up the original. The details are excruciating and heart wrenching, yet I love this book all the more."

4. A digital copy of **A Lancaster Amish Home for Jacob**, the first of the bestselling Amish Home for Jacob series. This is the story of a city orphan, who after getting into a heap of trouble, is given one last chance to reform his life by living on an Amish farm. Reader Willa Hayes loved the book, explaining: " The story is an excellent and heartfelt description of a boy who is trying to find his place in the community - either city or country - by surmounting incredible odds."

5. A digital copy of **False Worship 1-2**. This is the first complete arc of the False Worship series, retailing at

99c. Reader Willa Haynes recommends the book highly, explaining: " I gave this book a five star rating. It was very well written and an interesting story. Father and daughter both find happiness in their own way. I highly recommend this book."

You can get all five of these ebooks **for free** by signing up at

FamilyChristianBookstore.net/Rachel-Starter

Or via TEXT MESSAGE send

READRACHELS to 1 (678) 506-7543

ENJOY THIS BOOK? YOU CAN MAKE A BIG DIFFERENCE

Reviews are the most powerful tools in my arsenal when it comes to getting attention for my books. As much as I'd love to, I don't have the financial muscle of a New York publisher. I can't take out full page ads in the newspaper or put up billboards on the highway.

(Not yet, anyway.)

But I have a blessing that is much more powerful and effective than that, and it's something those publishers would do anything to get their hands on.

A loyal and committed group of wonderful readers.

Honest reviews of my books from readers like you help bring them to the attention of other readers.

If you've enjoyed this book, I would be very grateful if you could spend just 3 minutes leaving a review (it can be as short as you like) on this book's review page.

And if, *YIKES* you find an issue in the book that makes you think it deserves less than 5-stars, send me an email at RachelStoltzfus@globalgrafxpress.com and I'll do everything I can to fix it.

Thank you so much!

Blessings,

Rachel S

ALSO BY RACHEL STOLTZFUS

Have you read them all?

AMISH SEEDS OF CHANGE SERIES

Struggle. Resentment. Love.

Book 1 – Amish Seeds of Change

Amish teen, Emma Lapp has had a lifelong struggle with weight. Worse, Jacob, the man she wants desperately to court with only sees her as a friend. Caught between the loving excess of her mother's care and the desire to make a change, Emma feels overlooked and left behind. But when a terrible accident forces Emma to face hard truths about herself and her relationship with her sister, will this be enough for Emma to seize her dreams? Read More.

Book 2 – Amish Courage to Change

After Emma Lapp's weight loss surgery, her sister, Barbara, will do anything to make her sister fail. Tempting foods. Too large portions. But with the support of her long-time friend and true love Jacob, Emma perseveres. Seeing Emma's success, Barbara risks her marriage and her sister's good name in one, final act of ultimate betrayal. Will Barbara succeed in driving her sister away? Or will Emma find the courage to change herself, her family, and her community? Read More.

Book 3 – Amish Time of Change

Coming July 2017 – Get notified the moment it's released when you join Rachel's Readers Club at http://familychristianbookstore.net/Rachel-Starter.

AMISH OF PEACE VALLEY SERIES

Denial. Redemption. Love.

The Peace Valley Amish series offers a thought provoking Christian collection of books certain to bring you joy.

Book 1 - Amish Truth Be Told

Can the light of God's truth transform their community, and their husbands' hearts? Or are some secrets too painful to reveal?

Book 2 - Amish Heart and Soul

A lifetime of habit is hard to break, and for one, denying the truth will put not only his marriage, but his life, at risk. What is the price of redemption? Can there truly be peace in Peace Valley?

Book 3 - Amish Love Saves All

Can the residents of Peace Valley, working together, truly move past antiquated views in order to save themselves? (In Kindle Unlimited until 6/26/17)

Or SAVE yourself a few bucks & GET ALL 3-BOOKS in 3-Book Collection.

LANCASTER AMISH HOME FOR JACOB SERIES

Orphaned. Facing jail. An Amish home is Jacob's last chance.

The Lancaster Amish Home for Jacob series is the story of how one troubled teen learns to live and love in Amish Country.

BOOK 1: A Home for Jacob

When orphaned Philadelphia teen, Jacob Marshall is given a choice between juvie and life on an Amish farm, will he have the strength to turn his life around? Or will his past mistakes spell an end to his future?

BOOK 2: A Prayer for Jacob

Just as Jacob's life is beginning to turn around, his long, lost mother shows up and attempts to win him back. Will he chose to stay go with his biological mom back to the Englisch world that treated him so poorly or stay with his new Amish family?.

BOOK 3: A Life for Jacob

When orphaned teen Jacob Marshall makes a terrible mistake, will he survive nature's wrath and truly find his place with the Amish of Lancaster County?

BOOK 4: A School for Jacob

When Jacob's Amish schoolhouse is threatened by a State teacher who wants to sacrifice their education on the altar of standardized testing, will Jacob and his friends be able to save their school, or will Jacob's attempt to help cost him his new life and home?

BOOK 5: Jacob's Vacation

When Philadelphia teen, Jacob Marshall goes on vacation to Florida with his Amish family, things soon get out of hand. Will he survive a perilous boat trip, and Sarah the perils of young love?

BOOK 6: A Love Story for Jacob

When love gets complicated for Jacob, what will it mean for his future and that of his new Amish family?

BOOK 7: A Memory for Jacob

When anger leads to a terrible accident, will orphaned Philadelphia teen, Jacob Marshall, regain the memories of his Amish life before it's too late?

BOOK 8: A Miracle for Jacob

When Jacob Marshall makes a promise far too big for him, it's going to take a miracle for him to keep his word. Will Jacob find the strength to ask for help before it's too late? Or will pride be the cause of his greatest fall?

BOOK 9: A Treasure for Jacob

When respected community leader, Old Man Dietrich, passes on, Jacob discovers that the old man has hidden a treasure worth thousands on his land. Can Jacob and his two best friends solve the mystery and find the treasure before it's too late? Or will this pursuit of wealth put Jacob in peril of losing his new Amish home?

SIMPLE AMISH LOVE SERIES

Friendship. Betrayal. Love.

The Simple Amish Love 3-Book Collection is a series of Amish love stories that shows how the power of love can overcome obsession and betrayal. Join the ladies of Peace Landing as they hold onto love in Lancaster County!

BOOK 1 – Simple Amish Love

She's found love. But will a stalker end it all?

After traveling for rumspringa, Annie Fisher returns to her Amish community of Peace Landing ready to take her Kneeling Vows and find a husband. And when handsome Mark Stoltzfus wants to court with her, it seems like everything is going to plan. But when a stalker tries to ruin Annie's relationship, will she be strong enough to stand up for herself? And will her fragile new romance survive?

BOOK 2 – Simple Amish Pleasures

A new school year. A new teacher. A hidden danger.

Newly minted Amish teacher, Annie Fisher is ready to start a new school year in Peace Landing. Having been baptized over the summer, Annie is excited to begin her life as an Amish woman. And when the Wedding season arrives, she and Mark will be married. But there is a hidden danger that threatens everything Annie wants, everything she's worked for, and everything she loves. Can Annie face it, and if she does, will it destroy her?

BOOK 3 – Simple Amish Harmony

She's in love. With the brother of the woman who betrayed her best friend.

Jenny King is elated with her new love, Jacob Lapp. But a cloud hangs over their developing relationship. Jacob's sister betrayed Jenny's best friend, Annie Fisher and has now been cast out of the church. What happens next could spell the end of Jenny's future plans, and the simple harmony of her dreams.

Or SAVE yourself a few bucks & GET ALL 3-BOOKS the Collection.

AMISH COUNTRY TOURS SERIES

A widow. A new business. Love?

Join Amish widow, Sarah Hershberger as she opens her home for a new business, her heart to a new love, and risks everything for a new future.

Book 1: Amish Country Tours

When Amish widow, Sarah Hershberger, takes the desperate step to save herself and her family from financial ruin by opening her home to Englisch tourists, will her simple decision threaten the very foundation of the community she loves?

Book 2: Amish Country Tours 2

Just as widow, Sarah Hershberger's tour business and her courtship with neighbor and widower, John Lapp, is beginning to blossom, will a bitter community elder's desire to 'put Sarah in her place' force her and her family to lose their place in the community forever?

Book 3: Amish Country Tours 3

Can widow Sarah Hershberger and her new love John Lapp stand strong in the face of lies, spies, and a final, shocking betrayal?

Or SAVE yourself a few bucks & GET ALL 3-BOOKS in the Collection.

AMISH COUNTRY QUARREL SERIES

Friendship. Danger. Courage.

Join best friends Mary and Rachel as they navigate danger, temptation, and the perils of love in the Amish community of Peace Landing in Books 1-4 of the Lancaster Amish Country Quarrel series.

BOOK 1 - An Amish Country Quarrel

When Mary Schrock tries to convince her best friend Rachel Troyer to leave their Amish community and move to the big city, will a simple quarrel spell the end of their friendship?

BOOK 2 – Simple Truths

When best friends, Mary Shrock and Rachel Troyer, are interviewed by an Englisch couple about their Amish lifestyle, will the simple truth put both girls, and their Amish community, in mortal peril?

BOOK 3 – Neighboring Faiths

Is love enough for Melinda Abbott to turn her back on her Englisch life and career? And if so, will the Amish community she attempted to harm ever accept her?

BOOK 4 – Courageous Faith

Before Melinda Abbott can truly embrace her future with her Amish beau, Steven Mast, will she have the courage to face the cult she broke free of in order to pull her cousin from their grasp?

Or SAVE yourself a few bucks & GET ALL 4-BOOKS in the Collection.

WINTER OF FAITH

Hardship. Clash of Worlds. Love.

Join Miriam Bieler and her Amish community as they survive hardship, face encroachment from the outside world, and find love!

BOOK 1: Winter Storms

When a difficult winter leads to tragedy, will the faith of this Ephrata Amish community survive a series of storms that threaten their resolve to the core?

Book 2: Test of Faith

When Miriam Beiler, a first class quilter, narrowly avoids an accident with an Englischer who asks her for directions to a nearby high school, will this chance meeting push Miriam and her Amish community to an ultimate test of faith?

Book 3: The Wedding Season

When another suitor wants to steal John away from Miriam, who will see marriage in the upcoming wedding season?

Or SAVE yourself a few bucks & <u>GET ALL 3-BOOKS in the Collection</u>.

FALSE WORSHIP SERIES

A dangerous love. Secrets. Triumph.

When Beth Zook's daed starts courting a widow with a mysterious past, will Beth uncover this new family's secrets before she loses everything?

SAVE yourself a few bucks & <u>GET ALL 4-BOOKS in the Collection</u>.

AMISH FAIRY TALES SERIES

Cinderella. Sleeping Beauty. Snow White.

Set in a whimsical Lancaster County of fantastic possibility grounded in strong Christian values, join sisters Ella, Zelda and Gerta as they struggle to find themselves and their places in a world fraught with peril where nothing is as it seems.

SAVE yourself a few bucks & GET ALL 4-BOOKS in the Collection.

OTHER TITLES

A Lancaster Amish Summer to Remember

When troubled teen, Luke King, is sent for the summer to live with his uncle Hezekiah on an Amish farm, will he be able to turn his life around? And what about his growing interest in their neighbor, 16-year-old Amish neighbor Hannah Yoder, whose dreams of an English life may end up risking both of their futures?

ABOUT THE AUTHOR

Rachel was born and raised in Lancaster, Pennsylvania. Being a neighbor of the Mennonite community, she started writing Amish romance fiction as a way of looking at the Amish community. She wanted to present a fair and honest representation of a love that is both romantic and sweet. She hopes her readers enjoy her efforts.

Made in the USA
Middletown, DE
20 September 2020